DARK VISION

Instead of blue skies dotted with puffy white clouds, this painting's backdrop was a variegated firmament, black and gray streaks careening haphazardly through a dominant splotch of orange. Around the well were half-figures, some sprawling, some upright, shadowy caricatures with vague features, save perhaps for the agony in their long conical faces. Painted in crimson and claret red, they seemed to mesh in a crisscrossing pattern, red paint trickling from them, from the larger bloated forms that were animals, and from the well itself, seeping through the stones, pouring over the mouth. And there were no wood posts, no pointed parasols.

Mesmerized by the painting, Greg dropped to his knees and stared into its three-dimensional depths. It came alive for him; the figures writhed, beckoning obscenely with their thin appendages, perhaps pleading. There were sounds, at first distant and unclear, then louder. Cries and shrieks of mindless terror, agonized moans rising, rising to an unimaginable crescendo. And a word (*padgett*) uttered amidst the cacophony in an emotionless, genderless voice. (*padgett padgett*) Over and over, again and again, until all the figures were prone, some segmented. (*padgett padgett padgett padgett*) And more red spilled from them, and more gushed from the well, spreading over the canvas, dripping to the floor of the studio. . . .

W THE ELL

Michael B. Sirota

SPECTRA™

BANTAM BOOKS
NEW YORK · TORONTO · LONDON · SYDNEY · AUCKLAND

THE WELL
A Bantam Book / June 1991

Bantam Books are published by Bantam Books, a division of Bantam Doubleday
Dell Publishing Group, Inc. Its trademark, consisting of the words "Bantam
Books" and the portrayal of a rooster, is Registered in U.S. Patent and Trademark
Office and in other countries. Marca Registrada. Bantam Books, 666 Fifth
Avenue, New York, New York 10103.

PRINTED IN THE UNITED STATES OF AMERICA

RAD   0 9 8 7 6 5 4 3 2 1

For Barney

PROLOGUE:

Vacation

Lassen County had none of those California tourist places that people flocked to in the middle of the summer.

For the Lowells it was a bleak, dusty anticlimax to the week preceding their drive up U.S. Highway 395. Towns with names like Doyle and Milford and Buntingville passed with invisible speed. Before all the chaparral and rocks, it had been Lake Tahoe, the gold country, the wine country, and Jack London Park. And Bodega Bay, where Hitchcock had directed *The Birds* and they still dug for horseneck clams on the mud flats.

But that day, for a couple of hours, it was Lassen County.

The Lowells, Greg and Janet, and their children, Mark and Allison, had not planned this vacation. A month earlier, it had been nothing. Vacation plans for that year were to fly east at Christmastime and visit Janet's family in Pennsylvania.

But on a particular Sunday in July, Greg and Janet knew they couldn't wait that long.

Traffic inched along the San Diego Freeway near Mulholland Drive. Janet and Greg, trying to get home to Van Nuys from a day at the South Coast Plaza shopping mall in Orange County, had traveled three miles in the last forty minutes. A stage-one smog alert was in effect in the Los Angeles basin; temperatures were in the nineties. Turn your air conditioning off, roll down your window, breathe it in. Or leave the air conditioning on and overheat, like dozens of cars along the shoulder.

"Great choice," Greg muttered.

"What'd you say?" Janet asked.

"Nothing. Just thinking with my mouth."

She looked at him. "You've seemed a little out of it all day. Maybe these seventy-hour work weeks are finally getting to you."

A dented Honda cut into the few feet of space between Greg's Camaro and the car in front of them. Greg braked three inches short of the Honda's rear bumper.

"It's not just today," he said. "I don't know what's bugging me lately. Just . . . *things*. Guess I shouldn't complain. Work is going well, although Jeremy Hunter's fourth novel is going to be late and I'm getting some flak over that."

Janet nodded understandingly. Greg was executive editor at Sabre Press, a small but successful publishing house in L.A. A few years earlier, he'd "found" Jeremy Hunter. Now, after three best-selling novels—all set during the gold rush period in northern California—Jeremy Hunter had proven to be a gold mine himself, one whom Sabre Press depended on heavily.

"We have the kids," Greg went on, "and the house. But . . . Hell, I don't know."

Janet indicated the stifling freeway. "*This* could do it to anyone. And you have to deal with it every day."

"Maybe." He glanced at her. "I wish we could get away from it for a week or two."

"A vacation." She nodded. "I was hoping you'd ask. Okay."

"Just like that? What about December?"

"We'll go. The hospital will let me work extra shifts. Even if I couldn't, I'd just as soon cancel December and do something with you and the kids now."

Greg leaned over to kiss her, ruffling her short dark hair. "Thanks. The day's getting better."

Allison Lowell, fifteen, thought a vacation was a great idea. She had always been Greg and Janet's "baby," but that wasn't going to last much longer. Although Allison described herself as plain, Janet knew she was changing. The pictures of Janet as a teenager could easily be mistaken for Allison. And Janet, at thirty-nine, was considered a "foxy lady," even by Mark's friends.

Mark Lowell, nearly seventeen, was less excited. The tall boy, an ardent athlete, had inherited his father's dark coloring and rugged features. A starting linebacker for Van Nuys Central High, he was already into informal scrimmages for next season. It was the lure of Bodega Bay—Mark loved horror movies—that won him over.

Two weeks later, they left Shanty, their terrier, with Robert Lowell, Greg's father, and started up Highway 101 in Janet's LTD station wagon.

At Susanville, the largest town in Lassen County, they picked up State Highway 139, which skirted the Lassen National Forest. It was a slower route, but more direct for Greg's destination.

"How far is Bonner from here, Dad?" Mark asked from the back seat, momentarily looking up from his new *Sports Illustrated.*

"An hour and a half, something like that," Greg said.

"I'm hungry," Allison said.

"We'll be there by lunchtime."

"Are you assuming Bonner has a restaurant?" Janet asked wryly.

"*You* should talk, coming from Oil City, Pennsylvania."

"*Touché.* What will you do there, seek out old haunts?"

"Old haunts? I was born in Bonner, but I was only a few months old when we left. Didn't I ever tell you that?"

"I guess not. Why did your folks leave?"

"I'm not really sure. Tough place to make a living, I suppose. Dad wasn't exactly the farming type. And they had only been there a short time. Sold a piece of land that belonged to my mother's family. Crazy Ben Padgett's old ranch."

"*Crazy* Ben Padgett?" Mark repeated.

"My great-grandfather."

"But why *crazy* Ben?" Allison asked.

"Ah, a sudden interest in our family skeletons." Greg smiled. "Okay, I'll tell you the unpleasant early history of the Padgetts . . . later. During lunch, maybe."

"Aw, Dad!"

They drove through the prehistoric stillness of Lassen County for the better part of an hour. Greg concentrated on the often-twisting road as well as the music pouring from the speakers. It had been his turn to choose the tape: Beethoven's *Choral Fantasia.* The full orchestra had just joined the solo piano, which had laid a sonatalike foundation for the piece. The quiet entry of the strings belied the thunder that would soon follow.

Ahead, they saw a road sign: ENTERING MODOC COUNTY.

Allison and Mark, debating some issue in the back seat, heard nothing. Janet, gazing at the stark volcanic tableland outside, was only half sure her husband had spoken. Soon she forgot it, for what she thought she'd heard made no sense.

There would have been no reason for Greg to say, "Almost home."

part 1

THE
DIGGING

1

The Settlers

By 1856, the first settlers had already come to the land of the Modoc Indians. Not to the forbidding lava beds farther north, but to the surrounding valleys covered with rippling meadow grass for their herds, where lakes and streams were choked with fish, and juniper woodland and mountainous pine forests were overrun with pronghorn antelope and black-tailed deer.

Elias Kolb and his family were the first of the indomitable pioneers to settle in a particular mountain valley, one that stretched from the base of green rolling hillocks to the facings of taller peaks. *Sayka loluk,* the Modocs called it. Fire Valley, in the white man's tongue.

David and Amanda Trimble, a young Ohio couple, followed. Next, Edwin and Kate Leary and their children; Calvin and Edna Hoyt and their only daughter.

Jason Bonner came, too, but with different expectations. The entrepeneur, who had won and lost fortunes from the paddlewheelers of the Mississippi to the mining camps of California, saw the potential of the area. He built a hotel and saloon just south of the valley. A mercantile store, blacksmith-livery, gun shop, and others followed. Soon, the cluster of stores became a town, which despite his protests, bore the name of its charismatic founder.

They came to stay, the white people. The hated *basdin,* as the Modoc Indians called them, came to rule in their beautiful *sayka loluk.* They brought their guns, and their diseases. Yet by the time Fire Valley was settled, the Modoc fought little, and no longer for his birthright, but for survival.

* * *

Five months after the first wall of Jason Bonner's Harmony House hotel was raised, a small wagon train of Oregon-bound settlers set off north from Susanville. At its head rode Amos Ezekiel Paine, a scarred mountain of a man in his forties. Paine proclaimed himself a wagonmaster, cavalry scout, and bounty hunter of Indian scalps. The latter was in keeping with his avowed hatred of the red man.

On the second day of the journey, the party was following a rugged trail across a broad plain of chaparral. Paine, fifty yards ahead, suddenly motioned for the train to stop. He lifted his head, sniffed the air, then urged his horse back toward the settlers.

Wallace Padgett sat on the bench of a sturdy Conestoga wagon between Rebecca, his wife, and Martha, their twelve-year-old daughter. He watched Paine's approach with disgust. Neither he nor the other emigrants cared for Amos Paine, who had quickly established himself as a distasteful traveling companion.

"Something wrong, Mr. Paine?" the New Englander called.

"Not sure yet," was the gruff reply. "There's injins out there, but I don't know how many or what they're up to. I kin guess, though." He pointed past the rear of the train at a small straggling herd of cattle.

"How can you be sure Indians are nearby, Mr. Paine?" Rebecca Padgett asked. "Did you see any?"

"Don't have to see 'em, lady. I kin *smell* the stinkin' red devils. They smell worse'n cowshit!"

"What do you want us to do?" Wallace Padgett asked.

"I'm goin' on ahead. You tell the wagons to tighten up. Make sure your brats keep the cows closer."

"My *sons* have been doing just fine," Padgett said coldly as he climbed down.

"Father, can I go with you?" Martha asked.

"Of course, dear."

Padgett helped her down, and they walked back to the next wagon. Paine watched them for a moment, then his lewd gaze turned toward Rebecca, who was busy with the reins as she shifted over on the seat. She was a striking, shapely woman. He knew what her prim high-necked dress and matronly bonnet concealed. He had sworn that on the journey to Oregon, he would have her—one way or the other.

"Havin' trouble, lady?" he asked.

Rebecca stared coldly at him. "I'll manage fine. You'd best go about your business."

"When I'm ready," he growled, and despite her defiance, Rebecca was afraid. "What's with you, lady? That scarecrow Padgett ain't no man. I bet you never had a *real* man before."

"Mr. Paine, if you don't get away from me—"

"Hey, what's that?" Paine suddenly exclaimed.

He drew his Colt .45 as a red streak flew out of the chaparral twenty yards ahead. Rebecca glimpsed a naked Indian boy, perhaps eight or nine years old, about the same age as her own Benjamin. Paine didn't hesitate. The boy's flight was stopped by a bullet in his head. He toppled forward, dead before he struck the dirt. Paine fired five more shots, all on the mark.

Rebecca leapt down from her wagon and calmed her startled team, then ran to the little corpse. *"Murderer!"* she cried back at Paine. "He was just a child!"

Paine holstered his weapon indignantly. "He was an Injin."

"What happened?" Wallace Padgett exclaimed as he and others appeared. "Oh God! Martha, get in the wagon!"

The girl obeyed as Padgett knelt by his trembling wife. Together they stared at Amos Paine, who sneered and said, "You folks make me sick, comin' west with your notions of right 'n' wrong. This ain't a human, it's *vermin!*"

"As my wife said, Mr. Paine," Padgett replied stiffly, "you are a murderer. Let's get some shovels. We'll bury the boy."

"The hell you will!" Paine bellowed. "Faster we get away, the better. And you'll be doin' the injins wrong by buryin' it. They cremate their dead. Now leave it there and let's go!"

The other settlers turned to the Padgetts. The Torgesons, the Archers, and the Hewitts all respected the strong-willed couple who dared defy the seething wagonmaster.

"Let us at least hide his body in the brush," Rebecca said. "The children shouldn't have to look at this."

"Make it quick," Paine grumbled, and urged his horse ahead.

Padgett dragged the corpse into the chaparral; Rebecca and Torgeson covered the streaks of blood with dirt. They set off again quickly, but none could leave behind the image of what they had witnessed.

There was no retaliation. But Paine, who had drunk too

much, was the only one who slept that night. And the next day, his head throbbing, he was relentless in his tongue-lashing of the weary emigrants.

"What a detestable creature," Wallace Padgett muttered to his wife.

"To think that we have to endure this all the way to Oregon . . ." Rebecca shuddered.

"What choice do we have?"

A few days later, the Padgetts found a choice: the *sayka loluk*. From the rough trail that led through a range of low mountains, they gazed across Fire Valley. They saw the Trimbles' rippling fields of barley and wheat; the combined herds of the Learys and the Kolbs grazing on ankle-deep bunch grass; the mountain streams crisscrossing the valley floor.

The Padgetts stayed. After learning land was available, after experiencing the hospitality of those who'd already settled the valley, Wallace Padgett paid off Amos Paine. They said good-bye to the Torgesons, the Archers, and the Hewitts, all of whom chose to continue to the promised land of Oregon.

Wallace and Rebecca Padgett, their daughter Martha, their sons James and Benjamin, had arrived, the last players in the drama that would come to be known as the Fire Valley Massacre.

2

The Sign

On the sunny spring day that the settlers gathered to raise the Padgetts' cottage and barn, an uninvited trio lay hidden on a nearby hill. Dark-skinned stocky men with deceivingly sleepy eyes, they were Modocs, the South Lake People. Once, this land had been theirs to roam freely. Now the *basdin* took what they wanted and were protected by other *basdin* in blue uniforms. The South Lake People could only stand by helplessly and watch.

Their hatred of the *basdin* was as vast as the sky.

Shar-kah, oldest of the three, broke the stillness. "More *basdin.* One day this valley will be spoiled by many."

"It does not matter anymore," Cho-acks said dully.

"Listen to the two old women!" A-ke-kis exclaimed. "Of course it matters, especially *here*! Or do you not see where these lodges are being raised?"

"We are not blind, A-ke-kis." Shar-kah glared at him. "From the time they first came, it has been inevitable, as the *La gi* feared. But there is nothing we can do."

"*I* can do something!" A-ke-kis snapped. "After dark, when the others are gone, I can slit their throats—"

"What we *will* do," Shar-kah interrupted, "is tell the *La gi* what we have seen. Let he and the shaman decide what is best."

"I, for one, cannot see the danger of their presence," Cho-acks said.

"Fool!" A-ke-kis spat. "Do you think we've been sent to watch this place all these summers without reason?"

"I know the reason," Cho-acks said. "But none have ever

done more than dent the earth with the rows in which they plant seeds. What danger can this be?"

"I agree," Shar-kah said, "but the final word is not ours. Now come!"

They rode their ponies north across hills and other sparsely inhabited valleys, through a forest, until finally they came to the lava beds, their Land of Burnt-out Fires. The volcanic wasteland stretched even farther north to the shore of Tule Lake, then around it into Oregon Territory. In winter, their village was near the lake. But now the wickiups of the seminomadic Modocs were along a fish-choked stream to the west.

Shouting children and yapping mongrels greeted the trio as they entered the village. After leading their ponies to a patch of shrub grass where they could graze, the young men continued on to the *La gi's* wickiup.

Kan-kush, the head of their tribe, was a sturdily built man of indeterminate middle age. His usually cross expression intimidated his people.

"You have something to tell me, Shar-kah?" he asked in a guttural voice.

"Yes, *La gi.* We have just ridden from the *sayka loluk.* More *basdin* have come. They . . . build lodges near the place that you taught us to watch."

Kan-kush scowled. "How near?"

"Near enough," A-ke-kis said. "No more than twenty paces from the one where they keep animals."

The *La gi* shuddered. "The shaman must know of this."

He sent a boy, who returned a minute later at the heels of Ha-kar-gar-ush, the tribe's shaman, a bent old man wearing a feathered red skullcap. A man feared and respected by the South Lake People. Behind him, with expressions of concern and curiosity, the people of the tribe began to gather.

"Shaman," the chief said, "these three bring word that—"

"The boy told me." The elder gazed skyward and lifted his hands. "Did you also hear, Kumush?" he intoned loudly in a sing-song. "Do you know, Our Father, where the *basdin* walk?"

As Ha-kar-gar-ush chanted toward the clouds, the others, except for A-ke-kis, fidgeted. "Old fool," the young hothead muttered.

"A-ke-kis, *ssss!*" Shar-kah warned. "The shaman—"

"The shaman will pray to Our Father until he becomes heavy with sleep," A-ke-kis retorted. "We waste time. *This* is the only way to deal with *basdin!*" He hurled his knife into the ground.

Snapped from his chanting, the shaman glared at A-ke-kis. Kan-kush sprang to his feet. "You are impatient and disrespectful," the *La gi* growled. "It is not your place to interfere while the shaman seeks council with Our Father!"

"Someone must interfere sooner or later," A-ke-kis said, "or Kumush will have no more people to cherish!"

A-ke-kis and the elders stared angrily at one another, then the shaman bolted toward the young man. Despite himself, A-ke-kis retreated a step.

"What would you do, great warrior," Ha-kar-gar-ush asked, "kill all the *basdin?* We are few against many and would be destroyed."

"It will happen one day anyway," A-ke-kis said.

The shaman shrugged. "Maybe so. But for now, they leave us alone, and we must do the same."

"I cannot agree with either of you," Kan-kush said. "Are not some of the *basdin* our friends?"

"Friends, *pah!*" A-ke-kis spat. "We are *tolerated,* and only on their terms. Look at our people! We wear *basdin* clothes, speak their tongue. In their towns we are treated like dogs! But do we care? No. Instead we sell our women to them for whiskey! Are these our friends, *La gi?* I say kill them, or at least die honorably!"

The young Indian gazed challengingly at the *La gi.* But Kan-kush, who had not become chief by indecision, grabbed A-ke-kis by the shoulders.

"Hear me well. There will be no killing. Not now, and with the guidance of Kumush, perhaps not ever again."

"Obey us, A-ke-kis," the shaman added threateningly.

The raging young man looked at his friends, who nodded, then at the other members of the tribe. Most looked away from him, toward the shaman. Reluctantly accepting that for the time being, his feelings were his alone, A-ke-kis relented.

"It will be as you say," he told the elders. "But what of those in the *sayka loluk?*"

"If not for your interruption," Ha-kar-gar-ush said, "I might have finished my council with Our Father. I will go to the water and await His sign."

People stepped aside to let the shaman pass. With Ha-kar-gar-ush gone, the *La gi* spoke to his tribe.

"Whatever the shaman learns," he said, "one thing is sure: The *sayka loluk* must be watched at all times. *It cannot be allowed to happen again.*"

The people nodded.

A-ke-kis said, "I will return tomorrow to begin the vigil. Surely you won't deny me this."

"You may go, A-ke-kis, but only with another, until the angry fires that burn within you have diminished."

The scowling brave shrugged. Shar-kah grasped his arm. "I'll go with you tomorrow, my friend," he said. "It is the best way. Now come, let's eat!"

All of the men, women, and children turned to leave, then froze as a piercing sound split the air. The unnerving howl of *Wa,* the coyote, echoed from the nearby hills a second and third time before the beast fell silent.

The Modocs turned their gaze westward where *subbas,* the descending sun, touched the shimmering horizon. They saw, and they knew. A-ke-kis glared at the *La gi,* then stormed off to his reed lodge.

The South Lake People knew the shaman had received his sign from Our Father. They knew it was the sign of death.

3

Drought

Those who returned days later to watch from the hill saw that the barn and cottage had been completed. Martha tended a small garden halfway between the two buildings. In the fields to the east, young James watched the small plump herd of grazing cattle. Inside, the cottage had become a home, thanks to Rebecca's touches.

The next day, Wallace returned from a brief trip to Yreka. He brought with him a prize Hereford bull, a massive creature weighing nearly a ton. The animal's surly appearance belied its gentle nature. The Padgetts quickly grew fond of the red-brown giant with the white face, but none more so than James. He assigned himself the care and loving of Baron, as he named the majestic bull.

The spring months passed. Those who watched, usually A-ke-kis and one or two others, became familiar with the daily activities of the Padgetts. The furor of Kumush's ominous sign had long since diminished. Even A-ke-kis wondered what impelled him to devote so much time to the vigil when he might have been hunting or fishing with his friends, or making love to Lac-el-es, his woman. But portents of death were not to be taken lightly.

The previous winter had been one of the mildest ever in that area, and hardly a drop of rain had fallen since March. By late July, with the sun beating down mercilessly day after day, the first settlers were worried, for they knew what effect a drought would have on their lives. The later arrivals, among them the people of Fire Valley, watched their barely realized dreams blow away with the dust rising from dried-up ponds and cracked streambeds.

One morning, A-ke-kis, who had stood the current vigil alone for five days, rubbed his parched lips with the last precious drops of water in his pouch as a man slowly rode his horse along the path that led to the Padgetts' cottage. A-ke-kis had seen the man—Elias Kolb—before and thought him important.

Kolb tethered his horse near the barn, where Wallace and Benjamin greeted him. Benjamin, at nine the youngest Padgett, went back inside to complete his chores. The two men walked toward the base of the hill where A-ke-kis lay. The Modoc strained to hear their words. He knew some of the *basdin* tongue from the time he had spent in Yreka.

". . . and died the other day," Padgett was saying. "She was the second this summer, probably better than the rest of you. But it'll only be the start if this keeps up."

"Do you have *any* water?" Kolb asked.

Padgett pointed northward. "One creek is still running . . . barely. We're taking all we can, but it's not enough."

Kolb shook his head, the unkempt locks of his black curly hair bouncing. "You have more than most of us, Wally."

"What are you going to do?"

"Ed Leary has an idea. He wants to dig a well on his place. There's supposed to be ice caves up in those lava beds, and he thinks they may feed underground streams in the valley."

"When's he going to start?"

"Tomorrow. Trimble's going to help. So's Hoyt and me."

"I'll come. It's crazy, but better'n anything I got."

They continued walking, and their voices faded, but A-ke-kis had heard enough. *They were going to dig a well!* True, it was on the land of another, yet what if they failed? They might choose to dig again somewhere else, maybe—*here!*

No, Kumush, he thought. *This will not be.*

No one could say what A-ke-kis might have done next. He might have gone to warn his people, or he might have climbed down to kill the *basdin*. But he did neither, for he was unable to move. Belly empty, throat dry, strength sucked from him, A-ke-kis could do no more than roll onto his back, an exhausting effort that drained him completely. Had he not been hidden in a dense thicket, his skin would have been blistered by the angry sun as he lay immobile the entire day.

When Cho-acks arrived to relieve him, A-ke-kis was near

death. He was half aware of something wet touching his lips; a thin trickle of warm life-giving water fell down his throat.

"How could you allow this to happen?" Cho-acks scolded. "Do you think this is the way to help our people?"

A-ke-kis raised a hand and feebly gestured over the hill. His lips tried to form words, but to no avail.

"What is it, A-ke-kis?" Cho-acks asked.

"They . . . they go . . . to . . . ," he gasped.

"What?" Cho-acks exclaimed. "A-ke-kis . . ."

But the effort was too much. A-ke-kis lapsed into what Cho-acks at first mistook for death. When assured that his friend still lived, he carried the limp body to the horses. Left without a watcher, the *sayka loluk* fell behind the thundering hooves as Cho-acks took his friend to the medicine man.

The next morning, all the men of Fire Valley gathered at the Leary ranch. Even Jason Bonner came. From the ragged clothes he wore in place of his usual rakish suit, it was clear he planned to work.

"Personally, I think this is a waste of time," he told Elias Kolb. "But who knows, maybe we'll get lucky."

"Let's hope so, Jason," Kolb replied. "What's bad for us ain't too good for you either."

They broke ground behind Leary's barn. By the middle of the afternoon, they had dug thirty feet. They stopped then, no longer able to endure the blistering heat with so little water.

"We started too late," Kolb said. "Let's meet at dawn and get some of it done in the cool of the morning."

They met again at sunrise and dug another fifteen feet. With the oppressive temperature still climbing, they struck a layer of volcanic shale.

Their efforts had been futile.

Rebecca had woken when her husband departed in the half-light of early morning. Unable to return to sleep, she sat by the window and watched the unwelcome but magnificent sunrise. Preoccupied, she did not hear Martha come in.

"Good morning, Mother," the girl said.

Rebecca whirled around. "Oh, you startled me."

"I'm sorry."

"No, it's not your fault." Rebecca smiled. "My mind was wandering. Come, dear, come and sit with me . . ." Her voice trailed off; her eyes grew blank. She trembled and gripped the chair arms, her knuckles white.

"Mother, what's wrong?" Martha cried.

The trembling lessened. Rebecca shook her head. "It's over, dear. Whatever it was, it just came and went."

"Do you want one of the boys or me to get Father?"

"No, I'm all right," she assured Martha.

Something *was* wrong, something Rebecca could not understand. An elusive truth hovered just beyond the grasp of her conscious memory. It puzzled her through breakfast and frustrated her as she began the day's chores. Then, hours later, the fleeting image became as lucid as the stifling heat. She ran from the cottage.

"Benjamin, James," she called. "Martha, come quickly!"

"Ma, what is it?" Benjamin asked as he and his sister emerged from the barn to join her near the garden.

"Where's James?" Rebecca asked.

"In the north field. Ma, is something—"

"Stay close to me," Rebecca interrupted. "I'm going to find water."

"Mother, what are you talking about?" Martha asked.

Rebecca walked past them without speaking, and they followed. She strode to the rear of the barn, then stopped, her back against the wall. Eyes closed, she began counting off long steps. At twenty, she halted and bent down, touching the brittle earth with a finger.

"There's water here," she said.

"Ma, how do you know?" Benjamin asked.

"There's water here," she repeated. "Benjamin, ride to the Leary place. Tell your father and the others that there's water beneath our land."

Benjamin saddled up quickly and rode to the Leary ranch. The men were in a foul mood, for they'd admitted failure only minutes before. Still they listened to what Benjamin said, then turned curiously to the elder Padgett.

"Is it true, Wally?" Hoyt asked.

Wallace shrugged. "Damned if I know. You say she even pointed to the spot, Ben?"

"But how can she be so sure?" Trimble asked.

Wallace smiled grimly. "You've heard about us New Englanders and our dark pasts. Seems to me Rebecca's great-grandmother was burned for—"

"Come on, Wally," Leary said. "That's not even funny."

"Ed's right," Bonner added. "But if Rebecca thinks she's onto something, it's worth a try."

"Couldn't do any worse than this," Hoyt muttered.

"All right," Wallace said. "Tomorrow. We'll try again."

The men of Fire Valley returned to their homes to await the hope of the next day. Rebecca was calm before her husband's half-curious, half-angry inquiries. She did not withdraw her claim.

At dawn, the thirsty settlers met once more. Another shaft was begun where Rebecca showed them. By the time the heat overpowered them, they had dug nearly thirty-five feet into moist earth. Despite their exhaustion, the men's spirits were high as they resolved to continue digging the next morning.

They believed they would find the precious, elusive water so desperately needed by Fire Valley.

4

First Blood

The summer lodges of the South Lake People were in the mountains to the east of Fire Valley. There the shaman admitted the dehydrated A-ke-kis to his wickiup, which was filled with the tools of his mystical trade. While Lac-el-es prayed, while Ha-kar-gar-ush worked with little rest, A-ke-kis remained near death for two full days.

Then, late in the afternoon on the third day, the shaman returned to his wickiup to find his charge sitting up. He told Lac-el-es, who ran to the *La gi*. He then knelt beside A-ke-kis and examined him.

"How do you feel?" he asked.

"Weak," A-ke-kis whispered. "How long have I been . . . ?"

The shaman told him, and the young man gnashed his teeth. "You sent someone back to the *sayka loluk*?"

"Cho-acks set off the next morning, but had trouble with the Paiutes. They stole his pony and he returned on foot."

"Then it has not been watched all this time?" A-ke-kis cried.

The shaman nodded. "Remember, A-ke-kis, I fear what could happen even more than you. But can a few days really matter?"

A-ke-kis related the conversation of the *basdin*. He did not have to offer a conclusion, for Ha-kar-gar-ush understood.

"Kumush!" the shaman moaned. "Our fears were well founded. Kan-kush has already told Shar-kah and Cho-acks to return there in the morning. I will see that they depart all the earlier."

"I'm going with them," A-ke-kis said.

"You will not leave here until I say so."

"I'm going with them," he repeated, and lay down to rest.

Two hours before dawn, A-ke-kis, Shar-kah, and Cho-acks rode from the village. In addition to the weapons of their people, they carried *basdin* pieces. Shar-kah had a carbine, A-ke-kis and Cho-acks each a Colt. They rode strongly, and by mid-morning approached the hills that rimmed the *sayka loluk*. After tethering their ponies, they climbed the familiar slope.

When they reached the top and looked down, the sight stunned them. A dozen or more *basdin* men, women, and children were gathered around a large mound of earth and a gaping hole in the ground.

"Our Father!" A-ke-kis gasped. "It has happened! They must be told! They must be warned!"

He started down the hill before Cho-acks or Shar-kah could stop him. "A-ke-kis, no!" Shar-kah cried.

"Basdin no dig!" A-ke-kis shrieked in the pidgin tongue. "No dig! Bad place! *No dig!"*

Shar-kah and Cho-acks instinctively followed. Still screaming, A-ke-kis fired two shots in the air. The startled settlers looked up and saw the three Indians running toward them.

"What the hell!" Calvin Hoyt exclaimed.

"Indians!" Amanda Trimble cried.

Guns went up. The settlers' first thundering volley silenced the only warning they would receive. A-ke-kis rolled to the base of the hill, dead. Shar-kah and Cho-acks dropped down and returned the fire. One bullet struck Hoyt in the leg; another grazed the arm of the Kolbs' youngest daughter. But moments later, the two Modocs lay by their fallen brother.

The women guided the sobbing, terrified children into the Padgetts' cottage, Elias Kolb leading the way with little Sally in his arms. David Trimble knelt by Calvin Hoyt, who was writhing in pain. Jason Bonner and Wallace Padgett, only now emerging from the shaft, stared in disbelief.

"Christ, what happened?" Bonner asked.

"Over there." Ed Leary pointed toward the hills. "Those three crazy bucks came down on us like—"

"Three?" Bonner exclaimed. "From below it sounded like the whole damn Indian nation!"

"What are they, Pit Rivers?" Wallace asked as they walked cautiously toward the bodies.

Bonner shook his head. "They're Modocs."

"Modocs?" Leary said. "The *great* fighters? What kind of attack was this, Jason? It was suicide!"

"Are you sure, Jason?" Wallace asked.

"I'm sure," Bonner replied peevishly. "What does it matter anyway? Don't you realize we got problems?"

"What do you mean?" Leary asked.

"The Modocs have been quiet for a while, but something like this may set them off again. And before you argue that the army will protect us, remember that they're also supposed to protect the Indians. Like Ed said, the Modocs have a reputation as skilled fighters, and the army will have a hard time believing the details of this . . . 'attack.' There's bound to be an inquiry, and if things don't go our way, we could lose our grants."

"You think the government'll take away our land for killing a few Indians?" Leary asked. "Won't they believe that we did it to protect ourselves?"

Bonner gestured across the valley. "Are you willing to take that chance?" The other two men were silent. "I didn't think so."

"But what'll we do?" Wallace asked.

"Every trace of this has to be done away with. We've got to hide the bodies where they'll never be found." Bonner thought a moment. "Ed, you haven't filled that shaft up, have you?"

"Wait a minute!" Leary snapped. "You're not thinking of burying them on *my* place!"

"What other choice do we have?" Wallace asked.

"You wouldn't agree so fast if Jason offered *your* land as a cemetery! And speaking of that, why not stick 'em right here in this hole? We ain't getting anywhere."

Bonner shook his head. "You're wrong, Ed. Before all hell broke loose, we were digging in even softer earth. I don't think we're too far from water."

"All right," Leary conceded. "But don't none of you tell Kate. It'll upset her."

"We won't tell any of the women," Wallace assured him. "But we'd better let Elias know what we're doing."

Elias Kolb, the patriarch of the valley, met the men near where Hoyt had fallen. Though grimacing in pain, Hoyt was conscious, and the good-natured Kentuckian told his friends not to worry about him. Their attention turned to Kolb, whose face was drawn.

"Sally's all right; just a flesh wound. The other kids are shaken, but the women are settling 'em down." He indicated the three bodies. "What are we going to do about that?"

Bonner explained their plan. Kolb nodded grimly and said, "It has to be done. But it's more important that my Sally and Cal here be taken care of."

"No," Hoyt insisted. "Go and do what you have to."

"We'll do both," Bonner said. "Remember the train that passed through here yesterday? There's a doctor on it. I met him in town last night. He and the rest are staying until to-morrow."

"Beats bouncin' all the way to Yreka," Hoyt said.

A bustle of activity followed. While some draped the corpses over the Modocs' retrieved ponies, others helped Calvin Hoyt into the bed of his wagon. The pale Sally Kolb was lifted in next, accompanied by her mother. Edna and Alice Hoyt climbed up on the bench seat, flanking Kolb.

Wallace, Bonner, and Leary, riding their own horses, and each leading a Modoc pony with its bloodied passenger, were well along the dirt trail through Fire Valley before the wagon left the Padgett ranch. All the animals were sweating heavily when they reached the Leary place. The men left their horses to drink from the sparse muddied water in a trough and led the others to the edge of the shaft. The dead Indians, their weapons, and belongings were dropped to the floor of the useless pit. Then, fearful that the ponies possessed a homing instinct, they shot them. But the shaft was too narrow for the carcasses. The ponies' limbs and heads had to be severed before the sickened men could seal the vertical tomb with tons of dirt and rocks.

Leary and Wallace returned to the latter's ranch while Bonner caught up with the wagon on the way to town. David Trimble and Rebecca Padgett had erased all hints of the encounter. Nothing indicated that a bloody battle had been fought there.

The Learys left for their home, followed by David and Amanda Trimble, who took the remaining Kolb children with them. The Padgetts returned to their cottage. Knowing Rebecca would ask sooner or later, Wallace told her what he and the others had done. She listened in silence and said nothing.

That night a tense calm fell over the *sayka loluk*. All the families were again under their respective roofs. Even Calvin Hoyt was home, for his wound was not as bad as some had feared.

They were still thirsty, the settlers of this drought-ravaged frontier. But their spirits were buoyed by the hope that the next day the deep hole they had dug would reach the core of some subterranean watercourse. They might have found it that day if not for the interruption, the incident that would remain a nightmare for all of them.

5

The Cold

The settlers gathered again at sunrise, and the almost festive air of the previous morning was gone. They came with serious intent, knowing their future depended on what they found at the bottom of the dark shaft.

Calvin Hoyt, his bandaged leg propped up, sat in Rebecca's rocking chair with a carbine across his lap. His interest was divided between the digging and the hills. With little delay, the first team—Bonner and Trimble —descended the precarious rope ladder. Not long after, the other settlers, both men and women, were hauling up endless buckets of dirt. By the time the first two men came back up, to be replaced by Wallace and Leary, they had extended the depth of the shaft to seventy-five feet. Still their efforts went unrewarded.

The sun, aflame in a cloudless sky, tormented the settlers. By midmorning, the valley was a scorching hell with waves of heat that could be seen as well as felt snaking across it. Those who labored made do with meager sips of water collected from the trickle of a creek that ran through the Padgetts' north pasture.

Noon approached. The settlers drove themselves, fearing there might not be another day granted them. Finally, from nearly one hundred feet below, they heard the rasping voice of Elias Kolb, digging down there with Jason Bonner.

"In case none of you noticed, you're haulin' up mud."

"We're standing in about an inch of water," Bonner added, "if you can call it that. Kind of dirty, but it's something."

"And we're hearin' a sound. It's below us. . . ."

"What is it?" Wallace called down.

"It's runnin' water, damned if it ain't!" Kolb cried.
"Come on, Jason, keep that shovel movin'!"

Declining to celebrate prematurely, the settlers hauled up
the pails with renewed energy. Kolb and Bonner kept up a
barrage of talk, mostly addressing each other, occasionally as-
suring those above that an end to their troubles was near.

The women felt it first. They paused in their work. The
men looked at them, irritated. Then they too were assaulted.
They stood rigidly, looking down.

A bone-freezing cold displaced the heat of the valley
swiftly and intensely. Not a wind, or an encompassing mist,
for the relentless sun still throbbed in a clear blue sky. Instead,
the cold was within them, piercing their marrow with a million prickles of ice. Barely perceptible shudders were the only
outward signs of the chill, though the terror they each knew in
the second that it gripped them was beyond the boundaries of
their reason and understanding. When it passed, so did the
tension. Their shoulders sagged. But still there was no sound,
not even a whimper from the youngest child.

The well was also silent. Rebecca realized it first and staggered to the rim. Kneeling, she called, "Jason! Elias! Are you
all right?"

No sound from the blackness within.

"Elias, for chrissake, answer me!" Trimble yelled, sending
a few of the children into fits of sobbing. "Jason, what's
wrong?"

"Quiet down, Dave, we hear you," Kolb answered.

"We broke through the last layer of dirt," Bonner said.
"There's a chamber down here, a narrow one, barely enough
room for a man to fit. Water's coming from cracks in one wall
and emptying at the other end under a layer of rock. I'm
standing knee-deep in it right now. If you toss some of those
buckets down, you'll have all the water you want."

The chilling enigma was forgotten as the settlers lowered
the oak-slatted pails. Minutes later, they were drinking deeply.
Children splashed one another happily, while others filled a
trough near the barn for the sorry-looking horses tethered in
the shade. The hopes of those who had come to live in Fire
Valley soared.

In the midst of the celebrating, Wallace noticed the rope
ladder swaying. "Elias, Jason," he called, "hold on. We'll pull
you up."

He and a couple of other men grabbed the ladder. They

pulled slowly, so that Kolb and Bonner would not be shaken loose. A minute later, two hands appeared over the rim. First Jason Bonner, then Elias Kolb scrambled out of the deep shaft.

Laura Kolb, waiting to greet her husband, screamed when she saw him. The others dropped the ladder and stared open-mouthed. The children, already enduring too much, began to cry.

Elias Kolb's curly black hair and Jason Bonner's thick shock of brown had turned chalk-white. Their faces were ashen, the flesh cold and glassy, without a sheen of perspiration. They were dead men risen from a tomb. It seemed wrong that they should move, or speak.

"Jesus, what happened down there?" Wallace exclaimed.

Kolb shook his head. Bonner dismissed the question with a shrug. "There's a couple of canteens on my saddle," he said. "Somebody fill 'em, so I can get the hell out of here."

James Padgett and his sister ran for the canteens. The rest closed around the two men. Laura Kolb and her children, past their initial shock, engulfed Elias.

"Someone should ride with Jason to town," Trimble said.

"I'll go," Wallace offered.

"No, I'm all right," Bonner said. "The walls of this shaft will have to be shored up, or else the dirt could fill it again. There's lumber in town. Some of you come by first thing and help me bring it out here."

"Jason, you don't have to work tomorrow," Wallace said.

"I want to help, Wally. Just one thing . . ." He gazed at the hole. "I'm not going down *there* again."

His canteens full, the pale figure rode off. The barrels on the Kolbs' wagon were filled. With Elias at the reins—despite Laura's protests—they set out for their ranch. The Trimbles, Learys, and Hoyts also took what they needed and left.

Though weary, the Padgetts worked at restoring order to their homestead and lives. The cattle were driven in from the meadows to their corral, where they found water to drink as well as a puddle to wallow in. Hours later, the Padgetts drew lots over first chance at the wooden bathtub, which had been empty for so long. James even scrubbed down his beloved Baron, then joined his family on the porch where they watched the sunset before dinner.

Despite the mystery that surrounded the well, despite their fatigue, Wallace and Rebecca Padgett were at peace as they rested in the comparative cool of the evening. Freshly scrubbed, innocent and sensual in her sleeveless white summer dress, Rebecca sat with her bare feet stretched out luxuriously. Long-dormant feelings stirred in Wallace as he glanced at her. But soon she changed. A pall of uncertainty engulfed her, a cloud that her husband wanted to dispel.

"You did real good, Bec," he said.

"What? I'm sorry, dear, I must have been daydreaming. What do you mean?"

"Telling us where to dig the well. You saved a lot of people from ruin. You did real good."

"Did I, Wallace?" She gazed past the barn, and a shudder rippled through her body. "I don't know. I just don't know."

6

Manifestations

The settlers of Fire Valley slept late the next morning. It was nine o'clock before Trimble and Leary rode into town to help Bonner with the lumber. Bonner had regained his color, but his long hair and pencil mustache were still mostly white. Saying nothing of the previous day, he led the others to the back of Harmony House, where they began stacking lengths of pine on the back of a wagon.

Amos Paine, between commissions at the moment, was in Bonner, gambling and drinking away his recent earnings. That morning, on his way to the livery after leaving the half-breed whore who had entertained him all night, he noticed the activity.

"You fellas are workin' pretty hard," he said. "I—shit, Mr. Bonner, what happened to you? Looks like you seen a ghost!"

"Yeah, that's it, Amos," Bonner replied vaguely, and told Paine what they were doing.

"The Padgett place, huh?" Paine said, conjuring a vision of the aloof woman who had driven him crazy with desire. "Listen, count me in. I got nuthin' better to do, and the water in this town ain't fit for humans anyway."

Bonner introduced Paine to Trimble and Leary. They had heard about him, and their first inclination was to refuse his offer. But with Hoyt injured, and Bonner—and probably Kolb —unwilling to go down the well, they needed all the help they could get.

Their children tending to chores, Wallace and Rebecca were the only ones at the well when people began arriving. First came the Hoyts, then Elias Kolb, alone. Not far behind him, Wallace recognized Leary, Trimble, and Bonner driving a wagon. He could not identify the fourth man with them. When the wagon drew close enough to reveal Amos Paine, neither Wallace nor Rebecca could mask their displeasure.

Ignoring Wallace, Paine touched the brim of his hat and leered at Rebecca. "Mornin', ma'am. Pleasure seein' you again."

"Mr. Paine," she said coldly.

"Uh, some weather we been havin', ain't it?"

"If you're partial to sunstroke. Excuse me. Wallace, I've things to do in the house. Let me know if I can help."

Wallace smiled understandingly. "We'll manage fine, dear."

She walked away, head lifted. Staring after her swaying form, Paine was disappointed. But soon the valley echoed the sounds of sawing and hammering, and Paine proved himself an asset, putting aside his thoughts of Rebecca—for the moment.

Ironically, it was cooler that day than it had been in a month. The men worked until dusk with only a few respites. Kolb refused to go down, leaving two teams, Wallace and Trimble, Paine and Leary, to handle the labors below. But there was plenty for all to do, and their cooperation was such that most of the work was finished by late afternoon. Fitted timbers shored up the walls of the shaft so tightly that nothing, save a severe earthquake, could force more than a trickle of dust into the water below.

The Padgett children, with Alice Hoyt and her mother, had spent the morning gathering large stones. The men mortared them into place around the hole to a height of four feet, an effective barrier, they hoped, against any of the little ones toppling into the well.

"Damned if it don't look like somethin' other than a hole in the ground," Calvin Hoyt said.

Wallace nodded. "I don't think it'll change much from here on. For now, it's functional. Let's call it a day. It'll be dark soon."

"Amen," Ed Leary said with a sigh.

Rebecca, who had appeared only twice all day to bring refreshments, emerged from the house as people were getting ready to leave. She thanked each of them, even the grinning Amos Paine. With their thirst quenched, the other settlers

rode off, leaving the Padgetts alone with the object that had
occupied all of their attention for the past four days.

"Bec, the men wanted me to ask you something," Wallace
began.

"What's that?"

"They wanted to know if you would walk their land and
find them water. I wasn't sure what to say."

Rebecca frowned. "What do they think I have, some kind
of divining power?"

"You found this, didn't you?"

"Yes, but I don't know how!" she said angrily. "It
just . . . happened. I don't know if I could do it again."

Wallace placed an arm around her and smiled. "Don't
worry, Bec. I'll tell them you'd rather not."

"I can try, I guess. It's only neighborly . . ."

"We'll talk about it later. Come on, I'm starved."

"So am I," both James and Benjamin said.

After dinner, while her husband helped Martha and Benjamin with the cleaning-up chores, Rebecca stood near the
barn and stared at the well, a silhouette in the light of the half
moon. Lines of puzzlement creased her face, making her look
older than her thirty-five years. She had no idea why she had
been drawn there. After a few moments, she tore her gaze
away. Pulling her shawl tightly around her shoulders to ward
off an unexpected chill, she hurried back to the house.

James had avoided washing dishes by insisting Baron needed
tending. His father had let him go, to the chagrin of Benjamin
and Martha. Carrying a pail with some leftovers, the boy
squeezed his slight frame between two rails of the corral. His
appearance startled one of the younger cows, and the animal
lowed as it scurried away. Laughing, James balanced his lantern on a post and skipped to the center of the enclosure.

"Hey Baron," he called. "Come 'n' see what I got for
you."

The huge Hereford emerged from the shadows. The boy
ruffled the curly white hair on his snout. Then, sniffing food,
the bull gently nudged his master. After teasing him playfully,
James relinquished the treats. While Baron noisily devoured
the food, James stroked his back with a coarse brush. He continued after the animal was done, to Baron's grunting delight.

"Didn't see you much today, did I, big fella?" the boy
said. "That's 'cause we were hunting stones to put around the

well. It's done now, and we should have enough water until some rain comes. That's good, ain't it?" The animal snorted. "Anyway, now that we got water, there's dishes to wash, and I guess I better help, else Martha and Ben'll beat the tar out of me. You rest good, fella. I'll come see you first thing."

James patted the animal on its rump, and it lowed mournfully as it ambled off. The boy walked toward the fence but paused halfway, his back rigid, his gaze darting around the enclosure.

"Dang, sure got cold all of a sudden!" he exclaimed. "Hey Baron, do you—"

The bull had also stopped. Pawing the earth nervously, it faced the boy. Across the shadowy distance, James saw Baron's eyes ablaze with a minatory fire that bewildered him. But his innocence and love for the animal overrode any fear. With a shrug, he approached the animal.

"What's wrong, fella? Something spookin' you?" he asked. "Hey, don't worry, I'll stay here with you for a bit."

Baron lowered his head, but the boy kept coming.

"Baron, what's the matter?"

Rebecca heard a muffled sound as she gazed into the darkness from the porch. "Who's there?" she called. Silence answered.

Wallace appeared in the doorway behind her. "Bec, what is it?"

"I thought I heard something." She looked past her husband at the children. "Isn't James with you?"

Wallace shook his head. "He went to look after Baron."

"James?" she cried. "James!" But again the night was still.

Her maternal instincts flaring, Rebecca leapt off the porch and ran across the yard, her family close behind. "James!" she screamed again. "Oh, why doesn't he answer?"

She slowed near the corral. Her steps were deliberate as she walked along the fence, but concern won out. Still calling her son's name, she entered the enclosure.

Her husband at her side, Benjamin and Martha behind, Rebecca approached the middle of the corral. Clouds blotted the moonlight, but from the glow of James's lantern, she was able to see Baron standing peacefully, as well as the still form on the ground nearby.

James's small body, what remained of it, lay in a spreading pool of blood that poured from numerous gaping wounds.

A black spurting pit had been left in place of one eye; the other stared up at the horror-stricken family. Two yards away, Baron stood quietly, his sad gaze upon them. The dagger tips of his curved horns were darkly stained; his milk-white face was spotted with red.

James was buried the next morning in a small plot near the base of the hills. Ed Leary read from the Bible as the people of Fire Valley looked on. Rebecca, supported by her husband and children, was silent during the service, but as the tiny pine box was lowered into the grave, she crumpled in a fit of sobbing. Wallace carried her to the house, where Edna Hoyt sat with her.

Wallace had emptied his rifle into Baron the previous night; in the heat of the morning, the carcass was beginning to putrify. Several men dragged it into a field and buried it there.

In spite of the tragedy, life in the drought-plagued valley went on. With the pall of death still hanging over the Padgett ranch, some of the settlers—at Wallace's insistence—returned later in the day to draw water from the well.

Ha-kar-gar-ush was worried. It had been three days since A-ke-kis and the others had ridden to the *sayka loluk*. At least one should have returned with some word. The shaman had sought the guidance of Kumush, but Our Father chose to remain silent.

"We should send others after them," he said to Kan-kush.

"They can take care of themselves," the *La gi* replied. "I'm certain their reason for not yet returning is a good one."

"How long will we wait?"

"A few days."

"Then you'll send others?"

"Yes."

Amos Paine had been on a roaring drunk for two days, and he'd spent some of that time in an outhouse behind the livery stable, which doubled as a jail. On the morning that Jason Bonner let him out, he smelled worse than the building that had held him. Bonner nearly puked as he stood before the repulsive man.

"What do you 'spect, Mr. Bonner?" Paine said. "Your guest quarters ain't exactly big on facilities."

"You think you can behave yourself, Amos?"

"Sure. Almost outta cash anyway. After I get cleaned up, I'm gonna find me that breed, and—"

"Please, spare me your itinerary. In any case, you're out of luck. The woman in question has moved on to Yreka. Something about it not being profitable here."

"Damn!" Paine bellowed. "What kinda two-bit town you runnin'? Now there ain't a woman within fifty mile worth lookin' at—" he paused, "'cept that Missus Padgett."

Scowling, Bonner told Paine of the tragedy that had befallen the Padgett family. The wagonmaster listened, but the story barely wiped the smile from his stubbled face.

"Too bad," he said. "Liked that kid too. Well, I better go and pay my respects. It's only proper, ain't it?"

He strode toward the rear door of the stable. Bonner, despite his misgivings, knew it would be futile to try to dissuade him. "Amos," he called, "don't give them any trouble."

Paine's grin broadened. "Not me, Mr. Bonner. I wouldn't think of it."

Dressed in black, Rebecca stood before the small grave, as she had done endlessly since the funeral. That morning she had hardly spoken a word to her husband, who approached her now.

"Come on, Bec, let's go back to the house," Wallace said. "It's too hot to be standing out here." Rebecca shook her head. "We'll come back later, I promise," he pleaded. Again, the brusque refusal. "Listen, Bec, the children are in the north pasture, and I've got to give them a hand. Promise me you'll go back inside soon."

She looked at him with eyes that could no longer cry. "I will. I'll go in a little while," she said softly, and he nodded, though he knew she was not telling him the truth.

Rebecca stood there for a half hour more until a biting cold sliced through the heat. Shivering, she turned and walked away.

Amos Paine, swigging whiskey as he rode through Fire Valley, sang a lusty song that would have made women cover their children's ears. But as he neared the Padgett ranch and spotted the small grave, he fell into a respectful silence.

"Guess I better get cleaned up," he said, spotting the well. "Don't want her to think I'm an animal—or worse, an injin."

After tethering his sorrel by the trough, he dropped a bucket into the deep blackness. His big arms were hardly strained as he retrieved a hundred feet of rope. Ladling water from the brimming pail, he drank deeply. He splashed his face to wash away the bleary look but disdained cleaning the rest of his body, for he was no longer aware of his own stench.

"Mr. Paine," a voice called. "Mr. Paine, I'm over here."

Startled, Paine looked around. He saw Rebecca standing in the doorway of the barn. She wore a sleeveless white summer dress and was barefoot. For the first time since he'd met her, she had loosened the austere bun at the back of her head, letting her long auburn hair fall over bare shoulders. A demure but promising smile lit her face, which was touched with rouge and lipstick.

"Uh, mornin', Missus Padgett," Paine said clumsily, walking toward her.

"Call me Rebecca. Were you looking for me?"

"Yeah, Mis—uh, Rebecca. Uh, that is, I heard about your boy 'n all, and I just wanted to . . . uh, ya know."

"Of course," she replied vaguely. "Come with me, Amos."

She turned and disappeared into the dark barn. Confused, Paine hurried after her. Not immediately seeing her inside, he called from the entrance, "Uh, Missus Padgett?"

"Rebecca," her voice answered. "And I'm back here."

Paine walked past stalls of snorting horses until he came to the last one where bales of hay were stored and Rebecca waited for him. In the dim light filtering down through the ceiling cracks, he saw that she had unfastened the buttons of her dress. As he watched, she withdrew her arms from the straps. The top fell away, revealing small pale breasts with dark lust-hardened nipples. She wriggled free of the garment. Paine, his throbbing manhood firm, hungrily eyed the dark patch between her thighs.

"You told me you were a real man, Amos," she said huskily. "Let's find out if you've ever had a real woman before."

She began peeling off his clothes. If she noticed their stench, she didn't show it. The bewildered Paine watched her work methodically until they were both naked. Then she pulled him to the ground and did things with her hands and mouth that he did not think were possible. Sucking him to near-explosion, she eventually guided his engorged member into the liquid softness of her body. When his flood came, she took some eagerly into her mouth and smeared the rest on her stomach and breasts. Finally, with impossible strength, she cupped her hands around his head and drew it insistently between her thighs. Her body thrashed as his tongue slid up and down, in and out. She moaned ecstatically for what seemed minutes until she crumpled, spent, in his arms.

"Amos?" she whispered after their heavy breathing had eased.

"Yeah, Mis—Rebecca?"

"You'd better go now before someone finds us."

"Kin I come see you again?"

"Of course."

Paine pulled on his clothes, and with a final look at Rebecca's sweating body, he left. Rebecca soon rose and, not bothering to dress, padded to the door. She stared across the yard toward the well where Paine, again washing his face, grinned at her. He waved and mounted his sorrel.

As he rode off, Rebecca's head snapped back. After an instant of white blindness, her vision cleared. When she again saw Paine, she shrank back but quickly realized he was leaving. What was that animal doing there? She wondered. Perhaps he had come for water. Then she looked down at her naked, semen-streaked body, which reeked from contact with unwashed flesh. Turning slowly, she peered into the dim barn, not seeing but sensing the reality of the last stall.

And she knew.

Her face a tight mask, she walked back into the barn and extracted a pitchfork from a mound of hay. Pushing the handle into the ground, she angled the fork end sharply upward. After pressing her neck against the barbed tines, she fell forward.

Wallace found her, still upright, an hour later.

7

The Meeting

Two days after Rebecca's funeral, the Trimbles sold their land to Elias Kolb and left for Sacramento. They had begged Wallace Padgett and his children to come with them, but the proud man, despite his grief, had refused. All of Fire Valley was sorry to see the Trimbles leave. But as before, life went on.

Ha-kar-gar-ush knew the *La gi* feared the wrath of Kumush. In light of Our Father's silence, he decided to bend the truth. "Others must be sent," he told the Modoc chieftain. "They must be sent *now*. Kumush has given me a sign."

"What kind of sign?" Kan-kush asked.

Evading the question, the medicine man repeated, "Others must be sent to the *sayka loluk*. When will this be?"

"In the morning. They will go in the morning."

"I will go too," Ha-kar-gar-ush said.

"Is it the will of Kumush?"

He nodded. "If something is wrong, I must be there."

"Tomorrow morning then, shaman."

That same day, Peter Kolb was bitten by his dog. It was not a serious wound, but his hurt was big, for he had raised the gentle animal from a pup, and it had never once bared its teeth. They thought it a one-time aberration, until it went for other children, fortunately with less success. Elias Kolb destroyed it.

Later that afternoon, Wallace, who had been working in the barn after visiting the cemetery, heard a commotion outside. He saw Ed Leary and Tommy, his nine year-old son, at the well. Leary, a religious man whom Wallace had never known even to raise his voice, was slapping the boy across the back of his head. His language was worthy of a gold-town saloon.

"Ed, what're you doing?" Wallace called, running toward them.

"This goddamn kid," Leary snarled. "How'm I goin' to make a man outta him? Can't even pull up a friggin' pail of water!"

"It was heavy, Pa," the boy cried. "I hurt my arm yesterday, and—"

"Dammit!" Leary roared, hitting Tommy again. "Don't give me none of that. Get up, you snivelin' brat!"

"Ed, leave him alone!" Wallace grabbed Leary's arm. "Why are you doing this?"

"That's between me and him," Leary said, pulling free. "Christ, Padgett, mind your own goddamn business. Just 'cause the well's on your land don't mean you run our lives!"

He mounted his horse and rode off. Tommy, refusing Wallace's help, clambered atop his pony and followed in the dusty wake of his scowling father.

Watching them go, Wallace wondered if he should try to talk to Ed later. Then he turned his back and shrugged. It was their business, he thought. He'd just mind his own, like Ed said.

He saw Martha and Benjamin coming from the house and met them near the barn. "Where were you going?" he asked them.

"To see you, Pa," Benjamin replied. "What was all that ruckus with Mr. Leary?"

"It's no worry of yours!" Wallace snapped. "Why in hell can't you keep your damn little noses—"

Martha, who had not yet emerged from the despair of losing James and her mother, broke into uncontrollable sobs at his outburst. Benjamin bit his lip and looked down. Wallace's anger faded into bewilderment, then concern. He drew the youngsters to him.

"God, I'm sorry!" he cried. "I'm so sorry. You're the last ones I would ever hurt. In the name of Jesus, *what's happening*?"

"Father, I don't want to live here anymore!" Martha sobbed. "Can't we go back home, please?"

"Or maybe to Sacramento, Pa, where the Trimbles went," Benjamin added.

Wallace nodded sadly. "You're right. We've lost too much already. I'll talk to Elias. Come on, let's finish our chores."

"Can we . . . see them first?" Martha asked haltingly.

"Of course," Wallace said. Wiping his eyes, he followed his slump-shouldered children toward the hills.

What was happening here? he asked himself again as they passed the well. His gaze fell upon the salvation of Fire Valley, and he stopped. As he stared at the well, blood-soaked images of the recent days assailed him. Suddenly, intuitively, he knew there was a link between them and the silent stone-walled shaft. He could not begin to understand, but he realized he and the others of Fire Valley must face it.

Soon.

Six sleek ponies stole away from the Modoc village in the predawn hours. At the head was Ha-kar-gar-ush, still an able horseman, despite his age and his having ridden infrequently in the past several years. Lac-el-es, the woman of A-ke-kis, and Skmea-chee, his little brother, were with the elder, as were three braves. They rode purposefully down mountain trails and through dry passes.

Much of their journey was done as the sun passed its zenith.

Elias Kolb had gone to Yreka the previous day. Knowing this, Wallace did not call the meeting of Fire Valley's settlers until three that afternoon. The people were puzzled when Benjamin delivered urgent invitations early in the morning to meet at the well, but they all agreed to come. Ed Leary, grinning as he chased the giggling Tommy and Ruth around the yard in a game of tag, was especially curious. Still he told Benjamin they would be there for the "social," as he called it.

On the way home, Benjamin's pony bolted. The boy was thrown and bruised in a few places but not seriously hurt. He watched as the animal reared and lashed out with its hooves, finally snapping one leg in a burrow. It whinnied in agony as it lay there, and was still suffering when Benjamin, after running the remaining mile and a half, returned with his father, who ended the creature's torment.

Elias Kolb and his family were the first to arrive. They were welcomed by a grim-faced Wallace Padgett, who stood near the well with his children.

"What the devil's this all about?" Kolb asked, scowling. "I just got back from Yreka a few hours ago, and I'm tired."

"Let's wait for the others," Wallace replied. "It'll be easier. Here, Martha made lemonade. Cool yourselves off."

The Learys and Hoyts arrived together. Jason Bonner could not make it, though his presence was not a necessity. Wallace noticed that all the families were heavily armed; but then he was also, for it had been common practice since the Indian attack. Ignoring individual questions, he motioned his neighbors into a half circle and spoke to them.

"We've been denying this. Now it's got to be faced. There's something wrong in Fire Valley, something real wrong. You all know it, unless you're blind and stupid." He gestured behind him. "Ever since we started digging the well—"

"The well?" Hoyt said. "What in blazes does the well have to do with this?"

"It has *everything* to do with what's happened here. Look at the facts. First, those Indians that attacked us. Why did they do it?"

Kolb shrugged. "Probably likkered up."

"No, we would've smelled it. And were they really attacking? They could have picked us off from the hills. We couldn't see it then, but now it's clear. They were trying to warn us."

"*Warn* us?" Hoyt exclaimed. "Warn us about what?"

"The well!" Wallace said impatiently. "They wanted us to know about the well!"

"The well again," Kolb said. "What about it?"

"You tell me!" Wallace snapped. "You were forty-four when you went down. Now you look seventy. Jason Bonner is, what, thirty-six, thirty-seven? He's an old man now too. What happened down there, Elias?"

Kolb shrank back. "I don't know," he said meekly. "We couldn't remember for a few seconds. It was cold, just—cold."

"Just cold?" Wallace challenged.

"Yeah, dammit! Just cold!"

"All right, let's go on. Baron was the gentlest animal this side of Sacramento. What could have caused him to do what he did to James? And what about my Rebecca?" His sweat mixed with tears; the others squirmed. "I know all of you heard about Amos Paine's drunken bragging. Well, it was true. From what I saw in the barn, it had to be!" Martha began crying softly. Benjamin held her hand. "But believe me, as God is my judge, Rebecca wouldn't have slept with any man, much less that pig. She was *made* to do it, and realizing what she had done, she killed herself. Don't any of you see it?"

"Wallace, we know you suffered a lot," Kate Leary said softly. "But see what?"

"There's evil here!" Wallace cried. "We've uncovered something evil, and it's starting to spread!"

"Evil?" Kolb repeated. "Wally, you're out of your head!"

Wallace whirled to face Leary. "What about you, Ed? Nearly beating Tommy to death yesterday. Was that of your own doing?"

"I—I don't know what you're talkin' about," Leary stammered.

"You *beat* our son?" Kate exclaimed. "Liar! You told me he fell!"

She slapped him once and would have a second time, but Leary grabbed her wrists. "Dammit, Wally!" he snapped. "Why'd you tell her that? I didn't do nothin' to Tommy."

"Whether you remember or not, Ed, you *did*," Wallace said. "It got to you, and it'll continue to get to all of us. We have to do something!"

"What'd you have in mind, Wally?" Kolb asked scathingly. "Fill up the well, maybe? That'll ruin us for sure!"

"Ah, this is a lotta horseshit!" Hoyt bellowed, waving his crutch. "If you don't like it, Padgett, take your goddamn brats and get outta the valley. We don't need your kind here!"

Wallace stared aghast at his friend's twisted face. "Cal, listen to yourself!" he pleaded. "Can't you see what's happening to you?"

"Yeah, shuddup, Cal," Kolb warned, "or so help me Jesus, I'll mess up your other leg!"

"You beat our son!" Kate Leary cried, breaking free and pummeling her husband.

"Son of a bitch, Padgett!"

"Pa, stop it!"

"Mother—!"

The Modocs approached the place where their missing brothers had last tied their ponies. Even from a distance they heard the din rising on the far side of the hill. They gathered around Ha-kar-gar-ush and awaited his guidance.

"I feel death," he said. "Death is in this place. And . . ." He frowned as he turned his head from side to side.

"Yes, Shaman?" Lac-el-es asked.

"I'm not certain," he replied. "We must get closer."

They ascended the slope and at the summit found signs that the dull senses of the *basdin* would not have detected, telling them of the recent presence of A-ke-kis and the others. Then, peering into the valley, they loosed a cry of horror that was drowned by the shouting men, screaming women, and sobbing children below.

"It has happened," the shaman gasped. "A-ke-kis was right. We waited too long. Kumush, oh Kumush, *it has happened again!*"

"But where *is* A-ke-kis?" Lac-el-es asked.

Ha-kar-gar-ush trembled. "A-ke-kis and the others are dead."

"*Dead?*" Lac-el-es cried, and she would have raised a mourning wail had one of the braves not clamped a hand over her mouth.

"Their spirits have not yet risen," the shaman said. "Their bodies are buried somewhere in the *basdin* way."

"Then the *basdin* killed them?" asked Wee-hum, one of the braves.

The shaman nodded. "Yes."

Grim-faced, Wee-hum drew his knife. "Then the *basdin* must pay!"

Ha-kar-gar-ush gazed again at the violent, frenzied people by the well. "The *basdin* will pay. Oh yes, Our Father, they *will* pay."

8

The Fire Valley Massacre

Jason Bonner finished his business earlier than anticipated. He rode quickly through the valley in an effort to reach the Padgett ranch before the meeting was done, for he was curious about the invitation. At four-fifteen, less than a mile away, he passed an Oregon-bound wagon train. Amos Paine, who had returned to Susanville after the business with Rebecca Padgett and immediately taken the new commission, rode at its head. He grinned and waved at Bonner, who ignored him.

Minutes later, Bonner left the main trail and angled toward the Padgett house, as yet invisible beyond some knolls. Once past them, he spotted the wagons of the visiting families. Except for the Hoyt rig, all were tipped over on their sides. Horses were scattered about the yard, two grazing, the others lying dead. A foreboding pall of silence shrouded the ranch, and Bonner shuddered despite the hot sun. Then his gaze found the well and what surrounded it. A hundred yards away, he reined his horse and tried to justify what he thought he saw as a mirage of the shimmering heat. But when he urged his skittish mount nearer, he could no longer deny the scene before him.

The settlers of Fire Valley were dead. They had died hideously. The dark stain of their blood spread for yards around the well. The bodies of men, women, and children were mutilated, most beyond recognition. Dismounting, Bonner nearly stumbled over a dismembered leg. Gore-spattered faces of terror stared at him from twisted limbs and ravaged torsos, these bloated mounds already attracting innumerable black beetles and other blood-hungry parasites. Only two corpses were apart from the others. One was Elias Kolb; the second was a brutally mangled woman, though its slight form indicated it to be Kate Leary. They lay on opposite sides of the well, their right arms, strangely untouched, stretching toward it.

Bonner staggered back to his horse and galloped to one of the knolls. Spotting the wagons on the main trail, he fired two shots in the air. A few minutes later, Amos Paine, with three of the new settlers, joined him.

"What's all the ruckus, Mr. Bonner?" the wagonmaster asked. "You skeered a buncha folk back there."

Unable to answer, Bonner led them to the well, where they absorbed the carnage in disbelieving horror.

"Jesus Lord A'mighty!" Paine cried.

One of the settlers, a frail midwesterner named Clemmons, fell to his knees and moaned loudly.

"Water," Bonner gasped. "Get him some water."

"Aw, just like a damn ole woman!" Paine bellowed.

"Do it, Amos!"

Caked blood adhered to Paine's boots as he walked to the well. The bucket was already down. He grabbed the rope and hauled it up quickly. It clattered over the rim, leaving Paine staring into the sightless eyes of Wallace Padgett. Padgett's severed head was jammed tightly into the bucket, and streams of blood seeped through narrow cracks between the oak slats.

"Son of a goddamn whore!" Paine yelled, and dropped the tainted bucket. It plummeted into the darkness and struck the water with a loud splash.

Hart and Ellis, the other settlers, carried the glassy-eyed Clemmons to a trough by the barn. Paine, now ashen, rejoined Bonner. "Butchers!" he snapped. "Friggin' goddamn butchers!"

"You know who did this, Amos?"

"Injins, who else?" Paine roared. "Filthy friggin' cutthroat bastards! Every mother's son of 'em should be hung!"

"Over here!" Ellis called. "There's someone in the barn!"

Paine and Bonner hurried past the mounds of death. They raced into the barn where Ellis was casting aside bales of hay to reach Benjamin Padgett. The boy, with hardly a scratch on him, stared straight ahead, not seeing, or at least not acknowledging, the presence of those kneeling before him.

"Hey kid," Paine said, "what the hell happened out there? C'mon, tell us . . ."

"Idiot!" Bonner snapped, shoving him aside. "Ben, hey

Ben," he said softly, "it's me, Jason Bonner. Ben, can you hear me?"

The boy did not respond, but allowed them to help him to his feet. He stood on his own. Bonner led him out the rear door, so that he would not have to look at what he had likely already seen. Paine went to get the horses. Soon all of them, including the recovered Clemmons, had gathered near the cottage.

Taking charge, Paine told the others, "What happened here was real recent. It's our duty to go after the bastards that did this. I hope yer all with me."

"But there could be hundreds," Hart protested. "Look at what they did, and without losing a single one of their own."

"First off," Paine said, "these injins don't leave their dead, not if they kin help it. Second, a handful of the sneakin' devils could wipe out five times their number 'fore anyone knew what hit 'em. But don't fret, I'm not partial to suicide. If there's too many, we'll back off 'n' report it to the army. Otherwise . . ." He spat on the ground as he fingered his Colts.

"What about the train?" Ellis asked. "We have to get to Oregon."

Paine glared at the easterner. "If the Modocs done this, we'd be crazy to go any more north. Clemmons, you up to leadin' the wagons back to town, or you gonna keep gettin' sick?"

"N-no, I'm all right."

"Ellis, you ride with him. Gather up more guns and the rest of the men. Here, take the kid with—hey, where'd he go?"

His back toward the men, Benjamin stood several feet away. His gaze was transfixed on the well. Bonner attempted to lead him to the horses, but this time Benjamin would not move. When Bonner tried to lift the small boy, he wasn't able to budge him an inch. Benjamin was riveted to the spot, inexplicably held to the object of his rapt attention. Bonner called to Paine to help him, and both men were red-faced as they lifted the boy onto one of the horses. His slight frame remained rigid as Clemmons and Ellis rode off with him. Only after they were nearly a hundred yards away from the well did he slump over, unconscious.

While awaiting Ellis's return, the others scouted the area. Paine quickly found fresh signs of Indians on the far side of the hills. When Ellis got back with four other men, the weapons were distributed. With a last look at the bloody scene,

Jason Bonner, Amos Paine, and five nervous settlers set off through the junipers.

A couple of hours of hard riding later, Paine motioned them to a halt and sniffed the air cautiously. "They're near," he muttered. "Go slow, and keep those damn horses quiet."

The thunder of gunfire reverberating off rock walls faded slowly. Bonner, Paine, and the other men stood at the edge of a gully, guns still smoking, too hot to holster. Below, six bodies lay sprawled grotesquely, each riddled with far more bullets than were necessary to kill. The settlers, for whom this had been a first, were congratulating one another.

"This is only the beginnin'," Paine said. "We'll call over the militia from Yreka, just like was done after that Bloody Point business a few years back. This time, we'll wipe out *all* the friggin' red bastards!"

The settlers voiced their approval, but Bonner said, "This is as far as it goes, Amos."

"The hell!" Paine snapped. "These murderin' devils—"

"What's done is done. If the Modocs are about to make war, then it's up to the army to stop them. But I got to believe that the massacre in Fire Valley was an isolated incident."

Muttering to himself, Paine waved the other men back to their horses. Jason Bonner, running his fingers through his white hair, took a last look at the bodies, which included a boy, a woman, and an old man. Shaking his head, he joined the others.

The settlers of Fire Valley were buried in the cemetery that first held James Padgett and his mother. The Indians were left where they had fallen. Within days, their remains were washed away by a drought-ending deluge that filled the gully. Benjamin, encased in silence, was sent to Sacramento to live with the Trimbles. The *sayka loluk* remained unsettled for some years, though the town of Bonner held its own and eventually thrived.

No evidence could be found linking the rest of the Modoc tribe to the Fire Valley Massacre, though most whites harbored their suspicions. The incident became part of the region's bloody history, and the South Lake People were left alone—for the time being.

part 2

FIRE
VALLEY

9

Bonner

Modoc County was not very impressive to folks from the big city.

The first town was Adin, population five hundred, give or take a few. After seeking directions at the Juniper Tree Motel, the Lowells followed a secondary road west to Lookout, which was even smaller. Then, north on Route 91 until the road split. A sign indicated the left fork to be the Bonner Highway.

Five minutes later, the LTD wagon rounded a curve. From the top of a ridge, near where the Padgett family had stood more than a century earlier, the Lowells had their first sight of Fire Valley. This time there were roads, telephone poles, power lines, and smoke curling from the twin stacks of a mill at the edge of the town below. In spite of this, they were impressed by the sprawling mountain-rimmed valley.

"Oh, it's beautiful!" Janet exclaimed. "Why did you say your folks left?"

"I'm beginning to wonder myself," Greg said.

They descended to the town sitting at the mouth of Fire Valley where Greg Lowell had been born. BONNER, CALIFORNIA, a sign announced. NICEST LITTLE TOWN IN THE WEST. POPULATION 3,217.

"Sounds like we're driving into Dodge City or something," Allison said.

Janet laughed. "Maybe they have a real ornery sheriff. Broad-shouldered, big black mustache, a pair of six-guns at the hips."

"A Clint Eastwood type," Mark added, "like in the spaghetti westerns."

"All right, you clowns," Greg said, looking in his rear-view mirror. "You're going to find out real soon, because we got him on our tail. Damn speed trap!"

He pulled off the road, and a white squad car, its blue lights flashing, followed. As Bonner's sheriff approached their car, the Lowells quickly discarded all preconceived notions.

Winn Staley was tall and wiry, fair-skinned and cleanly shaven, with a scholarly sort of face. He appeared to be in his early thirties.

"Afternoon, folks," he said, bending over. "Hot enough for you today?" His voice was crisp but friendly, with no discernible accent.

"Hello, Sheriff," Greg replied. "What's the problem? I didn't think I was going too fast."

"You weren't," Winn Staley said. "I noticed that your registration sticker expired last month."

"Darn!" Janet said, rummaging through the glove compartment. "It's right here. I just forgot to put it on."

"Sorry, Sheriff," Greg said. "We'll take care of it."

"You just passing through Bonner?"

Greg shook his head. "We might stay a day or so. Can you recommend a motel?"

"Sure. Then this is your first time up here?"

"Actually, I was born in Bonner. But it's been a long time—"

"You're kidding!" Winn said. "What did you say your name was?"

"Lowell, Greg Lowell. This is my wife, Janet, and our children, Allison and Mark."

The sheriff introduced himself. "Lowell, huh? I don't recall anyone by that name, and I've lived here since I was five."

"My parents stayed in Bonner for a short time, probably years before you got here. They had some property to sell that my mother had inherited. She was a Padgett."

"No!" Winn said. "Wallace and Rebecca Padgett were among the first settlers of Fire Valley. Then you're a descendant of theirs."

"My great-great-grandparents."

"This is incredible. I imagine while you're here you'll want to drive out and visit the site of the massacre. It's a historical monument—an old well out on Vern Greenwood's place. Vern's in his eighties, though you'd hardly know it, and he's lived out there forever. He may be the one who bought the property from your folks."

"What massacre?" Mark asked.

"The Fire Valley Massacre," Greg said. "I'll tell you about it later. The car's pretty hot."

Winn smiled sheepishly. "I'm sorry to hold you up. A couple of things. First, the motels around here are okay, but if you want to say you've been in Bonner, get yourself a room at Harmony House. It's on this road, in the middle of town. You can't miss it. Second, there's a social at the high school tonight. I'd be pleased if you came as guests of my wife and me. It's at seven, and there's always plenty to eat."

"It's okay with me," Greg answered. His family voiced their approval, though Mark was less than enthusiastic.

"Great," Winn said. "I'll see you then. Anyone can tell you where the high school is."

The sheriff touched the brim of his hat, and the Lowells drove off. Greg followed the main road—now called Juniper Boulevard—past about two dozen small vintage brick houses, some run down but most well cared for. On the edge of town, they saw the Juniper Mall: ten or twelve specialty shops, Stringer's Food Mart, and the inevitable McDonald's.

Finally, downtown Bonner, eight square blocks. A green triangular park with a large statue of the town's founder was an island amid older businesses, a hardware store, a boxcar diner called the Depot, a sporting-goods emporium. Rising above them all was the town's four-story skyscraper, Harmony House. The carved plaque over the awning-covered door read HOTEL, RESTAURANT, AND SALOON.

Stopping in front of the hotel, Greg said, "You register us while I get the car filled. We're running on fumes. I'll meet you back here."

"Don't get lost," Janet said.

"Ha!"

Mark unloaded their luggage, then Greg drove fifty yards to Ledbetter's Texaco, an ancient, three-pump station. After filling up, he noticed that the rear of the station was also the hotel parking lot. He left the LTD there and walked back the short distance.

The rustic lobby of Harmony House was surprisingly small. Its primary source of light was a wagon-wheel chandelier hanging between heavy crisscrossed wood beams on the high ceiling. Two plush leather couches stood back-to-back on a worn rug in the center of the room. Framed photographs of Bonner and the region, some dating back over a century, covered the paneled walls. A stone fireplace stood empty in one corner, waiting for another time of year.

On one side, a wide curtained doorway led to the Modoc Room restaurant, the saloon, and a gift shop. On the opposite wall, the first ten steps of a narrow wood stairway rose to a small landing, then turned and disappeared above. By the stairs was an elevator, a manual birdcage thing with a bent, grizzled operator who had probably been there when it was installed.

Greg strode across the wood floor to the front desk, behind which stood a smiling middle-aged man in a plaid shirt and string tie.

"Welcome to Harmony House," he said cheerfully in a voice larger than his slight frame. "You must be Mr. Lowell."

"Yes. Where's my family? You couldn't have gotten them registered *that* fast."

The desk clerk's smile broadened. "We aim to please," he drawled. "The missus is in three-oh-eight, the kids next door in three-ten. They're in a larger suite, with separate rooms. Go on. Luther'll take you up. Enjoy your stay at Harmony House."

10

Family History

It took nearly half a minute for the ancient Luther Wall—that's what the plaque in the elevator said: *To Luther Wall, for twenty-five years of dedicated service to Harmony House,* and *that* was over seventeen years ago—to urge the clanking apparatus to the third floor. The old man didn't say a word to Greg and mostly kept his eyes straight ahead. Once, between the second and third floors, he glanced at his passenger. His expression might have been one of curiosity, or maybe disdain. Greg couldn't tell for sure. When he smiled, Luther Wall quickly turned away.

At the third floor, Luther threw the brake, and when the door opened, Greg noted that the floor of the elevator and the carpeted hallway were perfectly level. He thanked the old man, who nodded somberly but didn't close the cage right away. As Greg hunted for room 308, which was near the end of the short corridor, he was certain the grizzled operator was watching him.

When Greg stepped into a well-lit spacious room, he saw Janet had already begun unpacking.

"Like it?" she asked.

"Nice," he said as he looked around.

A brightly colored quilt covered the king-size brass bed, which was flanked by a pair of identical nightstands, each supporting a tall lamp. In one corner two armchairs that were probably as soft as they looked sat by a hexagonal table. An eight-drawer bureau and its scroll-edged mirror matched the nightstands. The powder-blue carpeting was plush, the matching wallpaper flocked and elegant. A color television was bolted to the wall in one corner. An open door next to the bureau led into the adjoining suite. Another door revealed a homey bathroom.

Greg shook his head. "I'm afraid to ask how much."

Janet told him. He looked at her curiously. "For this *and* the kids' room? They made a mistake or something."

She shook her head. "We got the red-carpet treatment when we came in. Probably because Winn Staley called."

"The sheriff?"

"To let them know we were coming. That was nice of him."

Allison and Mark, both smiling, came into the room. "Wow, this place is rad!" the girl said.

"It really is," her brother added.

Greg laughed. "It must be, for you guys to agree on anything." He sank into one of the chairs. "I'll have to check out your rooms—later. Oh, this feels good."

"I'm starved," Mark said.

"Come on," Janet urged. "I'm hungry too. Clean up and change, and you'll feel better."

"Okay," Greg said, grimacing as he pulled himself up.

They rode down in Luther Wall's birdcage. This time, the old man glanced at Greg repeatedly, and before they reached the lobby, Greg sensed Luther was wrestling with some half-recalled memory, seeking a hold on some thought that hovered just beyond his grasp. It caused him to overshoot the landing by two inches, and Greg guessed that never happened to Luther Wall.

The Modoc Room was actually two rooms. In one corner was the saloon, walled on three sides and looking like a set from an old western movie, complete with a mustachioed bartender and brass spitoons. People could enter from the street through swinging doors. By contrast, the main dining area, with its massive crystal chandelier, was elegant. There were twenty-five or thirty tables, fewer than half of which were occupied.

As the hostess guided them to a table, Greg asked, "Is everything in here original?"

The woman shook her head. "Sorry to say, no. Harmony House burned to the ground about forty years ago, and just about everything was destroyed. It was a real tragedy, people killed and all. They rebuilt it a few years later, and the new owners tried to make it look like it once did. Some of the furnishings in the hotel are real antiques, but most are replicas."

"A shame," Janet said. "I mean about the fire."

The food in the Modoc Room was good, although Greg thought the contemporary jazz music playing in the background was out of place with so many Stetsons hanging on hat racks. The Lowells took their time eating, a trick Greg and Janet had managed to teach their fast-food teenagers.

When they were finished with their meal and had ordered homemade pie and coffee for dessert, Mark turned to his father. "Dad, you promised to tell us about the Fire Valley Massacre."

"*And* crazy Ben Padgett," Allison added.

Greg laughed. "All right. You have me cornered. I can't recall the exact date, but the Fire Valley Massacre took place a few years before the Civil War. There were only a handful of families living in the valley then, and for whatever reason, they had gathered on Wallace Padgett's ranch. This was right after Rebecca—the wife—and one son had died."

"How did they die?" Janet asked as the waitress arrived with their dessert.

Greg waited until the woman had left, then he shrugged. "I don't know. My grandfather, who told me about it when I was a kid, wasn't sure himself. He guessed that the Indians did it, the same ones who eventually butchered all the settlers."

"Indians?" Allison asked, fork poised over her pie.

"The Modoc Indians. In the case of the Fire Valley Massacre, not the whole tribe, but a small band of renegades who were immediately hunted down and killed."

"These Modocs must've been real savages," Mark said.

Greg shrugged again. "They were darn good fighters. Savages? I don't know. The Modocs had been here for a long time before the whites came. They were only trying to hold onto what was theirs. Same old thing."

"What happened to the Modocs?" Janet asked.

"That's a story I'll save for later, because there's something we should see while we're up here. As for Ben Padgett, well, he was the sole survivor of the Fire Valley Massacre. God, what he must've seen! He was sent to live with a family in Sacramento. It was said that he hardly ever spoke, and he had a wild, distant look about him—hence the name 'crazy' Ben. But in spite of that, he did marry late in life, and had one son."

"Your grandfather," Janet said.

Greg nodded and sipped his coffee. "Samuel Padgett. I remember him like it was yesterday, even though I was only eight when he died. He was as much a mother to me as a grandfather."

"What do you mean, Dad?" Mark asked.

"My mother died when I was two years old. Grandpa Padgett came down from Sacramento to stay with us while she was still alive. He helped care for me then, and even more so after her death, because my father was despondent over losing her."

"When did your dad meet Grandma Clare?" Allison asked.

"Clare Burns came into his life not long after my grandfather died. Until then he had not even looked at another woman, but Clare was a special lady. Heck, you guys remember her. I resented her at first, but not for long. She was really the only mother I ever knew."

"She was great," Janet said sadly. She pushed her empty plate aside and rested her elbows on the table, hands around her coffee cup. "You know, you never talk much about your mother's family. The Padgett history is a tragic one. But I'm still curious about the time your parents spent in Bonner."

"For some reason, that's always been a real sore point with Dad. After a while, I stopped asking him about it. Only the fact that Bonner was my birthplace kept it in my mind. As best as I can figure, they came here in late January, I was born in May, and they left in September."

"Do you really believe they came here just to sell the land?" Janet asked. "They could have handled a real-estate transaction from anywhere."

"Good point. Matter of fact, Samuel Padgett did it that way back in the twenties, when the old sprawling ranches were parceled off. He never set foot within a hundred miles of Bonner in his life, but he made some pretty good money from it. No, when my parents came here from Stockton, I think they intended making a go of it. But it didn't work out, and they probably jumped at the chance to move to L.A. They used some of the money from the sale to buy their first house and put the rest into my dad's business."

After hearing the story, both Allison and Mark were excited about seeing the old Padgett ranch. Greg had the lunch charged to his room, then they all started out to the car.

"Darn," Greg suddenly said as they crossed the lobby.

"What's wrong?" Janet asked.

"I left my wallet upstairs. Go on, I'll be right there."

Luther Wall, sitting on a stool in front of his birdcage, rose stiffly when he saw Greg. He waited around for other passengers—longer than he should have, Greg thought—then finally dragged the doors shut and started up.

The old man was trembling. His hands shook so badly that as he kept one hand on the stick that operated the contraption, the elevator actually shuddered. He was staring wide-eyed at Greg, his leathery face pallid. Greg feared the man might be having a heart attack.

"Are you all right?" he asked.

The old man's answer was a vague "Yuh." He managed to turn away but still shook, and when he braked the elevator to a stop, he was six inches short of the third-floor hallway. He pulled the doors open quickly, and Greg had to step up. With a last curious look at the man, he started down the corridor. He stiffened when Luther Wall's rasping voice trailed after him.

"Why . . . did you . . . have to . . . come . . . back . . . here?"

Greg turned but could not see the old man. Seconds later, the ancient contrivance was clattering down its shaft.

11

The Warning

Greg used the stairs to return to the lobby. Luther Wall and his birdcage weren't there. Still puzzled, if not disturbed, by the old man's behavior and strange question, Greg hurried outside. He said nothing about the incident to Janet.

She had picked up a local map at the front desk. After studying it, Greg drove out to the old Padgett ranch, nine miles north of town. Juniper Boulevard became the Bonner-Oregon Highway as they continued into the heart of the breathtaking panorama that was Fire Valley.

The natural irrigation from the valley's many streams, coupled with the adequate rainfall of the current summer, left dreamlike splashes of color: Wide patches of various crops tumbling into sprawling layers of lush ankle-high bunch grass. Plump brown cattle grazed on the land, as they had for decades. A few big farms and ranches remained, though parceling had cut most of the properties to between ten and fifty acres, still impressive to those from postage-stamp lots in the big cities and their suburbs. The side roads that led to the various homesteads intersected the highway every half mile or so. Once, the Lowells had to slow as a tractor leisurely crossed their path.

"Boy, this place is incredible," Allison said. "Look at those mountains!"

"Just beautiful," Janet agreed. "No wonder the Padgetts and the others chose to settle here."

"No wonder those who were already here chose to fight for what had always been theirs," Greg said. "But you're right, it is something else."

They were halfway to the Padgett ranch on an empty

stretch of highway when three men suddenly appeared, standing abreast in the middle of the road, not twenty yards ahead.
They were stocky dark-skinned men with straight black hair.
Their torn garments of buckskin were soaked with the blood
that poured from countless wounds. Wide-eyed, their faces
pleading, they waved their arms, warning the Lowells to stop.

"Jesus Christ!" Greg yelled, jamming on the brakes. The
tires squealed, rubber burned. The LTD skidded off the road,
its front half across the shoulder, the rear still on the highway.
Greg heard Mark swear as he and Allison bumped heavily
against the back of their seat. Janet looked too scared to speak,
her hands braced against the dashboard. Another screech of
brakes assaulted them, then the deafening blast from the air
horn of the produce truck that had been following them at a
safe distance.

"Asshole!" the driver shouted as he passed them.

Greg ignored him. "Are you guys all right?" he frantically asked his family.

"I'm okay," Allison said, though her voice was shaky.

"I jammed my finger," Mark muttered.

"What the devil did you do that for?" Janet snapped.

"Are you serious?" Greg exclaimed. "Didn't you
see . . ."

"See what?" she asked.

"I didn't see anything," Mark said.

"Me neither," Allison added.

Greg turned and stared at the empty road, marred only
by the careening lines of his own tires. "What the hell . . ."

"Greg, what is it?" Janet asked. "What did you see?"

"Nothing, obviously," he answered, waving his hand disgustedly at the road. "I thought there was a—big pothole. You
know, I've been behind the wheel too long. Jan, will you
drive?"

"Sure. Greg, are you okay? You look—"

"I'm all right. Let's go."

"Is that what you two want?" she asked Allison and
Mark.

They nodded. "We'd like to see this place," Mark said.

Greg stepped out of the car, and Janet slid over behind
the wheel. He continued to stare at the road as he walked
around to the passenger side. A minute later, he was still looking in the sideview mirror, until he could no longer see the
spot where the three men had stood.

"How're you doing?" Janet finally asked.

"Fine," he answered. "Let's forget about what happened back there, okay? It was no big thing."

"Sure, babe," she said, and returned her attention to the road.

Greg gazed out the window at the mountains, trying to take his own advice and forget what he had seen. But he could not rid his mind of one thought. Why was he ignoring their warning? He turned back to the highway, expecting to see them again.

They did not reappear.

12

The Well

A few more miles of quiet driving through the magnificent valley brought them to another intersecting road. Two small signs, with an arrow pointing to the left: CEMETERY and FIRE VALLEY MASSACRE, HISTORICAL SITE.

"Interesting combination," Janet said, turning the LTD onto the narrow road.

"Probably didn't feel like hauling the bodies too far," Greg said.

Allison groaned. "Oh, Dad, *yuck*!"

They all laughed, and the pall that had ridden with them was lifted.

They drove past a couple of small farms and a larger ranch. Then, before reaching some juniper-covered hills, the road turned sharply to the right and became even narrower. It did not go far. On the left, fifty yards up, stood the arching wrought-iron gate of the Fire Valley Cemetery. Beyond it, half again the distance, the graded strip terminated at the entrance to Vern Greenwood's ranch, as evidenced by the nameplate on the mailbox. Another sign, hanging over the timber framework of the driveway, said simply: HISTORICAL SITE, COME ON IN.

"You weren't kidding," Janet said. "Nothing like having a cemetery in your front yard."

They drove in and immediately saw the well. Janet parked in the designated area, and they all got out and walked toward the monument. *(welcome home)* An overwhelming sensation of familiarity confused Greg for a moment. *(welcome home welcome home)* Not déjà vu, for he *had* been there before, but forty years ago, as an infant. What could he know?

He fell behind his family, who did not notice. *(welcome home welcome home welcome home)* But the feeling passed, and he caught up with them.

The well had been changed since the massacre. A pair of three-foot timbers rose opposite each other from the flat lip of the mortared stones. They were joined by a crossbeam and topped with a pointed parasol of overlapping shingles, lending the tragic monument a ludicrous wishing-well facade. There were no buckets. The shaft was sealed with a nailed disk of one-by-fours.

A bronze plaque hanging on one of the timbers told the grim story: *On this spot, August 13, 1856, a malcontent band of Modoc Indians brutally murdered and dismembered fourteen of Fire Valley's first settlers. The victims were Wallace Padgett, who owned the land, and his daughter Martha; Elias and Laura Kolb, and their three children; Calvin and Edna Hoyt, and their daughter; Edwin and Kate Leary, and their two children. Retribution for this heinous act came quickly as a party of men, led by Jason Bonner, hunted down the Modocs and destroyed them in a bloody confrontation.*

"An unpleasant tale," Janet muttered, shaking her head.

"Look," Allison said. "Someone's coming."

Across a dusty yard indented by tractor tires, a man in overalls emerged from an old barn. He was thin and gray-haired but walked with a strong step. The tired-looking German shepherd that followed could hardly keep up with him. As he neared, Greg noted that his smiling ruddy face showed hardly any wrinkles. If this was Vern Greenwood, he thought, then the sheriff wasn't kidding about his not looking in his eighties.

"Afternoon, folks," he said amiably. "Anything I can tell you about this place, jest ask. Lord knows I been here long enough."

"Good afternoon," Greg said. "Are the Padgetts buried in that cemetery?"

"Yep, the whole family, and all the others who died in the massacre. For that matter, most everyone who lived in this area since back then are there. How come you wanna know about the Padgetts?"

"My mother was a Padgett," Greg replied. "I'm sorry, I should've introduced myself. My name's Greg Lowell. This is Janet, Mark, Allison."

"You say Lowell?" Vern Greenwood said. "I bought this

place from, uh . . ." He paused as the names he groped for did not come.

"Robert and Katherine Lowell," Greg said. "My parents."

"Then you must be the little fella who was born here that spring."

"Yes, that was me."

"I'll be damned!" The old man pumped Greg's hand firmly. "I remember your parents. Nice man, your dad, and your mom, real pretty woman. Uh, they still around?"

"Dad lives in Encino, near L.A. My mother died less than two years after you met her."

"A shame."

"Did you get to know them at all during that time?" Greg asked.

"Had a few nice chats with your dad," Vern said. "It was him I dealt with on the ranch. Your mom was . . . sorta quiet. I suppose it was because she was sick most of the time."

Greg looked at the old man curiously. "My mother was sick?"

Vern nodded. "First time I met her was a month or two after you were born. She seemed okay then, maybe a mite frayed at the nerves. But a couple of months later she was thin, godawful pale, and her eyes were . . . ya know, sunk. She'd always be holdin' you tight, and wouldn't say nothin'. I —hey, maybe I shouldn't be tellin' you this."

"That's all right," Greg said vaguely.

"Greg, what is it?" Janet asked.

"Nothing." He shook his head. "It's just so frustrating not knowing about any of that. Mr. Greenwood, do you know why they wanted to sell this place?"

"Call me Vern. Everyone does. Your folks had a rough time makin' ends meet. The ranch was pretty run-down, and your dad, well, he didn't have much luck restorin' it. He seemed more the college type."

"He was—is," Greg said. "But I still believe they came here to stay."

"Thought they did. Couldn't say for sure, though. One thing I know. They were in a hell of a hurry to get away from Fire Valley. I paid good money for this place, but I'll tell ya, they coulda got plenty more if they held out. No, toward the end, all they wanted to do was sell it. Didn't even live out here the last couple of weeks. Stayed in town, at Harmony House—till it burnt down, anyway."

"They were there during the fire?" Janet asked, appalled.

"They and your husband, Miz Lowell. Among the few survivors, they was. Left the next day, bang! Had to finish the deal by phone and wire."

"There's something strange about all this," Greg said. "When we get back, I'm going to confront my father. However painful it might be, this time he's going to tell me about the skeletons, or whatever, in the Lowell closet. Mr. Gr—Vern, sorry about the questions, but I would never have known otherwise." He shook off the agonizing webs of the hurtful unknown past and brightened, at least on the surface. "I wanted to ask about—"

"Wait a minute," Janet interrupted, laughing. "Hey, you two, I hope that dog doesn't bite your heads off."

Allison and Mark had been petting Vern's German shepherd. Lying flat on its back with its legs extended, the dog whined and snorted in ecstasy as the two stroked its belly and neck.

The old man's chuckle turned into a brief spell of coughing. He finally said, "You don't have to worry 'bout Rudy. He'd never hurt nothin', especially folks doin' that to him. Now, what'd you want to ask?"

"The well," Greg said. "How come it's boarded up?"

"It got dried out, and I guess they did that to keep kids from fallin' in. That's how it was when I bought the place, 'cept for the top part. My Jenny and me did that. No real need for a well, with plumbin' and all."

"Jenny was your wife?" Janet asked.

Vern nodded. "Forty-six years we was married. No kids, just Jenny 'n' me. Worked side by side every day on this place." He pointed past the barn. "Her and me built that house over there, right where the old Padgett cottage used to be. Lord, she was a good woman! Died ten years ago this April. She's not in the old cemetery. Buried her in a small plot north of here, near the hills."

"I'm sorry," Janet said sadly.

Greg walked over to the well and knelt for a closer look at the stones his great-great-grandfather had helped lay. That odd sense of familiarity suffused him once more. *(welcomehomewelcomehome)* His hands shaking, he rose unsteadily *(welcomehomewelcomehome)*, though he managed to hide his confusion from the others.

In the midst of his delight, Rudy suddenly scrambled to his feet. His gaze found Greg. Dusty fur prickling, a deep growl rumbling from his throat, he bared his teeth.

Mark and Allison swiftly backed away as Vern commanded the dog to settle down. "He's never done this in his life," the old man added.

Greg took a step toward the dog. "Hey, boy, what's the matter? I'm not going to—"

Rudy yelped, as though shot. With his tail between his legs, he raced to the barn and disappeared inside.

Vern shook his head as he started after him. "Fool dog," he grumbled. "Better see what's got into him. Can you folks wait?"

Still looking at the barn, Greg replied, "I think we'll go now, but we may stop back tomorrow, if you don't mind."

"Course not. Be happy to have you. Maybe you can come over to the house."

With a final wave, the old man hurried to the barn. The Lowells started back to their car.

"Do you really intend coming back here?" Janet asked Greg.

"Yes, I want to. I feel bad about spooking his dog. Can't imagine what I did. Anyway, we have to pass by here to get to the place I want to show you."

"Why don't we go now?"

"Because it's not *that* close, and I'm beat. We'll do it in the morning. I'd like to go back and rest. You guys can do whatever you want."

Allison and Mark climbed into the back seat of the station wagon; Janet slid behind the wheel. Greg stood frozen by the other door, his gaze on the tragic monument. *(welcome home padgett welcome home padgett)* For a moment, something kept him there. But the hold was weak, and he pulled free.

"Greg, are you sure you're okay?" Janet asked.

"I'm tired, Jan. I'd like to crash for a little, so I can enjoy the party tonight."

She placed a hand on his arm. "Kind of rough, hearing about your folks like that."

He shrugged. "I guess. Jan, I want to talk to Dad as soon as we get back."

"Sure. Come on, let's get going so I can turn on the air. It's hotter than heck!"

"Oh?" Greg said. "I thought it was . . . comfortable."

The LTD bumped along the narrow dirt driveway, finally passing through the timber framework of the main gate. *(welcomehomepadgettwelcomehomepadgettwelcomehomepadgett)* Soon they turned onto the secondary road, and the entrance to the old Padgett ranch fell from sight.

13

Around Town

"You were right, Jan, it *is* hot!" Greg said as they rejoined the Bonner-Oregon Highway.

Janet glanced wryly at her husband as she turned on the air-conditioning. "Oh, that's better," she said as cool air poured from the vents.

Leaning back, his eyes closed, Greg asked, "What'd you guys think of the old Padgett well?"

"Kind of creepy," Allison replied, "knowing all those people were killed there."

"I thought it was neat," Mark said.

His sister scowled. "You would!"

Janet looked at Greg. "Feeling better?"

"Uh-huh. Trip's beginning to wear on me, I guess."

"It's been fun, but maybe it's time to head back. How about Monday or Tuesday?"

"We'll see. Why don't we play it by ear?"

"Sure. Greg?"

He glanced at her. "Yeah?"

"I'm really glad we did it."

Greg nodded, then closed his eyes again, the splendor of Fire Valley making no impression on him at the moment. The miles to Bonner fell behind uneventfully, although Janet slowed at the spot where Greg had run them off the road earlier, hoping to see what he thought had been there. At last they entered Bonner and inched along a business loop that bustled with campers, pickups, and an assortment of other vehicles.

As they stepped into the Harmony House elevator, Greg was relieved to see a young Mexican man at the controls.

"What time is it?" Janet asked as they rode up to their floor.

"Past three," Greg replied. "What are you guys going to do?"

The birdcage rattled to a stop, and the question went unanswered until they reached the room. "I think I'll check out that little shopping center we passed," Janet said.

"Me too," Allison said.

"You going with them, Mark?"

"No way. I'm gonna find the high school and see if anyone wants to throw a ball around."

"In this heat?" Allison exclaimed. "You're nuts."

"What's it to you?"

"You'd play football in the middle of an earthquake! Jeez, Mark, I never . . ."

The discussion continued as they walked into their adjoining suite. Janet smiled at Greg, who shook his head. While she freshened up in the bathroom, Greg switched on the television and found a baseball game. He sprawled atop the soft bed.

When Janet returned a few minutes later, he saw she had washed her face and put on fresh lipstick, but hadn't changed from her short-shorts, tank top, and sandals. Boy, she looked good, he thought, holding out a hand. She took it. He pulled her gently onto the bed, his lips finding hers before she could say a word. For a moment, she succumbed, her body pressed tightly against his. Then, reluctantly, she scrambled to her feet as Allison's voice reached them from the other room.

"Mom, we're ready," the girl called.

"Okay, meet you in the hall." She added to Greg, "Hold that thought."

"Count on it."

She smiled. "You're feeling better. Love ya. Bye."

"Have fun."

Greg tried to watch the game but couldn't concentrate on it. A thousand meaningless images raced through his brain. He sensed they had something to do with all that had happened since he had seen the three blood-soaked figures on the road. They were there, he told himself. They *were* there. Or perhaps with Luther Wall's strange behavior.

Now some of the visions took form. He saw ethereal faces full of pain; faces he couldn't recognize. No, some *were* familiar, but they passed by too quickly, as if he were trying to focus on them from a wildly spinning carousel.

Then a voice, faint, hollow, like a distant echo . . .

(. . . base hit to right, second hit off . . .)

No! Greg cried silently. *That's not it! Be quiet!* He couldn't hear!

(padgett go away)
What?
(padgett go away please)
I can't hear! I can't—

(. . . first and third, one out . . .)

No!

(padgett go away please padgett go away please)
What is it? Who are you? Who—
(WELCOME HOME PADGETT)

The images faded into a red haze, then blackness. Only one voice now (. . . sacrifice fly brings in the first . . .) then a silence to match the void of darkness into which Greg was falling.

Bonner High School was half a mile west on Yellow Pine Road, which intersected Juniper Boulevard two blocks south of Harmony House. Janet found it easily. After dropping Mark off near the playing field, she and Allison drove to the Juniper Mall. Like the rest of Bonner, it was busy.

"Where to first?" Janet asked as they looked around. "Hey, there's a boutique."

"Mom, I think I'd better stop at the supermarket first. I'm out of tampons."

"You can borrow some of mine."

"No. I hate those things."

"All right. You have money?"

"Uh-huh. I'll meet you in the boutique in a couple of minutes."

Allison went into Stringer's Food Mart, a clean and well-stocked store where locals filled up shopping carts and campers stood on express lines with the few items they had neglected to bring. Not quite Vons or Lucky, but large enough for her not to find immediately what she was looking for.

Billy Douglas worked full-time in Stringer's during the summer. The sandy-haired teenager was tall, two inches over six feet, and thin, and had pleasant boy-next-door looks. The girls in his class said he reminded them of Rick Astley, the singer.

Billy was pricing cans of pork-and-beans in aisle three, but laid his pricer down when he heard someone address him. He stood quickly and turned, but the nearest customer was at the other end of the aisle, his back to Billy.

Perplexed, Billy looked around. His gaze fell on his pricer, yet he did not go back to what he'd been doing. He had to be in aisle five. He strode rapidly to that aisle, too intent on getting there to question the impulse. Quite a few customers milled along the aisle, among them one confused girl, holding her hands up in frustration. He walked right over to her.

"Hi," he said. "Can I help you find something?"

"You sure can. Where would I find the tampons?"

Billy's usual shyness abruptly reasserted itself, and he blushed. It seemed that his whole body turned red. He glanced around furtively to see if anyone had heard. Finally he managed to blurt out, "Aisle four, next one over, near the center."

Allison looked at him curiously. "Hey, sorry if I shook you up."

"That's all right," he mumbled.

Trying to be friendly, she said, "I'm Allison Lowell."

"Billy Douglas. Uh, I've never seen you in here before. You a tourist?"

"Yeah, I guess. We're just staying for a day or so."

"Figures."

"What?"

"Uh, nothing. Sorry." His face reddened again. "Listen, I gotta get back . . ." He seemed distant for a second or two, then again looked at Allison. "Uh, there's this party tonight, at the high school . . ."

"The social, right? Sheriff Staley invited my family and me."

Billy's stomach jumped nervously. At his age he had yet to ask a girl to do anything, but the urge to ask Allison overrode his anxiety. "Uh, I was wondering, I mean . . . uh, about tonight . . . Oh, hey, here comes Mr. Stringer! I can't talk anymore."

He whirled and nearly ran down the aisle. "Billy?" Allison called after him.

He halted, his sneakers squeaking, and glanced back. "Yeah?"

"I'll see you there tonight."

He nodded, almost relieved to note that her face had also reddened. "See you."

Smiling, Allison went off to search for tampons in aisle four.

The football field needed mowing. The grass stood half a foot high, with spotty brown patches. Save for a lone jogger on the rimming track, Mark saw no one. Not an unexpected thing, considering the 94 degrees that flashed on the side of the Wells Fargo Bank in town. Mark had brought two footballs and his shoes, and contented himself by practicing placements off a low tee.

Mark did not fancy himself a kicker. His first two soccer-style efforts, from forty yards, fell short. But from twenty-five, he made three out of four, and the next pair, from thirty, were both good, one barely hooking inside the left post.

On his way to gather the balls, Mark noticed the sweat-soaked jogger waiting for him. The tall athletic man, in his mid or late thirties, rested on one knee and flashed an approving smile.

"Your form isn't too bad," he said. "You must take the game seriously to be practicing in this heat."

"Yes, sir."

The man rose and extended a hand. "I'm Craig Morley."

"Mark Lowell. You're not the Craig Morley who played tight end for the Cardinals, are you?"

Craig grinned. "Guilty. I'm surprised anyone remembers me."

"What do you mean? You were great! Boy, wait'll my dad hears about this. What do you do now?"

"I'm coaching at Bonner High. This'll be my fourth year here. Say, are you local?"

Mark shook his head. "No."

"Didn't recall seeing you before. Where's home?"

"Van Nuys."

"Central High?"

"Uh-huh."

"Then you play for Dale Porter. We're old friends. Doesn't know diddly about offense, but he's a defensive wizard."

"If you don't mind me asking, Mr. Morley, why are you coaching in a little town like this?"

"I like Bonner. This is my part of the country. I was born

and raised in Medford, Oregon. As for coaching here, Bonner
High's one of the top small schools in this part of the state.
Went eight and three last year, two of our losses to Division
One schools. Might do better this year. As far as rewards, in
the past two years I sent nine boys out of here on full scholar-
ships. Four went to the Pac Ten, another to the Southwest
Conference."

"Wow!"

"What's your regular position, Mark?"

"Middle linebacker. Coach Porter has me penciled in as
third-string quarterback for this fall, but fat chance."

"You like quarterbacking?"

Mark nodded. "I played that from all the way back in
Pop Warner."

"Well, let's see what kind of an arm you have."

They retrieved the balls and walked onto the field. "What
first?" Mark asked.

"Fly pattern, deep," Craig replied, crouching. "Right up
the middle. Bet you can't overthrow me."

Mark took an imaginary snap and dropped back. Craig
Morley raced down the field with the graceful strides that had
personified his pro career. Setting himself, Mark launched the
ball. It spiraled perfectly in a low arc. Craig, one arm raised,
slowed for an instant as he looked over his shoulder. Surprised, he sped up. The ball hit the ground five yards in front
of him, nearly sixty yards from where Mark stood.

"That was . . . great!" Craig gasped as they met near
midfield. "Let's see some more."

They ran a dozen or so plays, slant-ins and -outs, sidelines, deep drops. Mark's deliveries were crisp, almost always
accurate. Craig was impressed with the boy's ability.

Soon drenched and exhausted, Craig called a halt to the
workout. "If Dale doesn't take advantage of you, then he's
nuts. I'll tell you this, Mark. I have a top-notch quarterback,
Kevin French. The college recruiters have been drooling over
him for years. From what little I've seen of you, I don't know
why you couldn't be just as good. Too bad I'll never have a
chance to work with you."

"Thanks, Mr. Morley," Mark said. "I really appreciate
that."

He clapped the boy on the shoulder. "Call me Craig,
okay? Come on, let's grab a shower, then we'll go get a cold
drink. My treat."

14

The Social

It was nearly six when Janet returned to their room. Greg, showered and dressed, rose from one of the armchairs and turned off the old movie he'd been half-watching.

"Hi," she said, kissing him. "You look a thousand times better."

"I feel it. You guys have a good time?"

She nodded. "There are some nice shops here."

"Allison next door?"

"Uh-huh. She's . . . ah, been acting kind of funny all afternoon, walking around with this big grin."

"I don't understand."

Janet smiled. "I do. She didn't say so, but I believe she met someone today."

"Who?"

"A boy."

"We-ell, glad to hear it. I wondered if she'd ever get over her terminal shyness. When Stu Berger brought his nephew along for the Memorial Day barbeque, I didn't think she'd come out of her room."

"She even bought a new top for tonight. Swore she didn't have a thing to wear. I think he's going to be at the party."

"Whatever the case, it'll be one of the shortest budding romances on record."

Janet sighed. "I know. But I hope she enjoys herself anyway."

There was a frantic knock on the door. "Hey, Dad! Dad, open up!"

Greg unlatched the door, and his breathless son burst in. "Dad, I —oh, hi, Mom. Listen, you'll never guess who—"

"Whoa, wait a minute," Greg said. "You need to get ready so we can go to the party. We'll talk after."

"Okay," Mark said, grinning as he opened the connecting door and disappeared into the suite.

"What's with him?" Janet wondered.

An hour later, they were driving along Yellow Pine Road, their windows down. The day's scorching heat had already given way to the anticipated coolness of the evening. Mark was rattling on about his day above Allison's feigned yawns.

"Anyway, Craig gave me some great tips. We must've sat in the drugstore for over an hour, just talking!"

"Drugstore?" Janet said.

"Yeah, near the hotel. They have this old soda fountain there."

"*That* I have to see," Greg said.

"You'll meet Craig tonight, at the social," Mark went on.

"Oh, I can hardly wait," Allison muttered.

"Will you shuddup?"

"Greg, it's only five of seven," Janet said. "Think we're too early?"

"I don't think they know from 'fashionably late' here."

The majority of parking spots near the high school gymnasium were filled. Dozens of men, women, and children strolled to the main entrance where others were already milling.

"Still think we're early?" Greg asked, parking the LTD. Janet shook her head. "Guess not."

"Hi, folks, glad you could make it!"

A smiling Winn Staley, out of uniform, approached their car. He carried a large foil-covered plate, as did the woman with him.

"Hello, Sheriff," Greg said as he stepped out of the car. "Nice to see you."

"It's Winn, please. I'd like you to meet Carol, my wife. Honey, these are the Lowells. Now, let's see how good the memory is. Janet, Greg . . . uh, Mike?"

"Mark."

"Sorry. And you're Allison? Well, three out of four."

Carol Staley was a slim attractive woman with lustrous brown hair that cascaded down to the pockets of her jeans. Although nearly a foot shorter than her husband, she wore flat sandals. Seeing her made Greg think of Woodstock and anti-war protests.

"I'm glad to meet all of you," Carol said warmly. "I hope you enjoy the party."

"I'm sure we will," Greg said.

As they walked toward the gym, Janet asked Carol, "Do you have any children?"

"Two girls, four and two. They're home with a sitter."

"And we'd better enjoy getting out alone while we can," Winn said.

"What do you mean?" Janet asked.

"He means," Carol explained, "that Annie Stringer, who's been sitting for us since our oldest was born, is leaving for college next month. Good sitters are hard to find. I suppose I'm just too picky."

Greg laughed. "Hey Allison, here's a steady job for you— if you don't mind the drive."

"Right," she said.

"Don't you have any family in Bonner?" Janet asked.

"Just my mom," Winn said. "But she isn't up to that sort of thing, not with her heart problem. Carol's family all live around San Jose."

"Is that where you're from?"

Carol nodded. "Born and raised there."

"Where did you meet Winn?"

"At Berkeley. We were both sophomores. Fine arts and criminology; great combination. We were married in our senior year and lived near campus a couple of more years after that while Winn did his postgraduate work. I had a job in San Francisco."

"How come you settled in Bonner?" Greg asked.

Carol smiled. "My family wondered the same thing. Winn brought me here to meet his folks before we were married. I fell in love with the place. He would've stayed in the Bay Area, but I wanted to come here. It's a whole different way of life, but I haven't been sorry."

Inside, the surprisingly cool gym was gaily decorated with bunting and balloons. The Staleys deposited their plates of Carol's brownies on one of five long tables piled with other dishes of food. Winn and Carol then introduced the Lowells to many friends and acquaintances, each time mentioning the Padgett link. For a brief time, Greg and his family were the center of attention, to his embarrassment.

Sensing his guest's uneasiness, Winn said privately to Greg, "Listen, it's not every day we're visited by descendants of the first settlers, considering that not too many of them survived even to *have* descendants. You're not going to be in town long, and I didn't want these folks to miss the opportunity to meet you. I'm sorry if—"

"It's okay, Winn," Greg assured him. "Actually, it's kind of fun."

They finally got around to dinner, filling their plates with seconds and thirds of fried chicken, casseroles, corn on the cob, and several other homecooked foods. While eating, they listened to a country-western band playing on a dais along one wall.

"They're pretty good," Janet said.

Carol nodded. "Real good, for amateurs."

"Are you serious?"

"That fellow second from the left?" Winn said. "Les Curry, one of my deputies. He strums a mean banjo. They do it for fun."

Eventually Mark broke away to search for Craig Morley. Allison was intercepted by a smiling heavyset girl.

"Hi, I'm Stacey French," she said.

"Allison Lowell."

"Yeah, I heard. Come and meet some of the kids."

Stacey introduced Allison to Cindy Barnes and Lisa Cunningham, both sixteen. Allison felt at ease with them, though the observant Lisa could not help but notice how often she glanced around the hall.

"Who are you looking for, Allison?"

"Uh, a boy I met this afternoon."

"Fast," Cindy said. "Who is he?"

"Billy Douglas."

"Oooh, Billy Douglas!" Stacey said.

"Did he actually *talk* to you?" Lisa asked.

"Uh-huh. Not a lot, but we talked."

"You're way ahead of us," Cindy said. "He hasn't said a dozen words to me in the three years he's lived here."

"How come?"

"He's just shy. Drives all of us nuts, 'cause he's really cute. But he doesn't date any other girls. Small consolation."

"Hey, there's Billy," Stacey said, "over by the bandstand."

Allison saw him, too, and wondered how she'd missed

him, since she'd been watching the door all night. "Uh, listen, would you mind if . . ."

"Go on," Cindy said. "I don't blame you."

"Boy, you'd be tough competition if you lived in Bonner," Lisa said good-naturedly. "See you later."

Skirting the edge of the gym floor, where a few couples were dancing, Allison circled to the side of the platform and came up behind Billy, who was concentrating on the music.

"Hi," she said, touching his arm.

The boy jumped. "Oh, hi. I saw you over there before."

"Why didn't you come over?"

"You were, uh, with those other girls, and I didn't want to, you know, bother you."

"Silly," she said. "I was looking for you."

"Yeah?"

She smiled. "Yeah."

They stood together and listened to the music. When the band played a less frenetic tune, they danced. Allison felt at ease with him and barely noticed his awkward steps.

After the song was done, Billy looked down at his feet. "Uh, you want to walk around and see the campus? It's a nice night out."

"Sure."

They went outside. Her hand fell into his, and they walked away from the crowded gym.

Craig Morley, whose wife, Eve, was currently engaged in tracking down their eight-year-old son, stood before a semicircle of half a dozen eager youths, all but Mark Lowell members of Bonner High's football team. No one had to guess the topic of their conversation.

After Mark had outlined an intricate defensive pattern, Kevin French, a tall muscular boy and Bonner's reigning hero, turned to him. "Coach says you're pretty good. How about a pickup game with us? We'll see what you can do."

"Sure," Mark said. "When and where?"

"The field, Monday, about one," Dan Hillis, an oversized sixteen-year-old who played offense, replied.

"Hey, thanks," Craig said, scowling. "Nobody told me about this."

"We just, uh, figured you were too busy, Coach," Kevin stammered.

"I'll be over around one-fifteen, after I've finished a class. How about you, Mark?"

"We'll probably be gone by then," he said, disappointed. "I'll have to ask my folks."

"Well, hope you can make it," Craig said.

"So do we," the others added, and Dan warned, "Better bring pads if you have 'em. It gets rough."

Among the Staleys' closest friends were Adrienne and Eric Gordon, both in their mid-thirties. Had Adrienne dyed her auburn hair blond, she could easily have been mistaken for Lindsay Wagner. The bearded Eric could have posed in an ad for *Outdoor Sportsman,* except for his black-framed glasses. With the Staleys on the dance floor at the moment, Janet and Greg were enjoying a conversation with these new acquaintances.

"Anyway," Adrienne was saying, "I don't know how many times I've painted that old Padgett well. There's a different incredible background from every angle."

"You must be fascinated with the place," Janet said.

"Kind of morbid, huh? It's just a beautiful spot, one of the nicest in the valley. Hard to visualize what happened there. I tried to put it on canvas once, but couldn't. Not into violence much, I guess."

"Hey, how'd we get onto this subject?" Eric asked.

"Sorry. I just got carried away, meeting a real live Padgett."

Greg smiled. "That's all right. I'd like to see your work. Eric, what do you do?"

"I'm a stockbroker."

"In Bonner?"

Eric laughed. "You'd be surprised at the money there is up here. I'm in a branch office of Shearson Lehman, over in the bank building. I've been doing it five years, ever since we moved to this town."

"From where?"

"Sacramento."

"Wasn't it going well there?"

"Actually, business was great."

"Then how did you wind up in Bonner?" Janet asked.

"The price of success: stress, then an ulcer. It was even affecting our marriage. That was the clincher. We had to make some big changes. I remembered Bonner from when my father used to bring me here to fish. We drove up, found what we wanted, and stayed. And we haven't been sorry."

"That's an understatement," Adrienne said. "It's been great for all of us, especially our son Joey. We have a nice home, even a few horses."

Janet nodded. "Sure looks like it agrees with you."

"How about you two?" Adrienne asked. "Do you work, Janet?" When Janet said she was a nurse, Adrienne replied with a laugh, "You're lucky the Rubens aren't here tonight. Larry would probably try to recruit you. He's one of our two town doctors. His wife, Jill, is a nurse practitioner."

"I'm in labor and delivery," Janet said. "Before that, it was premature intensive care. But I don't suppose you can specialize in a small town."

Eric shook his head. "No way."

"Actually, that wouldn't be bad," Janet went on. "It's a great way to sharpen your skills."

"You seem enthusiastic about what you do," Adrienne said.

"Oh, I've flirted with burnout a couple of times. Thought about a sales or management position in the business world, far away from the hospital. But it's what I want to do, and I've never regretted it."

"Greg, what do you do?" Eric asked.

He told the Gordons; they were impressed. "I read the first *Gold Rush* novel not long ago," Adrienne said. "It was really good."

"Hey, I bet you two would enjoy meeting Donna and Burton Faraday," Eric said.

"Burton Faraday lives *here*?" Greg exclaimed.

"Isn't he the mystery writer?" Janet asked.

"Of course. We once lost a bid on some of his older works. I thought he was from the East."

Eric nodded. "Born and raised in Baltimore. But his wife Donna's a local girl. Met and married her about twenty-five years ago, and he never left."

"*I'd* sure like to meet them," Janet said. "Are they here tonight?"

"No," Adrienne told her. "They seldom come to socials like this. Burton's not reclusive, just . . . impatient with most people. But they'll be at our house tomorrow for a cookout. Why don't you two come?"

"That's a great idea," Eric said. "Starts at three, ends

whenever. Just a few friends, not this kind of madhouse. What do you say?"

"I'd enjoy that," Janet said to Greg. "But didn't you have plans for tomorrow?"

"Just for the morning. We'll be back early. Sure, we'll come, and thanks."

Mark appeared and after introductions, asked, "When did you say we were leaving?"

"We hadn't decided for sure," Greg said. "Probably Monday. Why?"

"Any chance we could leave Tuesday? Some of the guys on the football team are having a practice Monday afternoon, and they asked me to play."

"Up to you, Greg," Janet said. "I don't mind."

Greg nodded. "Why not?"

Mark ran off to tell Craig Morley and the others, and Greg and Janet turned their attention back to the Gordons. As they continued talking, discovering common interests, the two couples made their way to the bulging dessert table. Janet and Greg happily stuffed themselves. The band had given way to a deejay, and they danced, first gyrating to an upbeat Gloria Estefan tune, then gliding gracefully through a maze of other couples when the music slowed.

"I can't remember having a nicer time in years," Greg said, tightening his hold on his wife.

Janet laughed. "And I had to drag you all this way to get you to dance. But you're right. Everything is perfect."

"L.A. seems a million miles away tonight."

She put her head on his chest. "Let's leave it there for now, okay?"

While Craig Morley and Mark filled their plates at the dessert table, Kevin French and the other boys continued to talk football. Dan Hillis, who had helped decorate the gym earlier, noticed that a string of large balloons had come loose from one of the basketball backboards. They dangled a couple of feet above the floor where some small children were punching them.

"Damn," the boy said. "If they bust one of those, it'll sound like a firecracker." He strode over toward the backboard. "Hey, kids, leave 'em alone!"

The children scurried away. Dan gathered up the balloons as the others joined him. "What's the big deal?" Kevin asked.

"I put these up myself, but I had a feeling they wouldn't hold. It was hard reaching up there."

"Why don't you fix it?" Tommy Sinclair asked. "The ladder's right there in the storage closet."

Tommy and Dan brought out the ladder, positioning it beneath the backboard. Before Dan could climb up, Kevin grabbed his arm and said, "I'm taller than you. Let me put them up."

"I can do it," Dan said.

"Kevin, don't," Tommy warned. "Coach'll shit if he sees you up there."

"Just hold it steady, okay?" Kevin ordered.

He started up. On the fourth and final rung he took the string of balloons from Tommy. Stretching to his full height, he wrapped the end around one of the braces.

Across the gym, Craig glanced up from his large piece of lemon meringue pie to see that Mark looked ill. "Hey, what is it?" the coach asked. "Mark, are you all right?"

Pale, quivering, Mark stared blankly at Craig. "It's nothing," he said after a moment. "Just had the chills for a second."

It should not have happened. The floor was level, the ladder was sturdy, and Kevin's friends were anchoring it firmly. But the ladder toppled as though yanked from below, and Kevin French was thrown violently to the hardwood floor, striking it with the unnerving sound of shattering bones. The folded ladder fell on him but was quickly pulled off by Dan Hillis.

"Kevin! Oh, no, Kevin!" Dan exclaimed.

"My arm!" the boy cried. "God, it hurts!"

The music stopped. Several people, including Craig and Mark, rushed to see what had happened.

"Is Doc Ruben here?" Craig shouted as he knelt beside Kevin.

"He's on duty at the medical center," someone replied.

Craig gently laid his hands on Kevin's shoulders as the boy writhed in pain. "What about Rick Johnson?"

"I'm here," the paramedic replied, pushing through the crowd. "Come on, back away!"

"Oh my Lord! Kevin!" Ann French shrieked when she saw her son.

Johnson examined Kevin, then said, "We'd better get him in, quick. His arm is busted up pretty bad, among other things."

A stretcher was brought in from his van, and Kevin was lifted onto it as carefully as possible. Johnson and Winn Staley wheeled him out. Winn assured Janet, who had offered her help, that everything was under control. Ann French followed the stretcher closely, supported by her husband and daughter. Craig Morley, shaking his head in disbelief, ended the small procession.

"Christ, there goes the whole fucking season," Mark heard him mutter.

15

The Lava Beds

Kevin French's accident ended the social. The people who streamed out of the Bonner High gym just past ten-thirty were subdued, sharing the concern of the boy's family and the disappointment of Craig Morley.

Janet and Greg said hasty good-nights to the Gordons and Carol Staley, and walked to their car. Mark, shaken, followed.

"Really was a good party," Greg said. "Too bad about the boy."

"A shame," Janet agreed.

Allison was waiting for them by the car. They had spotted her a few minutes earlier across the parking lot, standing with a tall boy. The boy had left as the crowd began to emerge.

"Hi Mom, Dad," she said.

"Haven't seen you for a while," Janet said. "I assume you had a good time. Who was that young man?"

"Just someone I met."

"What's his name?" Greg asked.

"Billy. Billy Douglas."

"Douglas? We met some Douglases, didn't we?"

Janet nodded. "Ellen and . . . Jim, I think. Nice people. They mentioned their son."

"Uh, he asked me to a movie tomorrow night, but I told him that we might have to pack and get to bed early, if we're leaving Monday morning."

"We decided to stay till Tuesday," Janet told her.

Allison's face lit up. "Great! I'll call him tomorrow and say it's okay." She and Mark piled into the back seat.

Greg winked at Janet and said, "I don't know if I can get used to this."

She smiled and kissed him.

Greg woke his family at seven-thirty. During breakfast at the Depot, Janet reached into her purse.

"I almost forgot," she said. "I picked something up for you while we were shopping yesterday." She dropped a hard rubber bone on the table.

Greg frowned as he fingered it. "Gee, thanks. It's exactly what I needed for my teeth."

"Ha, ha," she said dryly. "It's for you to give to Mr. Greenwood's dog. I thought you might like to bring a peace offering."

"Hey, great idea," he said, pocketing the toy. "Thanks."

As they drove away from town, Janet asked, "Are you going to reveal the big mystery of where we're going, or do you intend to keep it a secret until we get there?"

"No secret. I'm taking you to see the lava beds."

"The what?"

"Officially, the Lava Beds National Monument. It's northwest of here, not far. Most of it's in Siskiyou County."

"Is that lava, like in volcano?" Mark asked.

"Uh-huh. But you won't see a volcano there, not like you're thinking of. Actually, this whole region sits on a sprawling volcanic tableland. Some of those mountains may have once served as primary vents, but during the last eruption—"

"Eruption?" Allison exclaimed.

Greg smiled. "It's been at least five centuries. When it happened, the lava and pumice escaped wherever it could. Most of it was covered over as time passed, but the lava beds stayed pretty much as they always were."

"Is that why the area was designated a monument?" Janet asked.

"Not for what it is, but for what happened there. When we were talking about the Modoc Indians, you asked me what became of them. Well, the incident that occurred in the lava beds pretty much marked their end.

"I mentioned that the Modocs fought to save their land. The Fire Valley Massacre was just one of many confrontations. But for a time thereafter the Modocs coexisted with the whites, adopted their ways. Things were comparatively quiet up here during the Civil War years.

"Then, the same old story. White man wanted *all* the land, wanted the Indians out of his sight. In 1864, the Modocs were moved to the Klamath Indian reservation in Oregon. The Modocs were actually kin to the Klamaths, but generations removed, and at that point not too fond of each other. Tensions grew, until one group of Modocs under Captain Jack left the reservation and returned to their ancestral land."

"Captain Jack?" Janet said curiously.

"A hell-raiser who became their chief. His real name was Kent-push, or something like that. The anglicized Modoc names were really colorful: Scarfaced Charley, Shacknasty Jim, Curly-headed Doctor. Anyway, Captain Jack led them home. They were brought back once, but jumped again. The second time, they were damned defiant over their right to exist. They even insisted on money from the settlers for living on their land. Things got pretty ugly again.

"Late in 1872, the army tried to arrest Jack and send the Modocs back to the reservation. Talk turned to violence. The soldiers burned their village, but the Indians managed to escape and headed for the lava beds. This was the start of the Modoc Indian War.

"The Modocs established themselves in an area of the lava beds called the Stronghold. You'll know why when you see it. From there, with fifty or so warriors, they held off anywhere from three hundred to a thousand soldiers for six months, killing more than their share. And they hardly lost any of their own. It was an unbelievable, courageous stand, and it received world attention, the best there could be at that time. There was even a surge of outrage and sympathy for their cause, until Captain Jack was pressured by his people into an ambush of some government representatives during a peace talk.

"Finally, the Modocs had to leave the Stronghold for water. The troops eventually rounded them up, though not before sustaining many more casualties. Captain Jack and his lieutenants were tried for the murder of an army general and a minister at the peace talk, then hung. The remaining Modocs were sent to a reservation in Oklahoma. After the turn of the century they were allowed to return here if they wanted, strangers in their own land."

They were all silent for a minute, then Janet shook her

head. "How could anyone do that? Man bursts on the scene, takes the land of another man who's been there for God knows how long, tells him to live where he wants him to live, do what he wants him to do. It's not right!"

"But how often has it happened?" Greg said. "And not just to Indians. It's an ugly part of our heritage." He shrugged. "Worst part is, do we learn from it?"

"Hey, there's the turnoff for the Greenwood place," Mark said. "Weren't we going to stop?"

"It's too early," Greg replied. "We'll catch it on the way back."

As they passed the farm road, Janet asked, "Greg, how do you know so much about the Modocs?"

He smiled. "Read a manuscript a couple of years ago that detailed all of what I just told you. The writing wasn't too good. I thought it was improbable, corny fiction, but I happened to mention it to Jeremy Hunter. He told me that the Modoc War, the siege in the lava beds, was for real. I checked it out for myself. That's one of the reasons I wanted to come up here."

They followed the Bonner-Oregon Highway farther north, finally turning west onto a graded road that wound through tree-lined hills on its descent to the Lava Beds National Monument. They knew when they had arrived, for the green valleys and cool forests were abruptly left behind. The grim Land of Burnt-out Fires stretched before them.

To nothing else could the appellation Badlands have been more appropriate. A sagebrush wilderness layered with jagged volcanic debris, ominous, cathedrallike buttes, spider webs of cracks and crevices that led into natural caves, and even deeper subterranean passages. A stark, brooding *malpais*, where an infrequent juniper pine dared to reach upward from the igneous rocks. A place that generations of Indians learned, of necessity, to coexist with, where the last of their kind to have tasted freedom came to relinquish that freedom.

Captain Jack's Stronghold, at the top of the monument, stood just south of Tule Lake, an inaccessible natural lava fortress. Seeing it, the Lowells had some inkling of how anyone, especially those who knew the land, could have withstood the onslaught of twenty times their number. From scores of natural pits, which the Modocs had fortified with stone walls, and from innumerable caves, they could pick off their attackers with impunity, as they crossed the open plateau that surrounded the Stronghold.

God, Greg thought, *if not for water and food, their children's grandchildren might still be here, resisting.*

Save for the outlying areas, reachable only on foot, the Lowells had seen a lot. They retraced their path and, pensive, drove away from the Lava Beds National Monument.

16

Vern Greenwood

The sun was high and hot as they headed south again. More cars dotted the highway than earlier, but most were going in the opposite direction. The Lowells reached Vern Greenwood's ranch quickly.

A few locals were visiting the cemetery, and two families from Washington State were looking at the well, but Greg saw no sign of Vern Greenwood or his dog. He was surprised, for he was certain the old man doted on welcoming tourists. He did not park where Janet had the previous day but instead drove the LTD along a jarring path toward Vern's home. He circumvented the barn, then stopped alongside a low picket fence that enclosed a vegetable garden in front of Vern's house.

The deceivingly large two-story colonial house was solidly constructed of wood and red brick. Window boxes decorated the first-floor sills, and gaily colored awnings shaded both downstairs and upstairs windows. A two-seat swing and long bench sat empty on a wide railed wooden porch. A narrow walkway, flanked by the vegetables on one side and rows of flower beds on the other, led to the house.

"Kind of like going back in time," Greg said as they climbed the three porch steps.

Janet nodded. "It's lovely. I remember homes like this when I was a girl."

"Hey, check out the view," Mark said.

Turning toward the eastern peaks, they absorbed scenery no less breathtaking than any they had witnessed in Fire Valley. Greg nodded admiringly. "No wonder Wallace and Rebecca Padgett chose to settle here. Imagine sitting every evening and looking at this."

"Who's out there?" a voice called. "Oh, it's you folks."

A tired Vern Greenwood appeared in the doorway. He wore dirt-covered bib overalls with only a T-shirt underneath.

"Good morning, Mr. Greenwood," Janet said.

"Vern, 'member? Forgot you folks mentioned you were stoppin' back."

"Listen," Greg said, "we can come back another time if—"

"Nah, that's okay. I'm happy to have ya. Just had a rugged night is all."

Greg took the rubber bone from his pocket. "Where's Rudy? I brought him something."

The old man's shoulders sagged. "Rudy died last night. Got finished buryin' him a few hours ago, over nexta Jenny."

"I'm so sorry," Janet said sympathetically.

Vern shrugged. "Rudy was old, and it was his time. Only thing was, he went so troublesomelike. Heard him yelpin' and snarlin' out toward the main gate, then found him thrashin' and foamin', like he had the rabies or somethin'. Didn't even know me. God, I almost got out the shotgun, but he finally died. Was rigid as stone when I dragged him there."

"Vern, why don't we leave you alone?" Greg said. "I can imagine how you feel."

"Tell ya the truth, I'd prefer company, especially all you young folks. Life's gone out of this place since Jenny died. I won't be around that much either, not at my age. Stay a bit, will ya?"

Janet managed a smile. "We'll stay."

Some of his burden lifted. "Come on, lemme show you the house. Then we can sit out here and visit."

They stepped through the doorway and into the past. Well-preserved furniture filled the large paneled front room: Three chairs, two of them straight-backed and the third matching the overstuffed sofa; two pairs of end tables, each on its own scatter rug. A small loom stood along one wall; opposite it was a stone hearth. Above the mantel hung an oil painting of a woman with an attractive face, knowing eyes, and a gentle smile. Many other small pictures, framed photographs, souvenirs, and colorful ornaments, covered the walls. A Tiffany lamp was suspended above the overstuffed chair, and two table lamps flanked the sofa. At the moment, the room was bright with the sunlight streaming in through the picture window, bordered by lace curtains. Other than the console television near the door—itself an antique of sorts—the room would not have been out of place in the time of Rebecca and Wallace Padgett.

"I love it!" Janet exclaimed.

"Rad," Allison said.

Vern beamed. "My Jenny's touch. The inside is all hers. I try to keep it up. That's her picture over there." He pointed to the painting over the fireplace.

"I thought so," Janet said. "She was very pretty."

The kitchen–dining room was a contrast of antique furniture and shiny harvest-gold appliances. The master bedroom was downstairs; three more bedrooms, all with "Jenny's touch," were above.

"We always had friends visitin'," Vern explained, "stayin' overnight or the weekend. But most of 'em passed away, and after Jenny was gone, well, I didn't bother anymore."

They carried tall glasses of lemonade out on the porch. Allison and Mark jockeyed for position on the swing while Vern and Janet settled on the bench. Greg leaned against the sturdy railing.

"We never got tired of lookin' at that," Vern said, gesturing eastward. "The tops of those peaks in the winter . . ." He shook his head in wonder. "Even stay white through most of the spring. There, see that shiny crack to the left? It's a waterfall."

He rambled on, telling them everything about his thirty acres of the world. The fields of barley and potatoes that he still maintained; the green rippling meadow, stretching northward to the perimeter of his land where his small herd of milk cows grazed; the shaded hillocks behind the house where the sun always set earlier and cooled the sultriest of days before the end of the afternoon.

The Lowells, absorbing the man's excited words and animated voice, found it difficult to tear themselves away from the tranquil setting. But it was already twelve-thirty, and there were other obligations.

"This time I can't say for sure that we'll be back," Greg told Vern as they walked to the car. "We're probably leaving Tuesday."

"Sure glad to have met ya," he replied. "Woulda been, even if you wasn't who you are. Yer welcome any time. I— hey, will ya look at that!" he suddenly exclaimed, pointing past the barn. "Must be a dozen people there, and me lollin' around. Gotta get some decent clothes on. See ya, okay?"

He scurried back into the house, unmindful for the moment of the pain caused by the loss of his dog. The Lowells piled into the car and followed the bumpy road back to the main gate, briefly slowing as they neared the well.

"Really are lots of folks," Janet said.

"Yeah," Greg replied vaguely.

For a moment, he stared at the enigmatic shrine that stood silently before a watercolor background. Then he drove his family away from the ranch.

17

The Paintings

"Got a message for you, young man," the desk clerk said as the Lowells entered the lobby of Harmony House.

"For me?" Mark asked, taking the slip of paper. He scanned it. "It's from Craig Morley. He and some of the team are meeting at two to visit Kevin French. He'd like me to come."

"You want to?" Greg asked.

"Sure, if you don't mind that I miss the cookout."

"No, go ahead."

Allison, who had been using one of the pay phones, joined them. "Billy gets off work at four. He'll pick me up at the Gordons' house."

"Let's go get ready then," Greg said, and glanced toward the elevator. Luther Wall was still absent from his post. Greg asked the desk clerk about the old man.

"Not sure if he's sick, or what," the clerk said. "Just up and took off yesterday. Oh, he does some funny things from time to time, Luther does. But heck, he's been here forever, so I guess he's entitled."

Mark left the hotel at one-forty, the rest an hour later, after they had washed off the dust of the lava beds. They drove up the Bonner-Oregon Highway for a short distance before turning right. A farm road led eastward for three miles until they reached the place indicated on the map Eric Gordon had drawn.

The Gordons' house stood a few hundred feet back from the road. Most of their four acres stretched behind it, the extreme edge bordering a wood. The house was a modern

California-style ranch, made mostly of stucco and with an attractive stone front. The wide semicircular driveway, rimmed by low bushes, led to a pair of oak doors. A red Firebird and a subdued black Mercedes were parked outside; the adjoining garage held a van and a Nissan Maxima.

Greg pulled up behind the Mercedes (MYSTREE, the license plate read) as Eric Gordon, in shorts and a San Jose State sweatshirt, emerged from the house to greet them.

"I'm glad to see you again," he said. "Hardly got in three words after the accident. The Faradays are here. So's Carol Staley. She and Adrienne and the kids are out by the stable. Winn'll be along later, after he gets off work. Hopefully the Rubens will make it too, although Jill called a while ago to say that Larry's been hit with a few emergencies. Emmett Nicholson's away, and that leaves Larry the only doctor in town."

Greg, Janet, and Allison followed Eric into the nicely decorated house and were introduced to the Faradays, both of whom were holding gin-and-tonics. Burton Faraday was an intense-looking man in his fifties, of medium height and build, with a startling shock of silver hair. His wife, Donna, five years younger, reminded Janet of Jane Wyatt when she played Margaret Anderson in *Father Knows Best.* Her warm, friendly demeanor contrasted noticeably with her husband's aloofness.

Burton Faraday was one of America's most popular mystery writers. Some of his novels had made it to the screen. One famous creation, the hard-nosed private investigator Tony Drew, had romped through three years of ladies with missing relatives, car chases, and beat-the-city-cops-to-the-busts on television. Burton's knowledge of the street, its language, and seedy denizens reflected his early life in Baltimore.

And again Janet and Greg asked, "Why Bonner?"

"I'm here because I want to be here," Burton told them in a clipped, formal voice. "It was hard back then. A father who ran out, a mother working herself to death, scarcely making ends meet. I worked too. I stole when I had to, got into trouble. But in spite of it, I wrote. I wrote my first three short stories in longhand and sold the third one. Not a lot of money, but more than I'd ever seen at one time.

"Not long after that, ironically, my mother died. I bought an old car and got away. Drove around the country for two years, earning a few dollars here and there, always writing. But I never stayed anywhere for long, until I came to Bonner."

"When we met," Donna said, "Burton was working in my father's hardware store and renting a small room above it. People could never figure how we got together—the tough city kid and the naïf from the sticks."

"But we were good for each other," Burton said, "and this part of the country was good for me. I found I didn't have to live in the sewer to write about it. Most of my books were written here. And within a year they began selling."

"We bought some land and an old house northeast of here," Donna went on. "Nancy, our only child, was born there. She's married now and lives in Phoenix. As things got better, we bought more property around the house. We have about sixty acres now, half of it wooded. We're in the middle of it. Burton needs the solitude for his work, and I like it. To be honest, I had planned on leaving Bonner some day, but that was before I met Burton. Only afterward did I realize what I'd always had. I've seen enough of the world since then. I'm always glad to come home."

"I really don't believe it," Greg said. "Yourselves, the Staleys, Adrienne, and Eric. You seem misplaced up here, yet you're all so settled. Are there many like you in Bonner?"

Burton shook his head. "Aside from the Rubens, Bonner is what you'd expect of a small rural town. But they're pretty decent people here. Honest, hardworking."

"You'd *better* say that," Donna said jokingly.

Eric grinned. "You're in a benevolent mood today, Burton. What happened to all your 'yokels' and 'rubes'?"

He sighed. "Marry one, become one."

When the good-natured laughter abated, Greg asked, "What about the Rubens?"

"Old Doc Jackson," Burton replied, "who might have come here with the settlers, died three years ago. Emmett Nicholson had a hard time handling the load by himself, but couldn't come up with another doctor to help him."

"He and the city council ran ads in some big-city newspapers," Eric went on. "You know, extolling the virtues of small-town life. Promised a decent income too. Larry Ruben was the first to reply. He'd spent the previous four years working for a large internal-medicine group in Portland. But his reasons for wanting to live here were quite similar to our own. He didn't have much trouble convincing Em Nicholson, who liked him from the start."

"Bonner got a real bonus in Jill," Donna added. "With

them, Doc Nicholson, and Rick Johnson, the new paramedic, things are usually under control."

"Then the Rubens are happy here?" Greg asked.

"Indeed," Burton said.

The patio door in the kitchen opened, and Adrienne Gordon entered. "Well, hello," she said. "I didn't realize what time it was. Honey, we'd better get the steaks going." She turned to the Lowells. "Hi, you must be Allison. We didn't get to meet you last night. Come on, everyone, bring your drinks on the patio. It's nice outside."

The room emptied. Out in the backyard, Greg lay on a comfortable chaise longue and discussed writing, editing, and classical music with Burton Faraday. As they spoke, Burton's precise speech changed into a streetwise lingo that raised visions of Tony Drew and dark, sinister taverns. He was at ease.

And Greg Lowell, immersed in the company of good people and surrounded by the magnificence of Fire Valley, was struck with the improbable thought that he could be comfortable in this place, with this kind of life.

At four-fifteen, everyone converged on the patio as Winn Staley, still in uniform, emerged from the house. Behind him came Billy Douglas, who had arrived at the same time in his old Datsun pickup. Adrienne and Eric deserted their grill on the side of the house to greet Winn, Carol Staley returned from the stable with her two small children and the Gordons' ten-year-old son. For a few moments, there was chaos as pleasantries were exchanged, then Adrienne took charge.

"Allison, Billy, why don't you have something to eat before you go? There's plenty, especially with the Rubens' not coming."

"They're not?" Donna asked.

Adrienne shook her head. "Jill called again about fifteen minutes ago. They're swamped. What do you say, kids?"

Allison looked at Billy, who said, "Uh, sure. Thanks, Mrs. Gordon."

They gathered around two cedar picnic tables. During dinner, Greg managed a brief conversation with Billy Douglas. The boy was nervous, but Greg, playing a new role, was personable toward this object of Allison's rapt attention. ("I'll kill him!" he used to bellow after Allison was born. "The first kid who comes to the house to date *my* daughter, I'll kill him!") He was pleased to find Billy a likable young man.

Allison and Billy left at five-thirty, promising to be back at Harmony House by eleven. A few minutes later, Annie Stringer, the Staleys' babysitter, came to pick up the two girls. Joey Gordon returned to the stable to feed and brush the horses; the others cleaned up the remnants of what had been a pleasant dinner.

As she helped Carol and Adrienne put the leftover food away, Janet asked, "Don't you miss big shopping malls, live theater, that sort of thing?"

"Of course we do," Carol replied.

"God, I'd lose my mind otherwise," Adrienne said. "But we have Donna's Beechcraft."

"Her *what*?"

"Her plane. A V-35 Beech Bonanza, to be specific. Seats six."

"Donna and Burton are licensed pilots," Carol explained. "We've gone on lots of one-day jaunts to Lake Tahoe, Portland, San Francisco. Shopping, shows, you name it. Even went to Vegas last year for a weekend."

"Incredible!"

"As a matter of fact," Carol said, "we're flying to Sacramento tomorrow. Adrienne has some business to take care of, then we're going to hit the malls! Jill Ruben's coming too. Want to join us?"

"We'll be back by dinnertime," Adrienne added.

"I've never flown in anything smaller than a seven-twenty-seven, but I'm game." She turned as Greg and Burton entered the kitchen, carrying even more dirty dishes. "Greg, do you mind if I go off to Sacramento with Donna, Adrienne, Carol, and Jill Ruben tomorrow?" She smiled, loving the sound of that and the startled expression on Greg's face.

Burton quickly explained about the plane he and Donna owned, and Greg nodded.

"Go on," he said. "It sounds like fun. I'll keep myself busy."

"Gregory," Burton said, "if you don't have anything planned tomorrow, how about joining Larry Ruben and me for golf?"

"If you can put up with a real stiff, sure."

Burton laughed. "Watch him hustle us out of our shoes."

"Hey, listen," Adrienne said above the laughter. "I'm going to the stable to check on Joey. Looks like you have it under control here."

"Adrienne, one thing before you go," Greg said. "I'd really like to see your paintings. Is your studio inside?"

"Matter of fact, it's right above the stable. Eric fixed it up for me. Come on."

"Jan, you want to see them?"

"Maybe after I finish up, okay?"

Greg and Adrienne walked to the stable, first over a manicured lawn, then along a dirt path patterned with U-shaped prints that led beyond the rear fence and into the wood. From outside the white building, they could see Joey hard at work and could hear him berating one of the animals.

"Uh-oh, I'd better see what the problem is," Adrienne said. "Those stairs on the side will take you to the studio. I'll be up in a minute."

Greg climbed the dozen or so steps and entered a converted loft. It was a bright room with two windows that nearly met in one corner and a large circular skylight. The tools of Adrienne's hobby were everywhere: an open storage cabinet bulging with tubes of paints and countless brushes; folded smocks; four easels, one containing an unfinished canvas. Paintings hung on every available inch of wall space, while even more were stacked upright on the floor.

Adrienne Gordon's work was good. Studying some of the landscapes, he could tell she was able to capture on canvas exactly what she saw. But there was little interpretation, no self-expression, a barrier between ability and creativity that hindered . . .

No, there *was* one' that broke that barrier. It hung just above the floor, along with others on the same theme. The well paintings. The grim shrine to the Fire Valley Massacre stood before different incomparable and colorful backgrounds, as Adrienne had described. But the one . . . Instead of blue skies dotted with puffy cumulus, the backdrop was a variegated firmament, black and gray streaks careening haphazardly through a dominant splotch of orange. Around the well were half-figures, some sprawling, some upright, shadowy caricatures with vague features, save perhaps for the agony in their long conical faces. Painted in crimson and claret red, they seemed to mesh in a crisscrossing pattern, red paint trickling from them, from the larger bloated forms that were animals, and from the well itself, seeping through the stones, pouring over the mouth. And there were no wood posts, no pointed parasols.

Mesmerized by the painting, Greg dropped to his knees and stared into its three-dimensional depths. It came alive for him; the figures writhed, beckoning obscenely with their thin appendages, perhaps pleading. There were sounds, at first distant and unclear, then louder. Cries and shrieks of mindless terror, anguished moans rising, rising to an unimaginable crescendo. And a word *(padgett)* uttered amidst the cacophony in an emotionless, genderless voice. *(padgett padgett)* Over and over, again and again, until all the figures were prone, some segmented. *(padgett padgett padgett padgett)* And more red spilled from them, and more gushed from the well, spreading over the canvas, dripping to the floor of the studio. More red . . .

"Hello there."

Adrienne Gordon stood in the doorway. She was naked, and wanting, the dark nipples of her perfectly formed breasts hard with desire. She'd made love recently, for her tanned body glistened with perspiration, and semen trickled down her chin as she ran her tongue across swollen lips. But she wanted more. She wanted Greg. As her tapered fingers played along the dark patch between her thighs, she said in her throaty voice, "Come and take me, Greg. Please, take me!"

Greg rose and walked toward her as she rubbed herself frantically, determined to have her before she succumbed to her own pleasure.

"Well, what do you think?"

"Wh-what? What did you say?"

"The paintings. How do you like them? Not exactly another Gauguin, am I?"

Adrienne, entering the studio, still wore her tennis shorts and yellow top, which adequately displayed her striking figure. Her auburn hair, clipped in a long ponytail, contrasted with her red face, flushed from the day's activities.

"These are really good, Adrienne," Greg blurted out. "I'm impressed. Especially this . . ."

He turned to the seven paintings of the Padgett well. They were all alike, only the backgrounds varying. The one he'd been staring at had been done facing west, and behind it were the verdant hillocks.

"Which?" Adrienne asked.

"These pictures of the well, all of them," he said, struggling with his confusion. "Having seen it, I know they're right on. The colors are great."

She shrugged. "I paint 'em as I see 'em. That's about the best I can do. But it's fun."

There were footfalls on the wood stairs, and Janet came in. "Mind if I join the tour?"

Adrienne showed them both around the studio, giving them a picture-postcard view of much of the inspiring Fire Valley, which she clearly loved. Soon they left, and Greg cast a final puzzled look at the cluster of paintings of the well.

Young Joey joined them downstairs, and they walked back to the patio. Eric was putting out platters of cut melon and other fruit. "Hope this is okay," he told his guests. "I had enough pie and cake at the social to last awhile."

"Amen," Carol said. "This is fine."

They ate and talked, and when darkness cooled the valley, they went inside and continued to talk. The Lowells felt comfortable with this unpretentious group, who had come to this "other" side of California to live—for them—a better life.

As much as he tried to join the conversation, Greg could not erase the images of Adrienne Gordon's studio from his mind. It made as much sense as the three men he'd seen—or thought he'd seen—on the road the previous day. Was he suddenly prone to daydreams? Or victimized by an overactive imagination? Not his style at all.

Eventually, the pleasant evening helped him put it all aside. When he and Janet left at nine-thirty, they both felt—though they did not say it—that they were destined to see these people many more times.

18

Night Caller

Mark was watching a movie when his parents returned. "Hi," he said, poking his head into their room. "How'd it go?"

"Great," Janet replied. "What about your day?"

"It was okay. We visited Kevin. We didn't stay too long, because he didn't really want to see anybody. Arm's busted in two places and he's got some cracked ribs and lots of bruises. He won't be playing ball for a long time."

"Too bad," Greg said.

"After that, Tommy Sinclair asked me and Dan Hillis over to his house. They're nice guys. Tommy's mother had us stay for dinner. They drove me back about an hour ago."

"Sounds like you had a good time," Janet said.

"Yeah, but wait'll tomorrow. I'm gonna show those guys how to play football!"

Mark went back to his room, and Janet and Greg turned on their own television. At ten of eleven, they heard raised voices next door and knew that Allison had returned.

"Settle down, you two," Janet said, stepping into their room.

"It's okay, Mom," Allison told her. "He couldn't make me mad tonight, no matter how hard he tried."

"You and Billy had a good time?"

"Yes!" she exclaimed.

"Come on," Mark said. "Can't I hear the end of this movie?"

"Let's talk in here," Janet said, and they went into Allison's bedroom. "What did you do?"

"We kind of watched the movie, but mostly we talked. The other girls told me how quiet he is. That's a laugh. We

talked each other's heads off! Billy's so different from most
boys. He's serious, but really kind and gentle."

"That's nice. Honey, you know that after tomorrow you
won't see Billy again. At least, maybe not for a long time."

"Yeah, I know. Boy, I wish we could live here."

Janet was astonished. "You don't really mean that."

"Sure I do."

"Tell you what, Allison. I know you're starting to grow
fond of Billy, but I want you to put that aside and think about
what you just said. Think about what you'd be leaving behind
if we actually did something like that. School, friends—you
know. Think about it until tomorrow night, then see how you
feel."

"All right, but I know I'll feel the same. Anyway, what
would it matter how I felt?"

"Good question," Janet said vaguely. "Listen, the rest of
us have plans for tomorrow. What about you?"

"I saw Lisa Cunningham at the movies. She has her own
car. A few of the girls are going over to some stores in Alturas,
and she asked me to come. That okay?"

"I just hope she's a careful driver. You know, something
just occurred to me."

"What?"

"Everyone ought to be in on this. Come on."

Mark, his movie ended, followed them next door. Greg
stood as they marched in. "What's up?"

"We all have a pretty busy day tomorrow," Janet said.
"Do we really want to start driving home on Tuesday?"

"Hey, let's stay till Wednesday," Mark said.

"Thursday," Allison added. "Or Friday!"

Greg laughed. "Whoa. Glad you're enjoying yourselves,
but let's be realistic. We'll leave Thursday."

"Sounds okay to me," Janet said. "Now let's get some
sleep."

*The man drew water from the well, cool and clear, as it always
was. He filled a second pail, picked both up effortlessly, and
started toward the cottage.*

*The girl worked in the garden on the side of the cottage.
The boy, leading the cows in from the meadows, was passing by
the whitewashed fence in front. At one window, the woman put
a loaf of hot bread down next to a pie.*

All three looked up at the man and smiled.
Behind him, the ground rumbled with laughter.

Janet had always been an incredibly sound sleeper. It had been
Greg's misfortune to be burdened with most of the three A.M.
feedings when Allison and Mark were infants. Janet had even
slept through a 5.3 earthquake that rattled the San Fernando
Valley a few years earlier.

At a couple of minutes past one, Greg was awake. Janet
lay curled up in the folds of the yielding featherbed, her
breathing barely audible. His lips near her face, he called her
name softly, but she did not respond. They had made love
earlier, enhancing the blackness that held her.

Greg dressed rapidly and slipped out the door. He used
the steps, pausing for a moment on the small landing that
overlooked the lobby. The desk was untended. The hardwood
floor did not betray his rubber-soled footfalls as he crossed the
empty lobby and went outside.

Vern Greenwood was having difficulty sleeping, despite his
weariness. He missed hearing Rudy's breathing at the foot of
his bed. It was just beginning to sink in that he was all alone.
He knew it would get worse.

Hearing the sound of a car engine, he sat up and glanced
at his clock. It was a quarter to two. Light shone through his
bedroom window for a moment, and when he looked out, he
saw that someone had pulled in through the main gate. The
car continued on to the well; then the headlights were turned
off. The motor continued to idle, though. Even with his glasses
on, Vern could not be sure if anyone had gotten out, for the
distance was too great.

"What the hell," he muttered. "Probably kids come to
neck, or . . . whatever."

He pulled a heavy robe over his pajamas and thrust his
feet into a pair of slippers. As an afterthought, he withdrew his
shotgun from the front closet. After checking the breeches, he
stepped out into the crisp night air.

Vern's soles crunched on the gravel as he walked past the
barn. He wished Rudy was with him. The beam from his flashlight swung back and forth, lighting his path. When he was
about twenty feet from the well, he turned the light on the
figure standing next to the memorial.

"Who are you?" the old man asked. "What're you doin' here so late?"

"Hello, Vern," a voice said. "Sorry about the hour."

The light found the face. "Oh, it's you," Vern said.

"You expected me back sooner or later, didn't you?"

"I don't understand."

"Sure you do, Vern. You have to."

"No, I don't! Crissakes, why are you here?"

"I'm here because I belong here. You know that."

Vern pulled his robe tightly around him. "Damn, I don't ever remember it bein' this cold in August."

"Come here, Vern."

"I—"

"Come here."

His flashlight and gun dropped to the ground as Vern Greenwood plodded mechanically toward the well.

19

Decision

"Greg?"

"Uumphh."

"Come on, get up."

"What time is it?"

"Six-thirty."

"Jeez, leave me alone."

"Greg, I'm supposed to be at the airstrip in an hour."

"You take the car."

"I thought you wanted it."

"Burton Faraday will pick me up."

"What time are you playing?"

"Ten."

"Are you sure about the car?"

"Yeah. Good-bye."

"Why are you so tired? Didn't you sleep well?"

"No. Feel like I went to bed an hour ago. Had . . . weird dreams."

Burton and Greg drove to the Bonner Municipal Golf Course, a rolling layout nestled idyllically amidst the juniper pines. In the clubhouse, Greg was introduced to Larry Ruben, an affable curly-haired man in his early thirties.

"I heard a lot about you and your family," Larry said as he shook Greg's hand.

"Same here. Sorry we weren't able to meet till now."

"It wasn't planned, that's for sure. This was a hell of a weekend!"

"I suppose you'll be lucky to finish nine holes," Burton said dryly.

"Nah, I'm here to play. See? No beeper. Emmett Nicholson's back, Rick Johnson's on duty, and so are both nurses. And the weekenders, bless 'em, are gone. Yep, this boy's free. Let's do it."

They played the course slowly, there being few others. The deceivingly stocky physician, a five-handicap golfer, impressed Greg with his long drives. Burton, with a twelve handicap, stayed reasonably close to Larry, but Greg, who had not played in years, was unable to find his game. The price of his thrashing was two rounds of beer. Still, he enjoyed himself, and even after stalking the greens for three hours, he regretted the game's ending.

After saying good-bye to Larry, Burton and Greg drove over to the high school to watch the scrimmage.

The day was cooler than the previous ones, yet the uniforms of the fourteen padded, helmeted figures, among them Craig Morley, were soaked with sweat. Still, they played with intensity, the popping sounds of their tackles echoing from the empty bleachers. And in the heart of it was Mark Lowell. Beneath the borrowed helmet of Bonner High's Mountaineers, he was a young man possessed, a ferocious stalking cat whose raw talent and potential were unrivaled by any on the field.

"I'll tell you something," Craig confided to Greg during a time-out. "If Mark were going to school here, he'd be my quarterback next month. He needs some coaching, but God, what natural ability. And his desire! Beats anyone I have to replace Kevin French. Would I love to work with him."

Burton left at three, but Greg waited until the workout was done, forty minutes later. Craig drove him and Mark back to Harmony House. As he dropped them off, he invited Mark to a more formal practice on Wednesday morning. Mark accepted gladly.

Back in his hotel room, Greg called Sabre Press and spent over half an hour talking to Stu Berger, his boss. Finished with that, he decided to take a walk around Bonner. He peeked into Mark's room to see if his son wanted to go. Clad only in jockey shorts, his hair still wet from his shower, Mark was asleep, his breathing loud, his face peaceful. Smiling, Greg turned off the television and quietly shut the door.

Stopping in the lobby, Greg killed some time first in idle conversation with the desk clerk, then in studying the old photographs on the wall. He'd looked at only half of them when Allison bounced into the lobby. She agreed to go for a walk with him, and talked excitedly about her day as they stepped outside.

Half a block from Harmony House, Janet honked at them as she drove past. They followed her to the parking lot, and Greg glanced at the packages in the back seat. "Looks like you bought out half of Sacramento. Had a good time, huh?"

Janet nodded. "The plane ride was incredible. And you wouldn't believe the scenery." She began handing bags to him and Allison. "I like Jill Ruben too. We have a lot in common." Carrying the last two bags herself, she slammed the door shut. "They're all such good people, Greg. And the way they let me be a part of them . . . I feel it's more than just a temporary display of hospitality. Adrienne came right out and said that she wished we lived here. Oh, and they invited me to play bridge tomorrow. They play once a week—"

"I hear you, Jan," Greg interrupted her. "As soon as we get to the room, I think the four of us ought to sit down and talk."

"About what?"

He smiled. "I think you know. Now, tell us about your day in Sacramento."

She could barely fill them in on all the details before they were upstairs. Mark, awake and dressed, was waiting for them.

"All right," Greg said, sitting on the edge of his bed. "I'll say it straight out: What would you think about living up here?"

His family stared at him in stunned silence for a moment. Then Janet said, "Greg, you can't mean—"

He held up a hand. "Hold on. I'll have my say last. Let's do it one by one. Allison, what about you?"

"Mom and I talked yesterday. She asked me to think about it. I did, lots, and I'd like to live here. Home is okay. I know I'll miss some of my friends and other things. But the girls I met here are real nice, and they seem to find plenty to do. The high school's pretty good. I asked. And there's . . ."

Greg smiled knowingly. "Okay. Mark?"

"I like it here, I really do. The guys are easy to get along with. And I think I'd rather play football for Craig Morley than anybody. I can learn a lot from him. He'll play me right off, too, maybe even let me start at quarterback. That's worth whatever I have to give up. Heck, back at Central, I'm just one of fifty or sixty guys. Yeah, Dad, I'd like to live here."

"No Dodger games, no Rams," Greg said.

Mark shrugged. "I know. That's okay."

Greg turned to Janet. "I really didn't think anything like this was possible," she said, "not after three days. Last week I said I was starting to miss home. Well, I haven't even thought of it recently, because . . . I've felt at home *here*. Don't look so surprised, Greg. I'm a small-town girl, or did you forget? Oh, I'd miss lots of things, especially Dottie. We've been friends for so long. But to live in this beautiful place, breathe clean air. To enjoy seasons again and have friends like Adrienne and the others . . . Greg, I'd be scared out of my mind, but I'd say—go for it!"

"Then it's settled," he said simply. "We'll start looking for a place tomorrow."

"Wait a minute!" Janet exclaimed. "It can't be as easy as that. What about you? You're not ready to retire yet. What are you going to do here?"

"Okay, my turn." He stood and began to pace around the small room. "I haven't said anything these past few days about my feelings for Bonner because I wanted to be sure of those feelings. All that's happened to us since we've been here seems to be telling us one thing: This is home. I have no idea why my folks left Bonner—although I'm going to find out—but I have no intention of repeating that mistake.

"I've thought about going back to the six-day, seventy-hour weeks, the freeway traffic, all the pressure . . ." He shook his head, stopping to face his wife. "I don't want to go after rainbows when I'm sixty-five, Jan. Life's too short. As far as I'm concerned, Fire Valley's one of the most beautiful places I've ever seen. I want to stay." He paused. "But . . ."

"But what?" she prompted.

"Good old practical Greg Lowell got to thinking: Is this a realistic decision, or a spur-of-the-moment emotional one? What if this isn't right for us? What if we hated it? I guess we could always go back, but it would be a lot harder with our bridges burned. So, a compromise. I called Stu about an hour ago and asked for an indefinite leave. He screamed, as you can imagine. But he finally gave in. He knows that Jeremy Hunter won't work with anyone but me. I'll continue working for Sabre, only up here. There are plenty of pending projects. Stu offered me two-thirds pay, which I thought was fair.

"Next, we rent the house. At what they're going for, we might even realize some income. Finally, we find a place to rent up here. We'll have time to see if this is our kind of life. If not, everything will still be there. What do you guys say?"

Janet threw her arms around him. "I guess you really meant it. I think it's a great plan."

"Rad!" Mark exclaimed.

"I can't wait to tell Billy!" Allison cried.

Three people rushed to two phones. Greg Lowell smiled to himself.

20

The Funeral

Tuesday morning, Allison left to spend the day with Billy. Mark, who had been unable to reach Craig Morley the previous evening, went over to the high school to tell him. Greg and Janet headed for the realtor's office.

Glenn Beechum Realty was a block from Harmony House. The smiling crew-cut Beechum, resplendent in a three-piece suit and Tony Lama boots, was surprised by their request. "Not too many folks interested in long-term rentals," he said. "Let me look into it and get back to you."

They were walking back to Harmony House for breakfast when Winn Staley, off for the day, drove up in a Blazer. "I was out last night," he said, leaning out the window to talk to them, "but Carol told me the good news when I got home. Can't think of anybody else I'd rather have coming to Bonner. But, you know, you guys really fouled things up."

"What do you mean?" Greg asked.

Winn laughed. "Here we were planning this going-away bash for you tomorrow night, and you decide to move here! Ah well. Party's still on. The Faraday house, seven-thirty?"

"We'll be there," Greg said, "and thanks."

"One other thing." Winn turned somber. "I don't know if you heard the news already. Vern Greenwood died yesterday."

"What?" Janet exclaimed. "We just visited him Sunday morning. Damn. He was such a nice man."

"How'd he seem to you when you were there?"

"Tired," Greg said, "and pretty down from losing the dog. But he perked up before we left, and I thought he was fine. What'd he die of?"

"Heart failure, Doc Nicholson said. Died in his sleep.

Otis Perry found him in his bed. He's Vern's best friend and works on the ranch a lot."

Janet shook her head. "At least he went peacefully."

Winn shrugged. "Did he? I got there before Doc and saw him. His eyes were still open, and his face . . . Well, he looked terrified. Like he'd been scared to death."

"When's the funeral?" Greg asked.

"Tomorrow morning."

"We'll come," Janet said. "How about family? Did he have any?"

"A nephew, Frank Wilson. Lives down in Sunnyvale. He'll be here today. According to Ted Broderick, who prepared Vern's will ages ago, the house and land belong to Wilson now. What little money Vern had in the bank he left to Otis Perry."

Greg sighed. "What a shame."

"Anyway, sorry to be so morbid," Winn said. "Janet, were you going to play bridge today?"

"Yes."

"Greg, why don't you meet me there, and we'll go on to Burton's. He wants to give me another 'tennis lesson.' Maybe you can do better with him."

"Count me in," Greg told him.

A rumpled man in his forties was registering at the front desk when Janet and Greg walked into Harmony House. Greg heard the clerk address the newcomer by name. "Wilson," he said to Janet. "That's Vern Greenwood's nephew."

Frank Wilson, a successful software designer, accepted their condolences with a curt nod. "I hope you don't think me cold," he said, "but I haven't seen Uncle Vern in over seven years. I suppose we should've been closer, me being his only family. Did you know him well?"

Greg shook his head. "Just enough to grow fond of him. Your uncle bought his place from my parents many years ago."

"I see," Wilson said.

"Maybe my timing is bad," Greg went on, "but have you thought about what you would do with the property?"

"Sell it, I suppose. We wouldn't want to live up here. Why? Are you interested?"

Janet understood what Greg had begun, and she explained their plans to Wilson. "It will give you a steady income," she concluded, "and should we decide to stay, then perhaps we'll be your buyers."

"Rent it." Wilson shook his head. "No way. I just want to arrange for the sale and get out of this burg."

Janet was disappointed. "Won't you at least think about it till tomorrow?"

Wilson shrugged. "I suppose, but it won't do any good."

"What a sweetheart," Greg muttered as Wilson carried his overnight bag across the lobby to the elevator.

"Oh, Greg, wouldn't that have been fantastic? To live on that beautiful land, your family's old place!"

He nodded. "Yes, it would have," he said vaguely.

A message was waiting for them after breakfast. Glenn Beechum had come up with two rental properties. They walked back to his office, and he drove them to see the homes. They weren't impressed.

"We'll let you know," Greg said when Beechum dropped them back at the hotel. The realtor sensed their lack of enthusiasm and promised to keep at it.

At one, Greg drove Janet to the Rubens', then he and Winn continued on to the Faradays' sprawling grounds. A private road took them to a surprisingly modest home nestled in the pines. Burton, currently between books, was eagerly awaiting them with racket in hand. Winn lost badly and quickly to the skillful Burton, but Greg gave him more than he could handle. Eventually he beat Burton in an extended match that left both men exhausted.

"Aside from Adrienne Gordon," Burton said as he handed Greg a cold beer, "there's been no competition up here for light-years. I'm looking forward to a rematch, Gregory."

That evening, Janet and Greg were joined for dinner in the Modoc Room by Jill and Larry Ruben. The physician and his wife, a tall black-haired woman, looked exhausted.

"The last few days have been unreal," Larry said. "Em Nicholson says he can't ever remember so much happening at one time. Accidents, fights, God knows what else. Worst of it was a head-on collision north of here, not far from the cemetery. Woman injured critically, a couple of others badly hurt."

"We're going back to the medical center after dinner," Jill said. "Em's about ready to keel over."

"I hope whatever it is passes before we get back," Janet said.

Larry nodded. "It will. This is rare for Bonner."

"Can I help at all?"

"No, we'll be all right," Larry said. "But Em said for you to see him as soon as you get back and are settled in. You want to work, you will!"

Janet smiled at Greg. "I think moving here may be the best idea we've ever had."

Greg smiled back. "I'm sure of it."

Frank Wilson knew his eyes were open, yet saw nothing but blackness. The room was dark, but not *that* dark. He should be able to see something. For a moment the unreasoning dread of sudden blindness struck him, and he held his hand an inch from his face. He could discern the outlines of his fingers. No, not blindness.

Just blackness.

A living, throbbing blackness that moved around him, through him. He felt cold at first, then he and the blackness became one and he felt . . . nothing.

As he sank further into the blackness, he sensed another presence, something large, misshapen. Not in the blackness, but *devouring* the blackness, sucking it in as though starved for its sustenance. And Wilson, who *was* the blackness, felt himself spiraling down toward a gaping red maw. . . .

One floor above, Greg sat up in bed. A sound, like a muffled cry, echoed from somewhere distant.

Greg nodded, then laid his head back down in the pillow's feathery softness.

Wednesday morning was gray. Rain started falling after eight. Why not? Greg thought. There was a funeral. Leaving Mark and Allison, he and Janet drove out to the ranch where others had already begun to gather.

At ten o'clock, the scheduled time, everyone was there. Winn Staley, the Brodericks, Emmett Nicholson, and about eight others, mostly elderly. And Otis Perry, Vern Greenwood's closest friend, a gnarled figure who looked older than the man they were burying.

Frank Wilson was waiting for Greg and Janet in front of the house. The man was pale, haggard; he looked ten years older than he had the previous day. Greg wondered why, since the loss of his uncle had not seemed to affect him too much.

"I decided to rent this place to you," he said sullenly.

"That's wonderful!" Janet said.

"There's still some legal matters to finish up. Ted Broderick will handle it on this end, since I'm heading back home today."

"Thank you, Mr. Wilson," Greg said.

"One thing. My inheritance stipulated that I look after Otis Perry, let him work around here like he always has, that sort of thing. Broderick told me that for a man in his seventies, he's anything but a burden. He can probably be a big help to you. Is that all right?"

"No problem at all," Janet said, and Greg nodded.

"Then it's settled. I'll introduce you to Otis after the service. You'd best talk to Broderick in the next couple of days."

"We're driving back tomorrow," Greg said, "so we'll do it later today."

Under a light but steady rainfall, they listened to the words of the Reverend David Stocker of the Bonner Presbyterian Church. Jenny Greenwood had belonged there, but not her husband, a fact evident by the minister's general references to the deceased. Otis Perry's brief but emotional eulogy was more inspired. Once he was done, the pallbearers lowered the simple box into the hillside grave alongside Jenny. Two workers with shovels stepped forward, and the service was done.

While Janet and Greg waited for Wilson and Otis Perry by the house, the rest of the subdued gathering walked back to their vehicles, which were parked near the well. Winn had been talking to the Reverend Stocker, but as they crossed the parking area, he realized the man was no longer listening to him. His hands outstretched, the cleric was staggering toward the well.

"Reverend, what's wrong?" Winn asked.

His body trembling, Reverend Stocker fell hard to his knees and screamed, "No! Oh no, dear Lord Jesus, *no!*" His jaw tightened; his face turned a sickly white. A voice came from his throat, but hoarse, barely intelligible, as he flailed on the ground. *"Can't . . . be . . . no . . . Je . . . sus . . . can't be . . . it . . . is here . . . oh . . . Je . . . sus . . . why here . . . Padgett . . . go . . . away . . . must . . . de . . . str . . . Jesus . . . why . . . Jessuuu . . ."*

The clergyman fell supine, terrified eyes bulging, a stream of blood trickling from where he had bitten his lip. Winn ran to the man, but for an instant found himself unable to touch the pallid shivering body.

Finally cradling the head, he cried, "Emmett! Come on, Doc, where the hell are you?"

"Right here," Nicholson said. "Move over so I can have a look."

The Lowells, Frank Wilson, and Otis Perry heard the commotion and ran to see what was happening. As they neared the crowd, Greg slowed. He glanced at the well *(padgett)*, the brooding monument, glistening in the light rain that fell. *(padgett padgett)* He stared at it without expression *(welcome home padgett)* and nodded. His attention then turned to the drama before him, where a pale Winn was emerging from the throng.

"Greg, quick," he said, "give Doc and me a hand with the Reverend."

"What happened to him?" Greg asked.

"Doc's not sure yet. But he's in shock, and we have to get him into town!"

They lifted the tall, heavy Stocker and gently laid him across the rear seat of Ted Broderick's Cadillac. Nicholson rode with him as Winn cleared their path to town. Minutes later, his urgent siren faded down the Bonner-Oregon Highway.

The rain stopped. The others got in their cars and drove off. Janet looked at Otis Perry.

"Are you all right?" she asked, noting his weary look.

"Yes, ma'am," he said. "Just too much happenin' in one day. Now don't you worry about a thing. This place'll be fine when you're ready to move in." He took Janet's arm and led her to the car. "Ya know, I'm glad it's you folks that're gonna be here. Vern was tellin' me about you the other day. It's kinda like you belong on this place."

They drove through the main gate of the ranch *(welcome home padgett welcome home padgett)* to the highway, and returned to town.

21

The Old Woman

Late in the afternoon, Janet and Greg met with Ted Broderick to discuss the lease. The matter was finished quickly, and after they returned to the hotel, Janet called the medical center to check on the condition of the Reverend Stocker.

"Still no change," Jill told her. "He's in deep shock. We're having him flown to Reno. Larry and Em thought it would be best. Listen, gotta run! See you tonight."

A little past seven that night, the Lowells headed for the Faraday house. Allison was dejected over Billy's having to work until nine, although he would be coming to see her afterward. But Mark, bruised and limping slightly, was elated over his first official practice with the Bonner High Mountaineers.

"Coach Morley told me I'd be starting the first game against Susanville in September," he said. "Isn't that great?"

"Whoopee." That from Allison.

"I have the playbook to study, but I wish I could make some more practices. When are we coming back?"

"After Dottie's wedding on Labor Day weekend, for sure," Janet answered. "School starts the following week. I checked today when I enrolled you."

"Can't I come up before? I can stay with Tommy Sinclair. He asked me."

"We'll see."

All except the Rubens were awaiting them at the Faraday home. Jill came ten minutes later. "Larry will be along in an hour, hopefully less," she said. "He just got back from transporting the Reverend to the airfield and has a few things to finish at the center."

"Winn told me about Stocker," Burton said. "How is he?"

"The same. Maybe they'll have better luck with him in Reno. But aside from the Reverend, things were slow today for a change. I don't know if that's any consolation."

"Hey, what is this, a wake?" Donna Faraday said. "Come on, grab a drink, chill out! Dinner'll be ready in fifteen minutes."

Larry arrived half an hour later and hurried to the buffet table. "Donna, if I'd known you were making your fried chicken, I would've beat them all here."

While they were eating, Burton asked Greg, "I suppose you're going to drive back to L.A. ?"

"Of course."

"I was thinking, why not leave the car up here, since you'll only have to drive it back? I'm flying to Oakland tomorrow for a seminar. I'll take you down there. You can catch an afternoon flight and be home by dinnertime. It beats driving a million miles."

"That's a great idea," Janet said. "What do you think, Greg?"

"Sure, we'll do it. Thanks."

"We get to fly in the Beechcraft?" Mark cried. "All right!"

"I think I'm going to be sick," Allison said.

While the others divided two strawberry shortcakes, Burton took Greg aside and guided him into his study, shutting the door behind them. "What's the mystery?" Greg asked.

Burton smiled. "I'll excuse the pun." He withdrew a thick envelope from his desk. "Here."

"What's this?"

"*Death Around the Corner.* One of my first novels. It got me a pile of rejections, but I always had a soft spot for it. For my own reasons, I never put it back on the market. I ran it through the word processor yesterday and made some changes, cleaned up the writing. It reads okay. Go ahead, have your people take a look. If you want to do it, give my agent a call. I'll let him know."

Greg leafed through the manuscript pages, unable to believe what Burton was doing. "Do you know what an unpublished Burton Faraday is worth? Stu Berger's going to shit! But why are you giving it to me?"

"First, I like you and your family, and I'm glad we're

going to be neighbors. Second, I respect what you're doing and admire you for it. You're making a big change, and that's a big risk, especially the way things are these days. Your boss is being reasonable now, but in four, five months? He may feel put upon, and despite what you think, he might convince this Hunter guy to work with another editor. Then where are you? This way, you're my editor too. Call it insurance."

"I don't believe it," Greg said, shaking Burton's hand. "Do you mind if I tell the others?"

"Of course not."

While the announcement of the potential new union between Sabre Press and Burton Faraday was being made, Allison sat outside in Billy's pickup. He had left the store early and come for her before nine.

"I'm gonna miss you, Allison," he said as they finished the dessert they had brought out with them.

"It's only for a few weeks, silly."

"I know, but I missed you today, and that's only since noon. Allison, I, uh . . ."

She smiled and touched his face. "You don't have to say anything. We'll have plenty of time."

They slid closer to each other. For the first time since they'd met, the two awkward teenagers kissed. It was brief, but satisfying. Allison put her head on his chest, and they listened to the radio until a quarter past ten when the party broke up.

By ten o'clock the next morning, the Lowells were ready to go. Burton was stopping by for them at eleven. Donna was coming with him to pick up the station wagon and drive it out to the ranch where it would stay until they returned.

"There's time for another cup of coffee," Janet said after checking the rooms one last time.

"Okay," Greg said. "But it occurred to me. When was the last time we called Dad?"

"From Tahoe. Lord, that's a week! Should we do it now or wait till we get home?"

Greg picked up the phone. "I'll call him. He gripes about the long distance, but he likes hearing from us."

"You going to tell him?"

"No way. We'll do that face-to-face."

Robert Lowell answered the phone after three rings. "Gregory! About time I heard from you."

"Hello, Dad. How're you feeling?"

"Fine, just fine. Where are you?"

"You'll never guess. We're in Bonner."

Robert was silent for a moment, then said in an apprehensive voice, "Tell me that again, Gregory."

"We're in Bonner, Dad. Surprised? I was always curious about where I was born—"

"Gregory, are Janet and the children all right?"

"They're fine."

Robert's voice softened, but Greg couldn't miss the coating of fear. "Gregory, I want you to do something for me."

"Sure, Dad."

"I want you to put your family in the car and get away from there."

"What?"

Robert Lowell exploded. "Get away from there now! Get in your car and—Oh Lord, Janet, the children!"

"Dad, we were just getting ready—"

"Get away from there! What could have possessed you—"

"Dad, listen to me! Settle down! We'll do as you say. Do you hear me?"

"Yes," Robert said after a minute, more subdued.

"But on one condition."

"What?"

"When we get back, you tell us about it."

"All right. But hurry!"

Greg heard a click and, bewildered, stared at the receiver before cradling it. "Jesus!"

"What was *that* all about?" Janet asked.

"I wish I knew. He must be living with some pretty bad memories of this place. How ironic."

"Dad, is Grandpa okay?" Allison asked.

"Sure, he's just eager to see us. Come on, I can use that cup of coffee."

Downstairs, Greg stopped at the gift shop to pick up a newspaper, while the others continued on to the Modoc Room. The papers were all sold out, though.

"Try the rack up the street, by the barber shop," the clerk suggested.

Still shaken and puzzled by the phone call with his father, Greg walked slowly up Juniper Boulevard to the newspaper rack. He inserted a quarter, withdrew the paper absently, and stood for a moment to examine the headlines. When he turned to go back, he nearly bowled over the person who was suddenly standing beside him.

"What the—!" he exclaimed, stopping.

The bent woman was dressed in a tattered gray coat, black stockings, and moccasins. She was old, her jaundiced face deeply wrinkled, unkempt white hair wispy. But her dark eyes were piercing and held Greg.

Thrusting a trembling finger in his face, the crone asked in a throaty voice, "You are Padgett?"

"I—I'm Greg Lowell," he stammered.

"You are Padgett," she said. "You are going away?"

He was compelled to answer her. "Yes, soon."

"But you are coming back?"

"Yes, to live here. Who are—"

"You must not."

"What?"

"You must not return to the *sayka loluk.*"

"The *what?*"

"Do not come back, Padgett, do not *(padgett go away please)* come back to the *sayka loluk.* Padgett, do you hear me?"

"I am . . . not Padgett!" he cried. "I am Gr—"

Her face was a blur, a milk-white background before which figures danced. They were the half-people of Adrienne Gordon's painting, but better defined, and more bloodied. Streams of crimson swirled through the cream cloud, dripping down into a hazy oblivion that Greg could not perceive. And their cries *(padgett go away please padgett go away please)* reached him, reverberating a hundred, a thousand times *(padgettgoawaypleasepadgettgoawayplease)* as the half-people floundered in the death where they had been drowning for lifetimes, until . . .

(WELCOME HOME PADGETT)

The visions exploded, leaving the pained, tired face of the woman. She hobbled past Greg and up the strangely deserted street. He turned to watch her go, wanting to run after her but unable to move.

Then he heard his name, and Janet was beside him.

"I wondered why it was taking you so long to buy a newspaper."

"Jan, did you see her?" he asked frantically.

"See who?"

"Her! That old woman!" He turned, pointing. "She . . ."

A father walked with his young son; an elderly man sat in front of the barber shop, swaying to a Kenny Rogers tune on his radio. Farther up Juniper Boulevard business people strolled into offices, shoppers into stores.

Greg looked at the paper in his hands, hiding his sudden fear from his wife. "I was reading this story," he said lamely, "about a fire destroying a retirement home. Guess I really got into it."

"Worried about your dad, huh?"

"Yeah. With his heart and all . . ."

She took his arm. "Come on. Burton will be here soon. If everything goes okay, we'll drive over to see Dad first thing in the morning. Maybe even tonight."

More than 130 years after the Fire Valley Massacre, Greg Lowell and his family left Bonner. The pall that had been cast over Greg by his father and the strange old woman lifted as Burton flew them over the incomparably beautiful watercolor of Fire Valley—the *sayka loluk* —including a dip over the ranch where they would live.

And the valley knew they would be coming back.

RESURGENCE

22

Preparations

Valerie Kelton, senior editor and woman-of-all-trades at Sabre Press, flagged down the red-faced Stu Berger as he returned from a harried lunch with an agent. "Can you take this call, Stu?" she asked.

"Not now," he said grumpily. "I got about a hundred things—"

"It's Robert Lowell."

"*Robert* Lowell? Right now I'd rather be talking to his son, the wilderness warrior! All right, put him through."

He closed his door and picked up the telephone. "Mr. Lowell, how are you?" he said jovially.

"Stu? Is that you?"

"Yes, sir. Haven't seen you in a while, not since the barbecue at Janet and Greg's on Memorial Day."

"I talked to Gregory this morning."

"Oh yeah? When are they coming back?"

"He said they were leaving today."

"Good. Were they still up there in Green Acres?"

"You mean Bonner?" Robert said coldly. "Yes. Then you knew they were there?"

"Sure. Greg checked in a couple of times."

"I figured as much. That's why I called you. Stu, when you talked with Gregory, did you get the feeling that anything was wrong?"

"Wrong? Hardly. Just the opposite. God, you'd think they'd found nirvana or something, wanting to *live* up there. Your son's *mishoogana,* Mr. Lowell, you know what I'm saying? But as long as they're happy—"

"Stu?"

"Yes?"

"Did you say they were going to—live in Bonner?"

"Damn, I thought they told you. Sorry. Yeah, they're serious. I'm giving Greg an extended leave, and as soon as everything's in order here, I guess they'll be going back. In some ways I can't blame them for wanting to get away from—"

Stu dropped the phone as a terrible keening sound nearly shattered his eardrum. He shook his head groggily, then scooped up the receiver, speaking into it. "Jesus, was that from your end?" He heard only silence, not even a dial tone. "Mr. Lowell, are you there? Hello? Mr. Lowell!"

After a routine flight from Oakland to Burbank, the Lowells arrived home by taxi before five o'clock. The phone was ringing as they opened the front door. Greg hurried to answer it.

"Hi, it's me," a woman said.

"Oh, hi, Dottie. Listen, we just walked in. Can Janet call—"

"No. I have to talk to both of you, now." There was an uncharacteristic urgency in her voice. "I'll be over right away."

Dottie Berger, Stu's ex-wife, arrived ten minutes later, bringing the Lowells' dog Shanty with her. While Allison and Mark took the ecstatic terrier out back, Dottie, her eyes red, embraced Janet and Greg.

"What's this all about, Dot?" Janet asked. "Why was Shanty with you? Something's wrong, isn't it."

Dottie looked at Greg. "It's your father. He . . . died this afternoon. I'm sorry."

"Oh, dear God, *no!*" Janet cried, sinking to the couch.

"Was it his heart?" Greg asked, his face ashen.

"Yes. He was talking on the phone with Stu and—"

"Talking with Stu?" Greg interrupted. "My God! Stu probably mentioned our moving to Bonner. I never thought to say anything."

"What does it matter now?" Janet said, sobbing.

"Dottie, tell me what happened."

"They were talking, then, nothing from your father's end. Stu called the paramedics. They got there fast, but there was nothing they could do. He'd had a massive coronary. Stu asked me to tell you as soon as got home. Greg?"

"What?"

"You're moving to Bonner?"

"Later, okay? Take care of Jan. I have to tell the kids."

Robert Lowell was buried on Sunday. Stu, believing his revelation had been the catalyst, if not the cause, of what had happened, was immersed in guilt. Janet tried to convince him otherwise. Robert had suffered two prior heart attacks, she reminded him. Greg was also adamant that it had been only coincidence, but in the back of his mind he had to wonder. He could not easily forget the thinly veiled terror in his father's voice when he'd last spoken to him. If news that his son and family were moving to Bonner had killed Robert, then why had the man been so afraid of that idyllic town? What had happened to Greg's parents during the eight months they had spent there forty years ago? Greg realized that—now—he would never know.

After the unpleasant task of settling his father's modest estate, the remainder of August passed quickly for Greg. He spent much of his time at Sabre Press, instructing Valerie Kelton in her new responsibilities, the rest discussing plans with Stu for his role in the ensuing year. The Faraday manuscript, which had snapped Stu out of his brief depression, was to be Greg's project. He would negotiate the contract with Burton's agent. Then, since Jeremy Hunter's next book would be late, Greg would edit Burton's manuscript after he returned to Bonner, write the cover copy, and outline the artwork before sending it back to Valerie.

Management of their house in Van Nuys was undertaken by Roy Heller, Dottie's fiancé. He quickly found suitable tenants, a professional couple with two young children. They were being transferred from Houston after Labor Day, which gave Janet and Greg more than enough time to finish their business.

At the end of August, Allison and Mark boarded a Greyhound bus for Sacramento. Adrienne had called a few days earlier to tell Janet that she was visiting family there and would be happy to drive the teens to Bonner the next day. Both Allison and Mark were elated over the prospect of an early return.

On Labor Day weekend, Dottie Berger married Roy Heller. It was a simple ceremony, attended by only a handful of people. Afterward, the Lowells drove the newlyweds to the airport for the start of their honeymoon in Maui.

"My associate Jay Lewis will be handling your tenants while I'm gone," Roy said to Greg before they boarded the plane. "Don't worry about a thing."

Janet hugged Dottie. "Not seeing you is going to be the hardest part of this. Promise you'll come up for Thanksgiving?"

"Try to keep us away!" Dottie said.

Janet and Greg had little left to do on the holiday weekend. With Allison and Mark gone, the house was as empty as they could remember. Even more so, for most of the furniture and boxes of belongings going to Bonner were already stacked in the garage. A truck would be coming for them Tuesday morning. Janet and Greg would leave right after, with a one-night stopover in Sacramento.

On Sunday, as he sat on the carpet among scattered sections of the *L.A. Times,* Greg was pensive. "What's on your mind, babe?" Janet asked as she handed him a cup of coffee.

"Just thinking about the last six weeks or so. Do you realize how much has happened?"

"It's been unreal, to say the least. You really miss your dad, don't you?"

"Yeah." He sighed. "His being gone is just starting to sink in. Shit! Why'd it have to happen now?"

"Doesn't seem fair, does it? You know, I've been thinking. Maybe his learning about our move *did* have something to do with his death. I mean, your dad never had a lot of friends. After Clare died, he's been alone, except for us. Maybe the thought of our leaving was too much for him."

"You may be right," Greg said. "Hell, I hope you aren't, since I was going to ask him to come with us."

Janet was surprised. "That would have been a great idea! But why hadn't you mentioned it to me?"

"I was going to talk to you about it on our way back. But after his reaction on the phone, I wasn't sure what to do. I decided to wait and play it by ear. Anyway, I'm sorry as hell that he's gone, and I guess we'll never find out why Bonner left such a bitter taste in his mouth, in . . . his life."

They were silent for a few minutes. Then Janet said, "Greg, are we really sure about this? Are we doing the right thing?"

"We each have to answer that for ourselves. I'll admit I was glad to get back home. But after a few commutes on the freeway, the crap at the office, that awful smog a couple of weeks ago . . . I must've daydreamed about Fire Valley a hundred times. The more I thought about it, the more I wanted to be there. Yes, I'm sure. At least sure enough to give it a try. What about you?"

"I feel the same. Like I told you once, 'you can take the girl out of the small town,' et cetera. Last Tuesday I was wondering whose house they were playing bridge at. And I'm already debating what to bring to the Homecoming social later this month."

He smiled. "You're hooked. Okay, the doubt is dispelled. Let's enjoy the rest of this weekend. What do you want to do?"

She shrugged free of her robe. She'd worn nothing underneath. "Same thing we've been doing," she said, smiling. "We won't be this alone again for a long time."

The moving van arrived early Tuesday morning and was gone by ten. When Jay Lewis stopped by for the keys, he told Janet and Greg that the tenants would be arriving on Thursday. He knew them personally and promised the house would be well cared for.

With the excited Shanty in the back of the Camaro, the Lowells took to the road. They reached Sacramento late in the day and enjoyed their last night alone with each other. The next morning, they rose early and drove straight through to Bonner. Shortly past noon, they were on the Bonner Highway, south of town. It was a clear day, and they couldn't resist stopping on the ridge to gaze at the stunning beauty of Fire Valley.

"We're home," Janet said.

23

Settling In

Before going to their new home, Janet and Greg stopped at Ted Broderick's office to sign the rental agreement. It was drawn up for a year, as they'd agreed. They could subsequently apply a part of the rent to the purchase price of the old Padgett ranch if they decided to buy.

Allison was waiting for them at Lisa Cunningham's house. There was no one home at the Sinclair place where Mark had been staying. They found him, as usual, on the football field, battered, sweaty, but happy over the past week, like his sister.

"What if we'd told you we decided to stay in Van Nuys?" Janet asked jokingly as they drove out of town.

"We'd say don't forget to write," Allison replied.

A cloudless deep-blue sky covered Fire Valley as they headed north on the Bonner-Oregon Highway to their house. With summer over in all ways but the calendar, there was no one at the well. Winn had said they would not see many visitors until next spring.

Greg pulled up behind their station wagon, which was parked in front of the house. He leaned on the horn to alert Otis Perry, but the old man did not appear.

"He's probably out working," Janet said.

The front door was open, and an enticing smell led them to a basket of fried chicken on the kitchen table. A note read: *Didn't think you'd feel like cooking after the trip. Talk to you later. Donna.*

"You know," Greg said, "we'd better get settled in quick, so *we* can do something for these people."

With Shanty excitedly exploring his new territory, the

Lowells unloaded both cars, then ate their late lunch on the porch. The crisp air heightened their appetites, yet they made little more than a dent in the large basket of chicken. Eventually they surrendered, content just to sit back and gaze at the mountains.

The distant sound of a motor reached them, and they spotted an old tractor rumbling across the meadow. As he passed by the house, Otis Perry waved to them. He returned the sputtering vehicle to the barn, then shuffled back to the porch.

"Hiya, folks," he said cheerfully. "Glad to have you back. Everything's been under control since I seen you last, Miz Allison."

"*Miz* Allison?" Janet asked.

"Lisa drove me out here a couple of times," the girl said.

"Yep, everything's been taken care of," the old man continued. "I gave away a lotta Vern's stuff, like Mr. Wilson said. Kept a couple of things for me. There's some furniture stored over by the barn. Oh, the electric and all that are in your name now."

"The place looks great," Janet said. "Sure you haven't been working yourself too hard?"

"Nope. Knock off every day around noon. Only reason I was out there today was 'cause the potatoes are near to harvestin'. Should have 'em up by the weekend."

"How about some lunch?" Greg asked. "There's plenty of chicken."

Otis climbed the steps. "I know all about that chicken. Smell near drove me crazy after Miz Faraday left it. I'd be glad to eat some."

Over Otis's protests that he could catch the three-o'clock bus on the highway, Greg drove him to Ledbetter's Texaco where his ancient pickup truck was being serviced. When he got back, Allison and Mark were debating hotly over who got the largest of the three upstairs bedrooms. Janet had decided to stay out of the fracas, which finally ended with a coin flip. Mark won. Allison, chagrined, made sure the empty room remained between them.

While Greg relieved her of the unpacking, Janet phoned their friends to invite them to a housewarming on Saturday night. She also asked Lisa Cunningham and her parents, Tommy Sinclair and his mother, and Billy Douglas's family. All but the Faradays accepted. Donna told Janet that she and

Burton were flying to Seattle on Saturday for a week's visit. She promised they would stop by on Friday.

An hour before sunset, Allison and Mark walked to the north meadow to lead the eight milk cows back to the barn, as Otis had instructed the girl. Greg and Janet went out on the porch to watch as the clamor of bells grew louder. They laughed as Shanty yapped at the animals and Mark tried frantically to hustle them along.

"Just keep them in line, dummy," Allison told him.

"But they're so slow."

"Mr. Perry says they'll get where they're going eventually."

With the animals secure, the family walked to a nearby hill and watched a fiery cloud-streaked sunset. The descending night chill urged them back inside, and shortly thereafter, they all went to bed. That first night in their new house, they slept peacefully.

By seven the next morning, Otis had already milked the cows and let them out to graze. Three shiny containers full of milk stood in the cool of the barn until he could drive them to the small dairy that had been buying milk and cream from Vern Greenwood for decades. By the time Greg peered groggily out the front window, Otis was seated atop the sputtering tractor. He was unable to catch the old man's attention before the vehicle disappeared across the field.

"Christ, he must've gotten up in the middle of the night," Greg mumbled, groping in a large bag for a tin of coffee.

Later, Janet and Allison drove into town to shop for food. Mark, with football gear, rode along. Greg stayed at the house and soon discovered there was little to do until the rest of their belongings arrived—with luck—the next day. He decided to walk to the north meadow.

As he stepped out of the house, he heard Shanty barking frantically. The dog raced toward the main gate before he could call to it. He started to follow, then saw someone standing by the well. It was impossible to distinguish features from so far away, but he felt certain the slight figure, dressed in dark clothing, was a woman.

It's her! he thought. And Shanty sees her too.

Greg ran across the yard and past the barn, noting that there were no vehicles in the parking area. Slowing, he walked by Shanty, who had decided to take up his now-quiet vigil five yards away. The woman was oblivious to his approach, apparently riveted to the well. She did not respond when he called a greeting, and he was unsure of what to do. Finally nearing her side, he said, "Hello, I'm—"

She spun around, startled. She was an old woman, but not the one he had seen downtown that morning. Despite her years, her complexion was smooth, the silver hair beneath the plaid kerchief full. Her surprised expression quickly changed, and she smiled at him.

"Sorry. I didn't mean to scare you," Greg said. "I'm Greg Lowell. My family and I live here. Something tells me you've been out this way before." The woman continued to smile, but said nothing. "How did you get here?" he continued. "I don't see a car."

Again she responded with silence. What was wrong with her? he wondered, just as Shanty resumed his barking. A battered old Buick Electra passed through the front gate, raising a cloud of dust. It stopped close to Greg, and the driver, a dark-haired man in jeans and a denim work shirt, climbed out. He was young, in his early twenties, of average height and stocky. A broad white grin contrasted with his swarthy face. He waved and clapped his hands for Shanty to come, but the dog kept its distance.

"Hiya, I'm Jeff Rand," he said, offering his hand to Greg.

"Greg Lowell."

"You're the new owner, ain't you?"

Greg shook his head. "We're just renting this place."

"Uh-huh. I see you already met my grandmother. Her name's Dora Waverly. In case you hadn't figured, she can't either hear or speak."

"I see. How did . . ."

Glancing at Dora Waverly, Greg realized she was disturbed about something. She and her grandson signed at each other. He pointed insistently at the well. Dora, frowning, turned to stare at it again.

"What was that all about?" Greg asked.

"No big deal," Rand said. "I usually wait outside the gate for her. She was wondering why I came in. Were you gonna ask me something?"

"I was curious about how she got here, but you answered that. What I don't understand is why."

"Why what?"

"Why she doesn't want you to come inside."

Rand's smile widened. "My grandmother's been coming

here every week for as long as I can remember, and for years
before that. Being part Modoc, I guess she's got a thing about
this place."

"She's a Modoc?"

"Her mother was full-blooded. That makes me one-
eighth. Anyway, she probably feels some kind of obligation to
be here. But ever since I've been bringing her out, she's asked
me to park down the road and wait for her there. I always
figured, what the hell, if it makes her happy, you know?"

"Sure."

"Uh, listen, old man Greenwood never minded her out
here, but what about you?"

"No, she's welcome. You tell her that."

"Yeah, thanks. Kinda funny anyway, 'cause—she doesn't
know this, by the way—I've been out here lots of times, doing
odd jobs for Greenwood. Even helped Otis a couple of times
last month. That's what I do, you know, odd jobs. Pretty good
too. Hope you can use me sometime."

"Maybe so," Greg said.

"Great. Hey, we'll get going now. She's been here long
enough."

Rand took the old woman by the arm and led her toward
the car. As they drove off, Greg set out to look for Otis. He
found him at the Greenwood plot. Fresh flowers lay by each
headstone.

"Just visitin' my old friends," Otis said sheepishly,
"tellin' 'em how things are. Kinda batty, huh?"

Greg smiled. "No, I understand. Are you finished out
here?"

"Yep. Got a few things to do in the barn, then I'm headin'
home. Unless you need me."

"No, that's fine. I'm just going to walk around."

"I'll be startin' to dig up potatoes tomorrow. Wanna
help?"

"Sure, as long as you tell me what to do."

"Nothin' to it. What about your family? We can use all
the help we can get."

"Mark and Allison have a school orientation tomorrow,
and Janet will be waiting for the truck to bring our stuff.
Maybe she can help after. What about using Jeff Rand?"

Otis frowned. "You met him, huh?"

"Yes. Is something wrong? I thought he'd worked here
before."

"Vern used him. I did, too, few weeks back. He's okay, I guess. Kinda slick young fella, awful cocksure. Part Injin, ya know."

"He told me."

"Anyway, I'll call him later. Not much other choice. The migrants up this way are all workin' steady."

The old man started up the tractor and rumbled off. Paralleling the low hills on his left, Greg walked to the north edge of the property, separated from the adjoining wilderness by a wire-mesh fence. On his way back, he cut across the meadow where the cows grazed on the high bunch grass, drank from a small creek, and lay under one of half a dozen low shade trees. Looking around at the rippling fields, the nearby hills covered with wildflowers, the distant pine slopes, he wondered, *Why am I here? Is this really happening?* But at the moment he wasn't interested in an answer.

On Friday, while Allison and Mark attended their orientation and Janet waited for the moving truck, Greg drove out to the potato field with Otis and Jeff Rand. Uprooting the potatoes was routine work, but hard on the back. Greg enjoyed himself, despite being unable to carry on anything more than a shouting match with his co-workers, who were scattered around the patch.

Janet joined them near eleven after the truck left. She wore a loose-fitting pullover top and cutoff jeans that showed her tanned legs. As she bent down to work about ten yards from Jeff Rand, she noticed the younger man gazing lasciviously at her.

On Saturday, Allison and Mark dug potatoes with Rand and Otis. By early afternoon, the patch had been picked clean. Greg gave Rand one bag and kept another; Otis sold the rest to Stringer's Food Mart. Greg paid Rand for two days, promising to call whenever anything else came up.

The rest of the day was spent in putting the house in order. All but a couple of boxes were unpacked, and those were stacked in the guest room. The furniture they had brought blended nicely with the Greenwood relics after they were shuffled around half a dozen times under Janet's discerning eye. The upstairs bedrooms echoed the busy sounds of their new occupants.

By the end of the day, the Lowells began to feel settled in.

24

Housewarming

The guests were scheduled to arrive between seven and seven-thirty Saturday night. Adrienne and Eric Gordon got there at five after seven, and within twenty minutes everyone else had arrived. Jessica and Walt Cunningham, as outgoing as their daughter Lisa, knew most of the people there and fit in comfortably, but not Norma Sinclair or the Douglases. Tommy's mother, divorced for years, looked sad and weary, and older than her age, despite heavy makeup. Ellen and Jim Douglas, proud farmers who had known bad times before coming to Fire Valley, were a serious couple, uneasy in crowds. Janet and Greg did all they could to make them feel at home.

Walt Cunningham, an insurance salesman, at first turned down Greg's offer of a piña colada. "Maybe you want something stronger," Greg said.

Walt laughed. "Hardly. I don't drink much. Tell you what, I'll try just a little bit of that, okay?"

Janet's dinner was a success. While they ate, Greg noticed that Walt's glass, which he'd emptied, had been refilled and was again being downed slowly. But he thought nothing of it until dessert when it was full once more. This time, Walt, glassy-eyed as he whispered to a frowning Adrienne, drained it quickly. When Adrienne walked away, he stumbled toward the table for another.

"That big jerk tried to proposition me," Adrienne muttered as she passed Greg. "He's drunk as a skunk!"

She joined Carol and Jill, who were standing near the fireplace. Greg watched as Walt, a new drink in hand, turned his attention to Norma Sinclair. His actions did not escape

Jessica, who watched him disdainfully as she talked with the Douglases.

"Poor woman," Greg mumbled.

Winn joined him. "Who?" he asked. "His wife or Norma?"

"You noticed too, huh? What's with this guy?"

"I swear to you, Greg, I've known Walt Cunningham most of my life, and I've never seen him loaded. Can't imagine why he's drinking tonight. I wish he'd leave Norma alone, though. She's had a rough life ever since her husband took a walk eight years ago. I'm gonna have to say something if he doesn't back off."

While the two watched Walt, Janet emerged from the kitchen and joined Adrienne and the others. "Hope you guys are having a good time," she said.

"This place is great," Carol said. "The things you've done in only a couple of days are terrific."

"It still needs plenty of work, but thanks."

"Janet," Adrienne said, "I once worked for an interior decorator in Sacramento. If you ever want help, just holler."

"After seeing your house, you're hired. Stop out next week. We'll throw some ideas around over lunch."

"Sounds great."

"The rest of you come too," Janet added. "I need all the help I can —Hey, maybe I'm nuts," she suddenly said, "but here we are in a roomful of people with a fire burning, and I'm cold!"

"I thought it was me, but I am too," Jill said.

"Maybe it's a draft from a crack somewhere," Carol said.

Janet shrugged. "I'll have to ask Greg to—"

A commotion across the room interrupted her. Jessica Cunningham had obviously tired of her husband's behavior. She was trying to pull him away from Norma, who, red-faced, retreated from the embarrassing scene.

"Take your hands off me," Walt told his wife in a loud slurring voice. "Whaddya think you're doing?"

"Walt, please," Jessica said, "let's leave."

"I woulda been screwin' old Norma if you hadn't butted in! Can't a guy have any fun?"

"Walt, will you *stop* it?" she pleaded. "Everyone's listening!"

"Everyone's listening," he mimicked. "Who cares? Fuck 'em all! Where'd that broad go?"

"Okay, Walt, that's enough," Winn said, walking over to the couple and putting a hand on Walt's arm. "Let Jess get you home so you can sleep it off."

"Always playin' tin badge, huh?" Walt said belligerently. "All right, I'll go."

"Janet, Greg, I'm sorry," Jessica said, swallowing back tears. "He's never acted this way in his life!"

"It's okay," Janet told her. "Just take care of him."

"Lisa, hey, Lisa!" Walt bellowed. "We're going home. Where's that chippy daughter of ours? Probably letting one of those young shits take a little—"

"Walt, shut your mouth," the sheriff warned, "or so help me, I'll throw you in the tank!"

Lisa, who had been up in Allison's room, joined Jessica, her eyes wide as she stared at her drunken father. The two hurried to the front door as Winn guided the now docile Walt behind them.

"You need any help, Winn?" Greg asked.

"No, I'll be fine. You have some fun. See you in a bit."

Greg walked out on the porch, watching until they were halfway down the path. He then turned and went back inside.

How did you figure that? he wondered as he joined Janet, who was sitting on the couch talking quietly to Norma. Greg was glad to see that the woman was smiling.

"Walt and I went to school together," she was saying. "He wasn't shy, by any means, but I never saw him like *that*! He hardly drank, not even beer, and—"

She gasped as they all heard loud noises from outside, then a woman cry out. Larry Ruben was first out the door.

"Walt, no!" Jessica screamed as the men ran down the path.

"Daddy!" Lisa cried.

Winn was on his knees, doubled over in pain where Walt had kicked him. Lisa straddled the hood of their car, flung there by her father. Jessica, cowering, gazed in horror at her husband.

"Bitch!" he shouted, slapping her face. "Who the fuck do you think you are? You goddamn—"

Greg and Larry wrestled him to the ground, but he broke free and regained his feet. They tackled him again before he could hit his wife another time. Eric silenced him with an effective blow to the back of his neck.

Larry hurried to assist Jessica, who had fainted. Jill and

Adrienne tried to calm the hysterical Lisa. Winn, still hurting but on his feet, eyed the scene in disbelief for a moment, then took charge.

"I'd better get Walt into a cell. Larry, how's Jess?"

"A bloody nose, a few cuts on the lip. I'll take her and Lisa down to the center as a precaution."

"Somebody help me put Walt in the back seat. Carol, you drive. I'll have to keep an eye on him."

The Rubens drove off with their patients, then the Staleys, Winn's prisoner breathing heavily. Janet and Greg said their disappointed good-nights to the remainder of the guests, all of whom left solemnly.

"Why did Walt Cunningham do that?" Greg asked as they watched the last car disappear through the gate.

Janet shrugged. "I don't know, but it sure as hell ruined a nice party. I hope Jessica and her daughter are okay. Coming in?"

"Right away."

Greg peered into the darkness. Even though he could not see the monument, he knew exactly where it was. He heard—or felt—hollow laughter and continued to stare until the night grew too cold.

25

Indian Summer

Greg phoned Winn early Sunday morning. The sheriff was still hurting, but he had already been to his office once and planned on working his regular shift.

"What about the Cunninghams?" Greg asked.

"Jess and the girl are both fine—physically. Funny thing."

"What's that?"

"Jess's biggest concern since she came to last night was for her husband. According to Jill, you would have thought someone else did this to them, the way she kept asking about him."

"That is strange."

"Walt was asleep—or unconscious—all night. I was there this morning when he got up. Couldn't believe where he was. Repentant as hell."

"They always are," Greg said dryly.

"No, there was something different about Walt. It wasn't like he was waking up from a drunk—you know, hangover and all. Before his eyes opened, he was carrying on a conversation with Eric about the stock market, one they'd been having at dinner last night. As far as he was concerned, he was still at your house. Only when I filled him in on what happened afterward did he remember. Boy, he cried like a baby. Called his wife and daughter immediately, said he'd talk to you and Janet later."

"Where is he now?"

"I let him go. Nothing to hold him on. Jess wouldn't file charges. In fact, she wanted Walt to come right home. Say, it was too bad about your party. Everyone was having a nice time."

"That's the way it goes sometimes. Are you driving down to Susanville for the game Friday night?"

"I can't. I have to work. But I won't miss the Homecoming game the week after."

"Good. Hope to see you before then."

"You will. Allison's sitting twice for us in the next couple of weeks, and I have to drive out to pick her up."

After he'd hung up, Greg told Janet what he had learned. While they were talking, the phone rang. It was Walt, as apologetic as Winn had said. He spoke to each of them for a minute. Afterward, Janet and Greg looked at each other.

"I still don't know what to make of it," Janet said. "He sounds so sincere."

"Yeah. Let's just forget about it, okay?"

The Lowells' first full week in Fire Valley was a busy one. After installing a phone in the small niche off the dining room that was now his office, Greg began working on *Death Around the Corner*. Janet interviewed with Emmett Nicholson on Monday morning and was hired. By Friday, she had worked three shifts. Allison, when not with Billy or her friends, found other baby-sitting jobs. Mark spent every day after school practicing for Friday night's opening game. In spite of their schedules, they managed to meet for dinner every evening.

On Friday night, Janet and Greg picked up the Gordons and drove to Susanville. Allison went with Billy and a recovered Lisa Cunningham and her boyfriend.

The game was a close one. Mark was nervous, and by his own estimation afterward, played poorly. But with Bonner down 10 to 6 halfway through the final quarter, he turned a broken play into a twenty-nine-yard touchdown run. The score held. The drive back to Bonner was a happy one.

On Saturday, Greg walked through the crisp early morning air to the barn. Otis, as usual, was hard at work. "You haven't missed a day since we got back," he said to the old man. "Don't you ever take any time off?"

"Nope. Wouldn't have nothin' to do. There's little enough out here now, what with the fields clean. You know I cut that patch of barley yesterday?"

"Janet mentioned it."

"Got a good price for it too. You sure you don't want any of the money?"

"Otis, we talked about that. Whatever comes from the milk and crops is yours. Wilson wants that, and so do I."

"Well, thanks. Listen, you sure you can drive that tractor now?"

"Yes. Why?"

"I'm gonna hook up the snow equipment soon. Won't be too long. You'll be needin' it, for sure."

Greg smiled. "Shoveling snow. See what I missed by growing up in southern California?"

Otis showed a brown-toothed grin. "Hey, you wanna finish milkin' this one? You and the missus learned real good yesterday."

"Janet did, anyway. At least she didn't squirt it on her foot. Sure. Move over."

Autumn arrived officially, but its formal coming went unnoticed in Fire Valley. It had been cool since Labor Day, the nights very cold, and the splashes of orange, red, and yellow that had inspired the valley's name were emerging. A trace of white had even appeared on the tallest of the far peaks. The scene was one of nature's finest hours.

On Tuesday, though, the weather changed as summer demanded a final bow. By midafternoon, the temperature was 86 degrees. The night brought some relief, but Wednesday's cloudless, fiery sunrise portended more of the same.

Janet was working at the medical center that day. Greg, doing his best to concentrate on Burton's manuscript, found his office too hot. At eleven-fifteen he gave up and went outside. Strolling around the yard, he considered—without much enthusiasm—moving his work to the shaded front porch.

Hearing noises from the barn, he decided to go see what Otis was up to. He found the elderly man in the walled-off back section of the barn that served as a storage area, tinkering with the tractor. The odor of grease and oil was unbearable in the heat, and he continued on, finally stopping near the well. Earlier that morning, he had seen Dora Waverly, still dressed in her heavy dark clothes, staring at the tragic monument.

What did she find so fascinating about the well? he wondered. Did something in her family history link her to it? Maybe one of her ancestors had been among those who—

(padgett)
"What?"
(padgett why did you take so long to come home)
"Who the hell—?"
(padgett why did you take so long to come home)
"I—I'm not sure. It wasn't the right time."
(i need you padgett)
"Need me?"
(you are home padgett)
"Yes."
(to stay)
"To stay."
(welcome home padgett)

The figure appeared on the hill. Greg first sensed rather than saw it. A stocky man in buckskin leggings and moccasins, his chest bare, a narrow band encircling his head of straight black hair. Terror etched his young face as he stared at Greg. He held a gun in one hand, pointing it skyward. His arm jerked, and puffs of smoke appeared from the bore, but there was no sound. Two similarly dressed men appeared over the ridge. The first one staggered. His gun fell down the slope, and he clutched at his body, now riddled with crimson holes. The others dropped to their knees as he rolled to the base of the hill, and they trained their weapons on Greg. The triggers were pulled. Gunfire erupted. Screaming, Greg dove to the ground by the well.

"Mr. Lowell!" Greg thought he heard a distant voice above the thunder. "Christ almighty! Mr. Lowell, you okay?"

He opened his eyes and saw Otis running toward him. Behind the old man was the tractor, still sputtering. The distant hillside was empty except for three scattered junipers.

"Mr. Lowell, what the heck happened?" Otis asked as he helped Greg to his feet.

"Nothing," he answered. "I was daydreaming, and when you started that monster up . . ."

"Scared the fool outta you, huh?" Otis said, and couldn't hide a smile. "Hey, I'm sorry. Just as long as you ain't hurt."

"I'm fine, Otis. Go on back to your work."

The old man did. Greg returned to his editing, and it was more comfortable on the porch. But he did very little.

26

Homecoming

Janet worked late on Thursday at the busy medical center. She was not scheduled, but one of the nurses had called in sick, and it was Rick Johnson's day off. Greg made dinner, and by the time she got home, Mark had already eaten and was upstairs doing homework, and Allison was baby-sitting for Joey Gordon.

"It looks great," Janet said as she saw the table. "Oh, my feet! I gotta get these shoes off."

"Tired?"

"Yes, but I'm really enjoying it," she said enthusiastically. Greg kissed her. "I'm proud of you."

She smiled. "Kiss me again."

"Okay." He did, this time harder.

"Want to skip dinner?" she asked huskily.

"Heck no! It took too long to make. You'll have to wait for dessert."

"How's the book going?" she asked a few minutes later as she tore off a hunk of garlic bread.

"Real well. I got a lot done today. It was too hot to work in here, so I took my stuff over to those trees on the hill past the Greenwood plot. You can see the reservoir on the other side. Beautiful spot. I have four chapters left. Then I'm getting together with Burton."

"Great. Anything else happen?"

"Otis finished loading up the loft with hay. He says there's more than enough to get us through the winter. He won't be out tomorrow. I think he's coming down with something. Looks like I milk the cows."

"I'll help," she said. "Oh, I asked about Reverend Stocker today."

"And?"

"He's still in Reno. They moved him to a sanatorium. Emmett says he can sit up, take food, even walk around a little. But he doesn't talk, just stares all the time."

"Too bad."

"His family moved down there a couple of weeks ago. They've already brought in a new minister."

"And they still don't know what caused it?"

She shook her head. "A severe shock. Only he can say what happened, and the secret may be locked up inside him for a long time."

The Bonner Homecoming weekend began on Friday afternoon when many of the town's prodigal alumni returned. A football game pitting past Mountaineers against current faculty was scheduled that night, followed by the varsity match Saturday afternoon. The festivities culminated with the Homecoming social later in the evening. In between were lots of less formal get-togethers.

Janet and Greg would have passed on the alumni game, but at the urging of Carol Staley, they went. "Winn's playing in it," she told them, "and he loves to show off. Besides, there's someone Donna wants you to meet."

The game was played for fun. By the third quarter, the score had grown to basketball proportions. About that time, Donna found the people she had been looking for all night, an attractive couple in their late forties.

"Marlene and Paul Bonner," she said, "meet Janet and Greg Lowell."

"Bonner?" Greg asked as he shook Paul's hand.

The well-dressed man smiled. "Jason Bonner was my great-grandfather. I've been looking forward to meeting you ever since Carol wrote us. It's been a long time since a Bonner and a Padgett crossed paths."

"I don't doubt that," Greg said. "Are you the last Bonner to live up here?"

Paul shook his head. "I left twenty years ago. My younger sister stayed until our mother died, seven years after that. She lives in San Diego now."

"And you?"

"We're from New Orleans."

"Great city," Janet said. "Is that your hometown, Marlene?"

"I was born and raised in Baton Rouge," the dark-haired woman said in a refined drawl, "but I went to school at Tulane University. That's where Paul and I met."

"Fell in love with Marlene *and* the city at the same time."

Donna left to find some other friends, and the Bonners and Lowells talked through the rest of the game. After the game—which the faculty won —Carol and Winn joined them, and they drove to Harmony House's crowded saloon.

Without Paul Bonner they might not have found an inch of bar space, much less a table. But Paul, attending his first Homecoming in three years, was an honored guest all over town. During their second round, he stood and excused himself. "I'll be back in a few minutes. I brought something for you, Greg."

"For me? I don't understand."

"Marlene, you know the story as well as I do. Fill them in, okay?"

He left, and Marlene explained. "Jason Bonner was a good friend to all the people who settled in Fire Valley. After the massacre, he went around to the ranches and gathered up everyone's belongings, storing them for safekeeping in Harmony House's attic. Maybe he hoped to return them to relatives. But somewhere along the way they were forgotten. They stayed in the same place for nearly a century, until the fire. Everything was destroyed—except a small metal chest that was pulled out of the ashes, a chest with *Padgett* inscribed on it. Paul's father took it home, but in the aftermath of the fire, it was forgotten again until Paul came back to settle the estate. He swore that someday he'd return it to a rightful owner. I guess that's you, Greg. We've never even opened it, although we're dying to know what's inside."

"Well, you're sure going to find out this weekend," Greg said. "That's really incredible."

"Oh, I'm excited," Janet said.

"Me too," Winn added. "Come on, Paul, where are you?"

"I have an idea," Greg said. "Marlene, when are you two leaving?"

"Monday."

"Great. I think we should do the unveiling up right. How about Sunday night, our place?"

"I doubt if I can wait that long," Carol said, pouting.

"I'll check with Paul," Marlene said, "but it sounds fine."

Paul returned with the Padgett chest, which was about fourteen inches long and half that in width and depth. Despite its size, it was heavy. A single latch with a large keyhole held it closed, and pieces of frayed but sturdy rope were tied around it. It had once been painted black, but most of that had long since peeled away, laying bare the cast iron and exposing a few rust spots.

Marlene told Paul the plan, and he agreed. Soon the three couples split up, the Bonners remaining in the saloon to visit with more of Paul's old friends. Janet and Greg took the chest home and placed it on a coffee table in the living room. This time, it would not be forgotten.

Prior to the game on Saturday afternoon, a violent storm ended the brief heat wave. Thunder and lightning cracked the sky, and rain fell in hard sheets. The downpour lasted for an hour, finally stopping before kickoff. Still, a distant rumbling continued throughout the day, and streaks of white fire wove webs in the gloomy overcast.

Dunsmuir High School had not been handpicked for the Homecoming game. It just happened to be the luck of the schedule. But Bonner had beaten Dunsmuir the past five years in a row and was again heavily favored. It was nice to know the chances of the subsequent celebration being dampened were slim.

Mark Lowell was brilliant in his first game before the hometown people, who received their new hero with loud approval. Most of his passes were aimed at Tommy Sinclair. Toward the end of the third quarter, his statistics were mounting, a testimonial to his skill and a sad commentary on the hapless Dunsmuir secondary. The score was 41–0. Mark, who knew that Craig planned to sit him down in the final quarter, cheered his teammates on, eager to see the Mountaineers get their shutout.

Rain began falling again late in the fourth quarter. Thunder echoed in the stadium; lightning flashed in the distance. A few spectators left, but most were determined to stay until the end.

"Come on, run it out, run it out," Mark called from the sidelines, clapping his hands. "Under two minutes now."

He watched as Scotty Blair, the second-string quarterback, ran Bonner's offense. The seventh play of a long time-consuming drive was another handoff to Dan Hillis, who had been running well all day. But this time he was tackled behind the line of scrimmage, leaving Bonner with a third and eight on their own forty-four yard line. Mark was sure Craig would call another running play, as he had all period. Failing to make the yardage, they would punt Dunsmuir deep into their end of the field.

A play was sent in. Bonner huddled, then lined up with three receivers on the right. Scotty Blair, to the surprise of everyone, dropped back to pass. His fists clenched, Mark heard Craig yell, "What the hell are you doing?"

Even disobeying instructions, the boy should easily have completed a pass to either of two wide-open receivers. But the ball was tipped as he released it, and it floated into the hands of an incredulous Dunsmuir defensive end, who stood alone at midfield near the sideline. A collective groan rose from the Bonner fans as they realized there was nothing but fifty yards of open field between the boy and the end zone.

Jimmy Michaels, six-three and 240 pounds, tucked the ball awkwardly under his arm and lumbered along the sideline, three Mountaineers angling across the field in futile pursuit. Mark, with his coach and the others, stepped an inch closer and watched helplessly as the boy passed them.

No, Mark thought. This couldn't be happening. He'd worked too hard. *This couldn't be happening!*

Hidden under the Mountaineers' gold helmet, Mark's face twisted with a rage that transcended the motivation. His body shaking, he fixed his malevolent gaze on the unknowing Michaels.

The zigzagging streak of white fire blinded the spectators as it hurtled to the ground from a dark cloud overhead. It struck Jimmy Michaels near the twenty yard line, incinerating him in a dazzling burst. The football bounced toward the sideline, rolling out of bounds. Many watched it for a moment before daring to look at the fused lump of bone and flesh, smoke curling upward from the core of a blackened patch of earth.

Silent for a moment, the stadium erupted in a crescendo of screams. Sobbing children were led outside by mothers who could barely stand. Others sat and stared in disbelieving horror. A few hurried onto the field.

Craig Morley was the first to reach the charred thing that

had been Jimmy Michaels. Overwhelmed by the smell of burnt flesh, he fell to the grass and vomited. The rain streamed down more heavily, weakening the odor somewhat.

Another streak of lightning hit the ground beyond the west bleachers. Shouting above the intermittent thunder, Winn ordered those on the field to disperse quickly and go home. Janet and Greg searched frantically for Mark, who had been standing ten yards from the doomed Jimmy Michaels.

"Mark!" Janet cried, weaving through a maze of bewildered players from both schools.

They found him standing in the same spot. His helmet was on; a stream of water trickled off it. His knees trembling, he looked as if he might collapse.

"Mark, are you all right?" Janet asked, grabbing one arm.

"I'm okay, Mom," he replied dully.

"Come on, son, let's get you out of here," Greg said, taking the other arm.

They turned away from the grisly scene, slowly following the crowd to one of the gates. Janet and Greg did not notice when Mark glanced over his shoulder, his expressionless gaze finding the scoreboard.

It read: Bonner 41, Dunsmuir 0.

The Padgett Chest

Bonner's Homecoming weekend was over—abruptly, tragically. The social was officially canceled, although no one would have attended anyway. Some of the returning alumni left before nightfall. The majority stayed through Sunday morning, but by midday, nearly all were gone. Among them were Marlene and Paul Bonner, who had called the Lowells the night before to tell them.

Jimmy Michaels's remains were returned to Dunsmuir. The funeral was scheduled for Tuesday. Bonner High School's principal announced suspension of classes for that day, urging all who could to travel to Dunsmuir with the football team, which had voted to attend.

The storm's fury had lessened during the night, but rain continued to fall Sunday afternoon. Janet and Allison were busy in the kitchen cooking dinner as Greg absently watched the final minutes of a football game. Mark was resting upstairs after a long and troubled night.

Concerned about his son, Greg called, "Jan, have you looked in on Mark lately?"

"About twenty minutes ago," she answered. "He was sound asleep."

"The Rams will be coming on soon. I wonder if I should wake him."

She appeared in the doorway. "I don't know, Greg. He really needs some sleep—"

Loud cries from above brought Greg to his feet. He climbed the stairs three at a time and burst into Mark's room.

The boy's eyes were still closed as he writhed and screamed, *"I killed him! I killed him!"*

"Mark!"

"I killed him! I killed him!"

"Mark, snap out of it!" Greg shouted, shaking him gently.

"I killed—"

"Mark!"

He opened his eyes and stared blankly at his parents, then at Allison, who hovered by the door. His body eased, and he fell back against the pillow, but the anguish on his face remained.

"Rough dream, ace?" Greg asked.

"I killed him," Mark said softly, staring at the ceiling.

"Mark, stop it!" Janet said.

"I killed him," he repeated.

"Why are you saying that?" Greg asked. "Killed who?"

"Jimmy Michaels."

"Jimmy . . . ? Oh, Mark." Janet sank onto the bed. "What are you talking about?"

"Mark," Greg said, his hand on the boy's shoulder, "I know what you must be going through, having been that close and all, but you didn't kill anybody. Know what I heard on the radio this morning?"

"What?"

"A farmer near Burney was struck by lightning in his field. Another was hurt over in Cedarville, and a couple of cows were killed somewhere else. That was a nasty storm yesterday. What happened here was a freak accident. Tragic as hell, but still an accident! I'm afraid that it'll leave you with an ugly impression, but we'll do whatever we can to help. Okay, ace?"

"Okay," Mark said, his eyes still averted.

"You want to come down? The Rams are on."

"Maybe later. I just want to be alone."

He leaned over and flicked on his radio, the blare of Bon Jovi punctuating what he'd said. His family went downstairs, Allison returning to the kitchen, Janet sitting next to Greg on the sofa.

"I'm really concerned about him," she said.

"Me too. But he's a tough kid. He'll bounce back. I just hope it's soon."

Two hours later, Mark came down to watch the end of the game but showed none of his usual enthusiasm. For the next two nights, violent outbursts interrupted his sleep—and his family's.

On Tuesday, though, he returned from the funeral in Dunsmuir seeming more like himself. At breakfast Wednesday morning, after nine hours of peaceful sleep, his thoughts were on the upcoming game Friday. Mark Lowell would not forget what he had witnessed four days past, but the worst of it seemed over.

Burton Faraday had been in monastic seclusion since the day after his return from Seattle when he began work on a new book. Greg had not even spoken to him. With *Death Around the Corner* finished, though, he had taken a chance and called Burton Tuesday night. The writer was eager to look over the editing. Greg offered to bring it out, but Burton, glad for the break, told him he would be by Wednesday afternoon.

Stepping in out of the soft rain that had been falling all day, Burton looked around the house. "You've really done some work on this museum. Hey, look at the old chest! A family heirloom, to be sure."

"I suppose," Greg said, "except that it's been in *this* family for only a few days." He related the background of the Padgett chest, which he and Janet had ignored during the recent troubled days.

"Well come on, open it," Burton said excitedly.

"No way. Janet would kill me if I did it without her. She'll be home later. How about working till then?"

"Oh, all right," Burton said, grumbling. "If we have to."

He read through the revised manuscript, agreed with most of Greg's changes, argued over others, rewrote a few paragraphs after making his point. They finished in under three hours and were discussing cover art when Janet arrived home, still in her white uniform.

"Ah-hah!" Burton exclaimed as she zipped off her boots. "Now we learn the ancient secret."

"Well, hello to you too," she said dryly. "What the devil are you talking about?"

"He wants to see what's in the chest," Greg said.

"Good. So do I, but I also want ten minutes to change."

Allison and Mark arrived while Janet was in the bedroom. When she came out, they were awaiting her impatiently. Greg first sliced through the ropes, then inserted the end of a screwdriver into the keyhole. A minute of twisting and jiggling resulted in nothing, and he was afraid he would have to snap the lock. But finally there was a click as the old mechanism yielded. With the rest watching expectantly, he raised the heavy lid.

The chest contained two objects. The first was a book, its thin pages bound in black leather. It had been wedged in tightly, but Janet managed to work it free. Beneath it was a string-tied pouch containing more than thirty gold and silver coins of various denominations. Everyone exclaimed in delight as Greg poured them out on the coffee table. Their face value totaled $473 and some change, probably the Padgetts' life savings. But as collector's items, their current worth was many times that.

While Allison and Mark examined the coins, Burton said, "I can understand why the money was locked up, but why the book?"

"Jason Bonner probably wanted something to keep the coins from jingling," Greg said. "You know, prevent temptation for anyone who might pick the chest up. The book fits perfectly."

"It looks like a Bible," Janet said.

Greg flipped through the pages. "It is. Probably an old family— Wait a minute." He extracted some folded sheets of paper. "There's something else in here."

"What is it?" Janet asked eagerly.

He opened the three sheets of yellowing paper and studied the microscopic scrawl. "Looks like a letter, a very long one. It's addressed 'Dear Grandma.' "

"One of the Padgett children wrote it, then," Janet said.

"Which one?" Mark asked.

"It's hard to read this," Greg said, "but there's something at the beginning about a doll."

"Martha, the daughter," Burton said. "I've seen her name on the well. How old was she when she died?"

"Twelve or thirteen, I think," Greg replied. "Look at the date on top. August fourth, 1856."

"That's not too long before the massacre," Janet said.

"And look farther down," Greg went on. "There are gaps, and later dates. I suppose with the mail service back then, people could spend weeks—even a month—writing a letter before sending it out. Oh, what tales this might tell. I only hope it's legible."

"Gregory, I envy your upcoming days," Burton said. "If it wasn't for my work, I'd be looking over your shoulder."

"I can't wait to write Marlene and Paul, and tell them what was inside," Janet said. "Actually, I wish we could do more for them, but they said they'd return anything we sent."

"Then we'll send something to their kids," Greg said. "How many did they say they had?"

"Three."

"We'll send each one a couple of the twenty-five-dollar gold pieces. I'll fix them up tonight and take them to the post office in the morning. Hey, I'd better get dinner going," said Greg. "Burton, can you stay?"

"No. Too much work to do. Promise you'll let me know when that thing's deciphered?"

"You'll be among the first," Greg assured him, and carefully placed the Bible and the letter back into the Padgett chest.

28

The Letter

Greg finished his work on Burton's manuscript after dinner and took it to the post office the next morning along with the package for the Bonner children. Afterward, he hurried home to explore Martha Padgett's letter.

The young girl had written with a quill pen. Her delicate stroke left gaps that had been further faded by time. In addition, ink had spattered, blotting even more words. But with patience—and a magnifying glass—Greg was able to read most of Martha's letter.

It began rather ordinarily:

August 4, 1856

Dear Grandma:

I'm sorry that I haven't written to you for awhile, but we've been very busy. Everyone is feeling fine here. I hope you are too. How are Uncle Will and Aunt Eleanor? I forgot to tell you last time that I almost lost the doll you made for me when we were crossing the desert, but James went back and found her. I named her Elizabeth.

Martha wrote at length about the friends she had among the settlers' children, the bull her father had purchased, the new curtains and tablecloth her mother had made, and other homey information. Then, the mood of her letter took a different turn.

You know how much it always rains in Worcester? Well, it hasn't rained the whole time we've been in Fire Valley. Today was very hot again. Some of the things in my garden aren't doing good. Father left early for Mr. Leary's place. They're trying to dig a well over there. Mother was sick or something when I got up, but then was better. Later she got queer again, and showed us where she thought there was water, out in the yard.

Greg wondered how Rebecca Padgett could have been so sure of where to find water, but Martha didn't say anything else about it. The next time she picked up her pen was on Wednesday, August 6, a couple of days later.

Three Indians attacked us today. They were Modocs, Mr. Bonner said later. They wounded Mr. Hoyt and Sally Kolb, who was standing next to me. The men killed them and took away the bodies. We weren't supposed to know, but James said they buried them on Mr. Leary's place. I was really scared, Grandma.

"Three Indians attacked us today," Greg murmured. Three Indians! Three Indians on the road, three Indians on the hill . . . God, what a thing for a child to have to watch!

The next day, Martha wrote, *It was cold for awhile today, but nobody cared, because they found water. Mr. Kolb and Mr. Bonner came up, and they were all white. But everyone was glad when they got to take water home.*

They were "all white" ? What the hell did that mean?

On Friday, August 8, Martha apparently sat down twice with her letter. *The men came back today to help Father shore up the well. Mr. Kolb said that Sally is feeling better. Mr. Paine, that awful man from the wagon train, was here too. I hate him.*

Baron killed James tonight. Baron killed my little brother. His horns were red.

Baron, Greg thought. The Hereford bull. Good Lord, James Padgett was gored to death!

What Martha wrote two days later was just as disturbing. *I saw Mr. Paine coming out of the barn this morning. Then I saw Mother. She was naked. I wanted to run and tell Father, but I was scared. He came later and found Mother. She was dead. She killed herself. Father said she wasn't in her right mind since what happened to James. I didn't tell him about Mr. Paine.*

Martha's words were becoming even harder to read. The writing was wavy, and the last page was stained with what must have been her tears.

I can't stop crying. Even when I write, I'm crying. Oh Grandma, I wish we were back home with you! I want to go away from here so bad. Mr. Leary beat Tommy today out by the well. He never did that before. Father yelled at Benjamin and me. I thought he was going to hit us too, but he didn't, he just cried. Then he said we would leave for good. Tonight he was queer. He said he was going to tell the others to come out here tomorrow, because it was our duty to warn them of what was out there in the well. He's going to send Benjamin around in the morning.

Greg read the paragraph a third and fourth time, but it made no sense. "Warn them of what was out there in the well"? Was Martha interpreting her father's words, or were they her own confused thoughts, drawn from the murk of her tormented mind? *Warn them of what was out there in the well!*

But the rest of the page was blank. The next day was August 13.

Martha Padgett never got back to her letter.

29

Walt Cunningham

Mark Lowell's first loss was hard to accept. No matter that Bonner had lost on the road to powerful Redding Manual Arts, a school one division removed from them, or that Mark had played well and that the margin had been four points. Bonner High had suffered its first loss, and Mark took it personally, brooding around the house most of Saturday.

The afternoon was cold, windy. Greg, not adjusting well to this kind of weather, was returning from the barn where he had been tending to the cows. He walked sidelong against the wind, his jacket collar turned up. Still, the wind bit through the down jacket, and he swore under his breath. Once he nearly stumbled, for his ankle still throbbed from having missed a rung on the loft ladder.

He slammed the front door behind him and strode into the living room. The warmth in the room didn't touch him. He left his jacket on. Mark was sprawled on the sofa, a forgotten book next to him. He hardly glanced at his father.

"Is that what you're going to do all weekend?" Greg muttered.

"Huh?" Mark looked up. "What'd you say, Dad?"

"Are you going to sit on your ass and feel sorry for yourself over losing a damn football game?"

"Dad—"

"Why couldn't you help me with those cows? You never help!"

"Dad, I helped Otis feed *and* milk them this morning!"

Janet, hearing her husband's irate voice from the kitchen, came in to ask what was wrong. Father and son were standing face-to-face. Greg's back was to her, but she could see his fists were clenched. Mark looked bewildered, and a little angry.

"Enough excuses!" Greg shouted. "When the hell are you going to take some initiative, start acting like a man?"

"Dad, please!"

Greg thrust a finger at the boy. "I ought to teach you—!"

"Greg, leave him alone!" Janet cried, walking toward them. Mark hurried up the stairs to his room, slamming the door. "What were you screaming about? You haven't raised your voice to him in years."

"It was between me and him," Greg said, whirling on her. "Why couldn't you keep out of it?"

Now she saw his face, red and twisted with fury. His cold eyes, his sneering mouth. And she was frightened.

Frightened of the man she had been married to for over eighteen years.

"Greg, what is it?" she asked, feeling compelled to retreat a step. "What's wrong?"

The strange mood swept away suddenly, and he shook his head in confusion. "Nothing, Jan. I . . . bruised my ankle in the barn. It still hurts like hell. Guess I was just irritable, and Mark was handy. I'm really sorry. I'll go and talk to him. Jeez, it's hot in here!" He peeled off his jacket and limped toward the stairs.

She started after him, wanting to help him yet still hesitating. "Greg, you sure you're . . . ?"

He turned and smiled. "I'll fix the leg after I've seen Mark. Be down in a while."

At dinner, Greg and Mark busily planned Sunday's football schedule as if nothing had happened.

But something *had* happened, and Janet could not let it go. A nonviolent man like Greg Lowell . . . What was it Martha Padgett had written in her letter?

Mr. Leary beat Tommy today out by the well. He never did that before. Father yelled at Benjamin and me. I thought he was going to hit us too . . .

. . . out by the well.

On the first Tuesday in October, rain fell steadily for the second day in a row. With Janet home in bed with a bad cold, Greg walked the aisles of Noble's Drug Store. As he hunted for the Nyquil, he saw Walt Cunningham near the front of the store.

"Greg! Hey, Greg," the big man called, smiling.

"Walt, how're you doing?"

"What a coincidence meeting you here. Look what I was buying." He held up a thick paperback book, which Greg instantly recognized as one of Jeremy Hunter's.

"I applaud your good taste," he said, grinning.

"It's the third. Jessica loved the first two. She may hook me."

"How is she?" Greg asked.

"Doing real good. We're . . . uh, trying to forget about what happened, start over again, you know? I'm taking her to Hawaii in a couple of weeks for our anniversary."

"That sounds great."

"Listen, gotta run. Nice talking to you, Greg."

"I might run into you later. I'm picking Allison up at your place in about an hour."

"I doubt it," Walt called over his shoulder. "I'm meeting a client right now, and that'll take some time. Say hi to Janet. Maybe we'll see you soon."

Walt paid for the book and some other things. Before leaving the store, he looked back at Greg, his expression strangely puzzled. His exit a few seconds later was furtive, as if he were fleeing from something dangerous.

Greg heard the bell on the front door. Turning, he saw the broad back of Walt Cunningham and scowled as he watched the salesman climb behind the wheel of his Continental. Then, as the car pulled away from the curb, he nodded and smiled.

The Cunningham house was on Whitehorse Road, a mile east of downtown. It was old but well cared for, the front porch separated from the tree-lined curb by a hundred feet of lawn that, having been sprinkled with rye seed late in the summer, still showed some green. Lisa's Toyota was parked at the top of the long driveway; her mother's Cutlass was in the adjoining garage.

The rain had stopped. Allison, who had driven home with Lisa to do homework, stood on the curb and talked with her friend while awaiting her father. The first car to pull into the driveway was a dark green Lincoln. Both girls waved.

"Hi, Dad," Lisa called.

Walt glanced at them but did not reply. When he braked to a halt, his front bumper was only inches from the Toyota.

"Wow, he almost clobbered you," Allison said.

Lisa smiled. "He drives like that sometimes, especially after a bad day. But I haven't lost my car yet."

Red-faced, Walt climbed out from behind the wheel and stomped into the house, completely ignoring the girls. He peeled off his damp raincoat and flung it on the couch, then called, "Jess!"

"I'm in the kitchen, Walt," his wife answered. He followed her voice and found her unpacking a bag of groceries. "Hi, dear," she said, looking up at him. "How did it go with Peterson . . ."

She saw his flushed scowling face, smelled the stench of liquor that engulfed him. The fear she had known only once before gripped her again. She backed away a few steps.

"Where's dinner?" he demanded. "Why the hell isn't dinner on the table?"

"Walt, did you forget?"

"Forget what?"

"You said we were going out to dinner tonight. The Modoc Room. You called this morning—"

"What kind of lie is that?" he snapped, coming closer. "Any excuse for not making dinner, huh? I *know* the truth, Jess! Someone's been fucking you all afternoon, right?"

"Walt!"

"I bust my ass, make us money, and you lie on your back all goddamn day! What're you running, bitch? A whorehouse?" He was inches from her now. "Is that cunt daughter of yours part of the stable too? *Huh*?"

Jessica knew what he would do. She knew it would be worse this time and was not going to let it happen. Reaching behind her, she slid open a drawer and withdrew a long sharp carving knife. She clutched it with both hands, her knuckles white, and waved it before her.

"Stay away from me," she said. "Stay away, or so help me, I'll . . ."

Her husband laughed. "You'll *what*? You spineless bitch! You're not going to—"

He took another step and she lunged awkwardly at him, the tip of the knife piercing his left shoulder. Stunned, he staggered back, grabbing his shoulder. A dark stain spread across his white shirt. He stared at the wound, then at her, his face distorted in anger. This time, he would not be stopped.

A raging beast descended on Jessica, swatting away her

meager defense. The knife clattered across the kitchen floor.
Unable to run, she dove for it. Walt's heavy shoe pinned her
wrist before she could grab it; her hand became discolored. He
released her, and while she writhed in pain, he picked up the
knife. His first thrust put four inches of steel into her stomach.
Jessica screamed, and screamed again when the blade sliced
through her right breast, and screamed again, and again . . .
. . . until it found her throat.

Greg was close behind Walt, arriving at the Cunningham's
three minutes later. "Hiya, girls," he called. "Why are you
standing in the rain?"

"Hi, Dad," Allison said. "It stopped raining, in case you
haven't noticed."

He grinned. "Yeah, I guess so. Ready?"

"See you tomorrow, Lisa," she told her friend as she
opened the passenger door. The haunting, funereal allegretto
of Beethoven's Seventh Symphony poured from the car.

"Okay," Lisa said. "Hey, weren't we supposed to watch
some of that new miniseries together?"

"How about Thursday and Friday?"

"Great."

"Why don't you two swap overnights?" Greg said.

"That's a super idea. Lisa?"

"I'll check with my folks and call you. Bye."

Lisa started up the walk as Greg made a U-turn. Before
driving off, he looked past Allison at the Cunningham house.
He smiled.

Halfway up the walk, Lisa thought she heard a sound
coming from the house. It was muted, unrecognizable, and
after a few seconds, it stopped. She hurried to the porch, but
inside, meeting silence, she hesitated.

"Mom? Dad?" she called. "Hey, where are you?" No
reply.

From the kitchen came a grunting sound that seemed
more animal than human. She thought it might be Rusty, her
Irish setter, who was usually out back. Smiling, she crossed to
the kitchen. In the doorway she froze, the scream in her throat
stifled by the horror she saw.

The kitchen was red. Walls, counters, table. Pools of red
on the tile floor. Her father, his penis bloated and erect, straddled what remained of her mother, a bloody torso with a head
half severed, an arm that had left a weaving trail as it slid

across the floor, a mound of raw flesh that might have been a breast. Drenched in red, his face still distorted with passionate rage, Walt stroked his manhood. As he looked up at Lisa, the semen flood came, the milky seed dripping down into the dark pool between Jessica's legs. It was still spurting as, grabbing the knife, he rose and lurched toward the girl.

"She was a good lay," he muttered in a voice Lisa had never heard. "No wonder they all wanted her. She was a good lay."

Unable to move, Lisa watched him stagger closer. He slid in a pool of Jessica's blood and, struggling for balance, fell forward. The kitchen knife penetrated his head directly between his eyes.

Then Lisa moved. Five minutes later, a motorist nearly ran her down as she crawled across Whitehorse Road, her scalp bleeding from the times she had pounded it against the asphalt.

30

From the Blackness

On the last Saturday of October, Janet and Greg invited their friends to the house for pizza. The timing was good, for that afternoon Mark had led Bonner High to their third straight win, a crusher against overmatched Burney.

Billy came at 6:45 to take Allison to a party at Stacey French's house. It was the girl's first social venture since the Cunningham tragedy, which had left her pale and without an appetite for weeks. That night, wearing makeup and a smile, she seemed to be recovering her spirit. She and Billy helped themselves to some pizza before leaving, putting to rest her parents' fears of her wasting away.

"Must've been tough on Allison," Burton said, "losing her friend in the wake of that mess. I understand Lisa's living with family back east."

Greg nodded. "An uncle and aunt from Virginia came for her last week. Yeah, Allison's been taking it hard. They had become pretty close."

"But what about poor Lisa?" Janet added. "Can you imagine the things she saw in that house?"

"I don't have to imagine it," Winn said, frowning. "Neither does Larry. God, it was an ugly thing!"

Larry shook his head. "Someone should've suspected after the first time. Why couldn't we see—"

"Larry, drop it!" Jill said sharply. "He's been agonizing over it since that day. *Nobody* could have anticipated something like that. Perfectly sane loving husband and father goes berserk. It happens. Not too often, thank God."

"Jill's right, Larry," Eric said. "How was Lisa doing when she left?"

"Physically, okay. Otherwise, not good. Withdrawn. You can imagine. Her aunt said that she'd receive good care when they got her home. I hope so. She's going to need that—and more."

Pretending great interest in her slice of pizza, Janet struggled to distance herself from the others without their noticing. Jill's words reverberated painfully in her head.

Perfectly sane loving husband and father goes berserk. It happens.

Perfectly sane . . .

Mr. Leary beat Tommy today out by the well.

It happens.

She glanced at Greg, who noticed her and winked. He was her husband. Yes, he was. Still . . .

. . . it happens.

The conversation soon turned to Martha Padgett's letter. Everyone knew its contents by then, and opinions over some of the words varied.

"I still contend," Larry said, "and no offense, Greg, that Martha was a little nuts when she wrote that last part, or maybe her father was, for saying it. What could there have been in the well besides water?"

Winn nodded. "He's right. The well was only a symbol, although an important one at the time. Remember, these people were plagued with drought, the threat of Indians, day-to-day hardships of frontier life. And it was worse for the Padgetts after losing two of their family. Who could blame a slip of the tongue, or the pen?"

"What do you mean?" Adrienne asked.

"The settlers were massacred out by the well. Don't you see? That's where Wallace Padgett assembled them to tell them what was on his mind. What he probably said the night before, or meant to say, was 'to warn them out there *by* the well.' Doesn't that make more sense?"

"But warn them of what?" Donna asked.

"Maybe Wallace had some knowledge of the pending attack. It might not have been anything concrete, just a suspicion that sooner or later the Modocs would try to get even for losing three of their warriors. Unfortunately, he was a day late."

Most nodded their agreement. One of the dissenters was Burton. "You're out in left field, Larry. I think that Wallace Padgett said exactly what he meant to say."

"That there *was* something in the well?" Winn exclaimed. "Uh-uh. That's crazy."

"Is it? Then what about the business of a week earlier, when two of the settlers came out of the well white? Have any of you figured that out yet? I have. I think they were probably covered with a mineral of some kind that they'd unearthed, something that was also in the water."

"Wait a minute, now I'm following you," Eric said. "You're saying that what he wanted to warn them about was the *water* in the well! *That* makes sense. What was it, poisoned?"

"I don't think so, since they all drank it for a week. It might have had some hallucinatory effects. Whatever the case, it was bad. It made normally calm people belligerent, even did the same to animals. Case in point, the bull."

"I still think Larry's right," Winn said doubtfully.

"Look," Burton said, "why would they have closed up the well if the water was good?"

"Are you sure that's why it was shut down?" Greg asked. "Vern Greenwood told me it was because it ran dry."

"Ah-hah!" Larry exclaimed.

"Greenwood couldn't have been sure of that," Burton said, "unless he looked for himself, which I doubt. I wouldn't be surprised if there was water down there right now."

"Only one way to know, and that's to check it out," Winn said. "Greg, do you mind?"

"Hell no, I'm curious too. Who's coming?"

"Not me," Janet said. "It's too cold and windy."

The other women agreed, and Donna said, "Don't you want to see that movie we talked about?"

"It's not on for another half hour," her husband replied. "Just save us some pizza."

"If you're lucky."

The five men trudged across the yard through the chilly night air, Greg stopping in the barn for a crowbar, some rope, and an aluminum milking pail. By the light of two battery lanterns, they pried loose the wooden disk, propping it against the side of the well. Burton dropped a stone down and they waited, but heard nothing.

"Damn whistling wind," Eric muttered. "Come on, let's try the bucket."

Greg tied one end of the rope to the handle and lowered it

into the shaft. A hundred feet were paid out before the line slackened.

"I've hit something," he told the others. "Can't tell what."

"Drag it around for a bit," Winn said, "then pull it up."

Greg complied. After retrieving a couple of feet of the line, he exclaimed, "Christ, it's heavy! There's something in it."

"Water," Burton said.

Larry shook his head. "A pail of dirt, or rocks. You'll see."

Greg pulled the load halfway up, then Winn took over. Burton, eager to prove his side of the argument, leaned over the rim of the shaft, his head and arms immersed in the blackness.

"Careful you don't fall in," Greg said.

"Don't worry. I can hear it scraping the walls. Doesn't sound too far down. Can't you pull it up any . . . Wait a minute, I think I see—"

A bloodied, leering face rose out of the darkness. Five cold coarse fingers encircled Burton's wrist in a viselike grip and dragged him into the well. His feet left the ground, but Larry saw that and grabbed his ankles, pulling him back.

"*Winn, let it go!*" Burton screamed. "*Jesus Christ, let it go!*"

Stunned, the sheriff released the rope, which sparked on the rim of the shaft as the bucket fell. Recovering himself, Winn set the heel of his boot on the other end of the coil, so that he wouldn't lose the whole thing.

"What the hell!" he snapped. "Burton—" He turned to the man, but his angry question was left unasked.

Standing unsteadily next to Larry, Burton was deathly pale. His jaw sagged; his hands trembled uncontrollably. Larry tried to help him, but he backed away.

"Didn't . . . any of you see it?" he asked breathlessly.

They shook their heads. "We didn't see anything," Greg said. "It was too dark, and you were covering most of the well."

"What is it, Burton?" Eric asked.

Burton shuddered as he relived the instant and knew that the nightmare could not be shared. "Uh, in the bucket . . ."

"What?" Winn asked impatiently.

Burton smiled weakly as some of the horror waned. "You

know, the four of you are looking like eight to me," he said. "I think I had too much Chianti. You wouldn't believe what I thought was in the bucket! Anyway, I know it wasn't water, so I'm willing to concede. Can we go back to the house?"

"Wait a minute!" Eric said. *"I'm* not willing to concede anything. If you're loaded, then how do you know what you saw?"

Winn nodded. "He's right. Let's pull it back up and see."

Burton's smile faded, then returned. "Okay."

The others surrounded the well again as Winn pulled the rope. Burton backed away, waiting for the discovery, and when Eric groaned loudly, he knew they too had seen it.

"Son of a bitch!" Winn exclaimed.

"Yuck!" Larry said.

"Burton, you weren't kidding," Greg called, turning around with the bucket. "This is pretty disgusting."

He flung the bucket at Burton's feet; he froze, staring. It had been half filled with rich brown dirt, which now poured out, along with a thick writhing mass of earthworms.

Larry laughed. "Fishing, anyone?"

"Hey, that's not funny," Eric said. "There should've been water in that bucket."

"Yeah, but there wasn't," Larry replied. "Satisfied now that Wallace Padgett was a little out of it toward the end?"

"I still think. . . ."

The debate raged as they returned to the house. Inside, they filled the women in on what had happened.

"Christ, you should have seen Burton," Larry said, laughing. "You would've thought the damn bucket of worms was trying to pull him in or something!"

"I didn't know worms had hands," Winn said, deadpan.

Larry grinned. "Which leads us to the old debate about whether clams have feet."

"Okay, I think you've picked on Burton enough," Jill scolded.

Soon the whole matter was finished, and everyone settled down to watch the movie. But Janet was aware that Burton had not fended off the good-natured teasing in his familiar mock-haughty way. While the faces of the other men were flushed from the cold, Burton's appeared pale.

Concerned, she followed him as he went into the kitchen by himself. She hesitated in the doorway, watching as, his back to her, he poured a glass of wine. His hands shook, the bottle ringing against the glass.

"Burton, can I—" she began.

The writer spun around. She could see he had rolled up the right sleeve of his sweater, revealing an ugly purplish bruise around his wrist. He quickly pulled the sleeve back down.

"Are you all right?" she asked.

"Fine. I'm fine. Just scraped the damn side of the well . . ." He smiled. "Come on, the movie's starting."

He carried his glass out, but Janet did not follow immediately. Despite the warmth of the house, especially the kitchen, she trembled.

What was it? she wondered. Why was she feeling that something was wrong? What had Burton Faraday seen?

. . . *warn them of what was out there in the well.*

It happens.

Several minutes passed before Janet could rejoin the others.

31

Jeff Rand

Light snow flurries introduced November. The tallest of the surrounding peaks were already capped with white, as were the high-country junipers. With temperatures falling into the teens at night, the ponds beginning to freeze, Fire Valley's first measurable snowfall seemed close.

November third was Allison's sixteenth birthday. Janet and Greg threw a memorable party for her. The only sobering footnote to the day was a card that came in the mail, signed in a hasty scrawl by Lisa Cunningham.

Later that week, the Lowells were in the stands with the rest of the town for Bonner's "big game" against Lincoln High School of Chico. They went crazy when Mark threw a touchdown pass to Tommy Sinclair in the fourth quarter, giving the Mountaineers a two-point win. Bonner High's talent, along with its 7–1 record, was beginning to turn some heads.

With school and two part-time jobs, Billy Douglas had few free hours. Still he and Allison spent as much time as they could together, and Billy became a familiar face to the people Allison baby-sat for.

With the revision work and editing of Jeremy Hunter's fourth book nearly completed, Greg spent time working around the ranch. Never much with his hands before, he learned a great deal from the crusty Otis Perry and from Jeff Rand, whom he employed for jobs either too strenuous or time-consuming for the old man. Semiliterate, often talking crudely about women, Rand was not stimulating company. But he did his work well, which was all Greg cared about.

Janet averaged three shifts a week at the medical center, and took extra ones when they were shorthanded or busy, which was often. She enjoyed the work, as well as her deepening friendship with the four women, especially Adrienne and Donna. Living in the country also stimulated her love of exercise. Previously a casual jogger, she became a familiar sight along Fire Valley's back roads. By November, she was doing four miles. Adrienne joined her at least once a week.

The skeletal trees and brown meadow grass stood out starkly against the snow-topped mountains and clear blue sky. It was the first morning of a new week. Deeply inhaling the cold air, Greg enjoyed the splendor of the silent landscape as he walked out to the barn to chop firewood. Jeff Rand, taking the place of a bedridden Otis, emerged from the double doors as Greg neared.

"Hiya, Mr. Lowell," he said.

Greg waved. "How's everything going?"

"Just finished up. Didn't get much out of Duchess today. Something wrong with her?"

"I'm not sure. That's the second day in a row. Maybe I'd better have the vet stop out. Are you dropping off the milk?"

"Already in the truck. Don't have to worry about keeping it cold. Anything else you want me to do?"

"No, I don't . . . Wait a minute. You know anything about plumbing?"

"Some. Whaddya got?"

"A kitchen sink that's clogged."

"Yeah, that I can handle. I'll get some tools."

"Just go on over. Janet's home. I'm going to chop wood for a while. Let me know if I can help."

Rand gathered up the tools and walked to the house. Janet let him in the back door. She was dressed in old jeans, a bulky sweater, and fuzzy orange slippers but still looked good to Rand. He smiled as he stepped into the warm kitchen.

"Hey, Miz Lowell, how're you doing?" he asked.

"Hello, Jeff," she replied coolly. "What do you need?"

"Mr. Lowell says your sink's clogged. I'll take a look."

"Oh, good, it's been driving me nuts. Let me move some things."

Rand peeled off his coat. "Jeez, sure is hot in here."

"I've got the furnace up and a fire going," she said. "Feels okay to me. There, now I can get out of your way."

"Oh, you're not in the way," he said with a leering smile.

Janet ignored the comment and returned to the living

room. She stood in front of the roaring fire, rubbing her arms, but still could not get warm. Maybe she was coming down with something.

Working under the sink, Rand began sweating profusely. He thought about saying something about the heat to Janet, then changed his mind. After all, it was her house.

As he worked around the copper pipes, he smashed a finger. He swore loudly, then, remembering where he was, barked an apology. It went unanswered. She must've gone into the bedroom, he thought. God, I'd like to go in the bedroom with her!

A few minutes later, Janet returned to the kitchen. Rand heard a soft rustling sound as she walked. It stopped, and he knew she was close.

"Jeff," she said softly.

"Yeah?"

He stopped his work. Peering over his chest, he nearly cracked his head on a pipe when he saw her smooth, bare legs and slim feet. He pulled himself out from under the sink and gaped. She had changed into a short filmy nightgown and lacy black panties.

Staring at her hard nipples, which pushed against the flimsy material, Rand felt his manhood suddenly burgeon. Oh Jesus, don't come! he thought. Don't come yet. She's gonna let me fuck her!

Janet took his hand and said in a husky voice, "I know what you want, Jeff. Come with me."

She led him into the living room, pulling him insistently to the couch. As she undid the metal buttons of his jeans, his penis, already moist, sprang free.

"Oh, look at *that*!" she said, and took as much as she could in her mouth.

Don't come yet, Rand thought desperately. Don't come yet! "Oh Jesus, don't come yet!" he blurted out.

She stopped, smiling. "What's the matter, little boy?" she asked mockingly. "This your first time? If it's too much for you . . ."

"Never you mind, Miz Lowell!"

"Janet."

"Okay, Janet. You just keep at what you were doing, and I'll show you!"

She sucked him hungrily, and his momentarily flaccid member hardened swiftly. He pulled off her scanty top and

massaged her nipples until she moaned with desire. Peeling
away her panties, she stretched on the couch. Rand, again
near explosion, deftly opened the beading mound and positioned himself to enter her.

Janet's head suddenly snapped back, her face a white
emotionless mask. A few seconds later, she opened her eyes
and saw Rand.

"Oh my God!" she screamed. "What are you doing? Get
away from me, you filthy pig!"

She slapped his face, and he backed away, stunned. "Janet, I—"

"Greg! *Greg, help!*"

"Oh, shit! What you wanna go and do that for? I was
only—"

"Keep backing up, mister," Janet warned, "or so help
me . . ."

Incredulous, Rand watched her leap off the couch and
scurry to a chair across the room where she'd discarded her
clothes. Pulling them on, she continued to glare at him. Rand,
his pants still down around his ankles, would have spoken, but
Greg burst through the front door.

"I thought I heard—*Jesus Christ!* What the hell is going
on here?"

"Mr. Lowell, listen—!"

"You fucking animal!" Greg dove at Rand, knocking him
to the floor. He began pummeling him, and though Rand tried
to defend himself, he was no match for the enraged man.

"Greg, stop!" Janet screamed. "You'll kill him!"

"I don't care! He tried to rape you, didn't he?"

"I didn't rape nobody!" Rand shouted, struggling to get
away. "She *asked* for it!"

"You lying son of a bitch!" Greg drove Rand's head
against the floor.

"Greg, leave him alone! Maybe he's right!"

Abandoning his assault, Greg stared at his wife. "What
are you talking about?"

"I—I don't know. I can't remember. One minute I was in
the kitchen. The next thing, we were over there—on the
couch. Honest to God, I don't know what happened!"

"She *wanted* it, Mr. Lowell!" Rand said, pushing himself
up. "I swear—"

"You shut up!" Greg knocked him down again, then

looked back at Janet. "None of this makes sense. Why the hell—"

"Oh, Greg, just let him go," she said disgustedly, her arms crossed.

"Shouldn't I call Winn?"

"No. Just get him out of here."

Greg backed off. Rand scrambled to his feet. As he buttoned his jeans, Greg told him, "I don't *ever* want to see you here again, understand? Next time, I might not listen to anybody."

Rand scowled. "Yeah, yeah, I'm going. Uh, my coat's in the kitchen."

"Get it, and get out!"

Rand stared at Janet, but she looked away. He disappeared into the kitchen, and a few seconds later they heard the back door slam.

Janet sat on the edge of the chair and gazed blankly at the wall. Greg, his body still trembling with rage, knelt before her.

"Jan," he said softly. "Jan, I . . ."

"Please, Greg, give me a minute. I'm trying to sort this out."

"Jan, listen, I know you wouldn't have tried to seduce him."

She looked at him. Her eyes were cold, but behind the veil of ice, they pleaded with him. "If I didn't," she said, "then what are those doing over there?"

She indicated the couch where the black nightgown and bikini pants he'd bought for her years ago at Frederick's of Hollywood lay on the floor.

"Rand wouldn't have found those in a million years," she continued. "I would have *had* to go and put them on."

In the distance, Jeff Rand's Buick roared to life, but neither noticed.

"Greg!" Janet cried, falling into his arms. "What the hell happened here?"

He stroked her hair. "I don't know. I really don't."

Early Wednesday morning, while Greg was in the post office mailing some material to Sabre Press, a woman backed into his Camaro in the parking lot. The worst of the damage was to the radiator, which would need work before he could drive again. Greg's temper had been short the past few days. Although it had been an accident, he harangued the woman mercilessly until both she and her small son were in tears. He stopped only after Les Curry arrived to write up his report.

Within a half hour, Pete Ledbetter arrived to tow the Camaro. The woman and her son had already gone. Greg would have walked over to the medical center for the LTD, but Curry offered him a ride.

"Hey, I don't mind," the deputy said when Greg protested.

They drove up the Bonner-Oregon Highway, Greg silent and moody, Curry filling in the conversational void. He continued to talk as they negotiated the muddy farm road, but stopped when they saw a car parked on the right side, about a hundred feet from the entrance to the ranch.

"It's Rand," Greg said disgustedly.

Curry nodded. "Thought I recognized that old heap. Yeah, that's Jeff Rand, all right."

He pulled up next to the Buick. Greg rolled down his window. "I told you to stay the hell away from here!"

Rand, who had been half asleep behind the wheel, glared at Greg. "I ain't on your place. You can't make me move, so fuck you!"

Greg was enraged. "You half-breed son of a bitch!" he shouted, enraged. He opened the door of the squad car, but Curry restrained him with a firm hand.

"Let it go, Mr. Lowell," he said. "I'm not fond of Jeff Rand either, but he's not doing anything wrong."

"You tell him, *Lester,*" Rand sneered.

Curry pulled the door shut and drove off as Greg and Rand traded a last round of obscenities. "What the devil was that all about?" the deputy asked.

Greg stared at the slight figure of Dora Waverly by the well and shook his head. "He messed up a job the other day. Not the first time either. I fired him, told him not to come around anymore."

"He's always been a troublemaker. Must be that Modoc blood."

They drove past the barn. Otis, his cold still lingering, poked his head out and waved, then went back inside with Shanty at his heels. As they approached the house, Greg felt some of his tension ease, and he smiled at the deputy.

"Les, I owe you an apology for the way I've been acting. It's been a rough week, and getting the car smashed up didn't help my disposition."

"Hey, no sweat, Mr. Lowell."

"How about a cup of coffee?"

The deputy looked at his watch. "Coffee sounds good. I guess I can squeeze ten more minutes. Nothing much happening today."

An overpowering fury slammed through Jeff Rand.

"Who the fuck does he think he is?" he muttered, pounding a fist against the dashboard. "He ain't got no goddamn right to tell me to move! The cocksucker and his bitch wife! That cunt asked for it. Sauntered right in and begged for it. Then what? Screams like I'm killin' her, watches him beat the shit outta me. Fuck her! Fuck 'em both!"

He continued to sound off until he was trembling with a cold and unquenchable rage. Eyes glazed, jaw firm, he extracted a .30 calibre carbine from under the front seat, checked the clip, and climbed out of the car.

Greg was pouring coffee when he and Les Curry heard muted gunfire. There were so many reports, they could not be separated for ten seconds until the echoes of the last shot faded.

"What the hell?" Curry muttered.

He pulled out his service revolver and followed Greg from the house. Standing on the porch, they looked around but saw nothing. They raced across the yard until, fifty feet from the barn, they saw Jeff Rand stalk through the double doors. Both men froze. Rand's face was contorted with madness.

"I'm gonna kill you, Lowell!" he yelled, raising his weapon. "I'm gonna—"

"Get down!"

Metal whined above him as Greg, reacting to Curry's frantic warning, dropped to the ground. Three shots cracked from the deputy's gun, any one of which would have been enough to kill Rand. His dark eyes bulged. Dropping the rifle, he crumpled.

Pausing for only a second to make certain Rand was dead, the two hurried into the barn. The horror of Rand's insane killing spree made Greg retch.

He'd shot Shanty and all eight cows. The latter had been destroyed execution-style, at close range. Most of their faces had been torn away. The blood that seeped from the rigid carcasses blended with the rich milk from the overturned pails, swirling obscenely on the sawdust floor.

Otis Perry was also dead, although his brain refused to accept that. His frail body riddled with bullets and drenched in blood, most of his face blown off, he somehow dragged himself across the floor to Greg and the deputy, who stood frozen. Mewling sounds escaped from him. Bony fingers wrapped around Greg's ankle, reflexively holding on after the shattered body finally succumbed.

Sickened, Greg pried the hand loose, then the two men staggered out of the barn. Once free of the charnel house, Curry recovered and ran to his squad car to radio Winn. Greg followed but paused for a moment to gaze at Dora Waverly. Still staring at the Padgett well, she was oblivious to what had happened behind her.

32

Day One

On Friday, Otis Perry was laid to rest in the cemetery by the well. For the first time since coming to Fire Valley, Greg saw the weatherworn graves of the Padgetts and the other settlers. An hour later, he and Janet sat by the fireplace, each sipping absently on a drink.

Janet had been unwilling to speak since the bizarre seduction-rape incident with Jeff Rand. She had immersed herself in her job, trying not to be alone with Greg until she'd had enough time to sort it out for herself.

Only now, as she faced the horror of Otis's death, did she grasp how close she had come to losing her husband.

Janet Lowell and Jeff Rand, she thought. Rebecca Padgett and . . .

Mr. Paine, that awful man from the wagon train . . .

I saw Mr. Paine coming out of the barn this morning. Then I saw Mother. She was naked.

She killed herself.

Mr. Paine, that awful man . . .

. . . killed herself.

"I think maybe it's time we talked, don't you?" Greg said.

She jumped, startled, then murmured, "Too close to home."

"What'd you say?"

"Otis and Rand. They . . . died *here*. On our place! And Shanty too." She turned to Greg, her expression that of a child who had just heard a terrifying ghost story. "Oh Jesus, I'm so scared!"

"Jan, it's over with," Greg said patiently. "That animal

Rand's dead. Believe me, I was scared too. But he can't bother us anymore."

"I don't mean just him. What about all the things that have happened since we came here? I thought Bonner was a sleepy little town."

"What things are you talking about?"

"You know what I mean. The Homecoming game, then the Cunningham business."

Greg shook his head. "An act of God, a man pushed over the brink, a hotheaded kid looking for revenge. What's the connection? And aside from Rand, what does any of it have to do with us?"

First the Padgetts, she thought. Now the Lowells . . .

It happens.

She shrugged. "I don't know, but . . ."

"But what?"

She looked at him with all the pain she was feeling in her heart. "Greg, why did I seduce Jeff Rand?"

"Jan, you didn't seduce—"

"Don't tell me that! I've thought about it a thousand times and tried to deny it just as much, but I can't! I *asked* Rand to make love to me! I led him to the couch!"

Greg shrugged. "Jan, I know that's not true."

"Listen to me!" she shouted. "I gave Jeff Rand head for nearly—"

He slapped her. Not hard, but enough to send her reeling backward, stunned. It was the first time he'd ever struck her. She stared at him fearfully, afraid the violent rage she'd seen twice before would resurface. It didn't. Shocked at what he had done, Greg dropped to her side and held her.

"Oh Jan, I'm sorry! Christ, I'm so sorry!"

She pulled away for a moment, then relaxed against him, allowing the tears she'd held back for days to fall. "Why did I seduce Rand?" she asked quietly. "Why did you do what you just did to me? Why have you bullied Mark and Allison the past month? And what about your parents? Why did they leave Fire Valley? Why was your mother so sick? Why did your father react so violently to our being here? Don't you see?"

Greg eased back to look at her. "See what?"

"Something is happening here, something we can't control! It's been growing worse ever since we came to Fire Valley. And it happened to your mother and father."

"I don't understand."

"Neither do I! It doesn't make a damn bit of sense! Yet how do you account for what's happened?"

"Jan, do you want to go back to L.A. ?"

"Yes. No!" Her shoulders sagged; she shook her head. "When you say it as plain as that . . . No, I don't want to leave. We have so much up here. But I can't get it out of my head that there's something wrong!"

"We've been big-city people for a long time," he said, stroking her hair. "Maybe we haven't eased up enough to enjoy this kind of life. Okay, things happened here, explainable or otherwise. But they're over. I think it'll be different, especially now that we've cleared the air. That's probably what we needed to do."

She took a deep breath. "Maybe you're right. This past week has been horrible."

"As for my parents," he went on, "I didn't forget how curious I was a few months back about the time they spent here. But after Dad died . . . I made some inquiries, yet aside from Vern Greenwood, no one seemed to remember them. I thought that old man who operated the elevator at the hotel might, but he must've left town, because no one's seen him in months. My mother was ill here, and things were rough, and my father probably hated Bonner because of those memories. You know, guilt by association."

Janet shrugged. "It makes sense . . . I guess. But what about the hotel burning down while they were here? Another coincidence?"

Greg thought about that for a moment. "I suppose. Bonner's probably had its share of bad things, both before and after the Harmony House fire."

She managed a meager smile. "I'll be okay, Greg. Thanks for talking. As far as I'm concerned, this is Day One."

"Day One," he repeated, and kissed her, long and hard.

The game that night against Alturas High School was supposed to be a laugher for the Mountaineers. But for whatever reason—an emotional letdown, Craig Morley would later say —the contest was close throughout. Going into the last quarter, Bonner was behind by four points. Dan Hillis had already hobbled off the field with a pulled hamstring, nullifying the running game. Most of Mark Lowell's passes were either uncatchable or dropped.

With nine minutes left, Bonner was driving for the lead. Tommy Sinclair had carried an end-around to the Alturas forty-two yard line, and a fine run with a screen pass by Arnie Frederickson had left them on the seventeen. After two short running plays, Mark found Tommy alone in the end zone. The pass was perfect, but the ball ricocheted off Tommy's fingertips.

Dejected, Tommy returned to the huddle. Mark harangued his friend cruelly, his bitter expression evident under the helmet. Tommy found it hard to meet his eyes.

"Hey, Mark, back off," Arnie Frederickson finally said. "We've all been screwing up tonight."

Relenting, Mark took his play from the messenger guard. Bonner lined up, and again he dropped back to pass. But Alturas threw a safety blitz, and Mark was blindsided. He cried out, more in surprise than pain, as he was hit and knocked to the ground. The ball popped from his hands, was kicked around, then recovered by an Alturas linebacker.

The Alturas fans went crazy; players jumped up and down and pounded pads. Mark, rising slowly to his feet, saw them through a red veil. With a low growl, more bearlike than human, he stalked number fifty-seven, the player who had tackled him. The boy's celebration was cut short as Mark dragged him to the ground and beat him savagely. Only his pads and helmet saved him from serious injury, for ten seconds passed before Mark could be pulled off, and it took four people to do it.

Mark was ejected from the game, which Bonner lost. Craig suspended him for the remainder of the season, although it was academic, for he had broken two fingers on number fifty-seven's helmet. Bonner lost its final regular game, then lost in the first round of the regional playoffs. The magic season had disintegrated into the dimness of mediocrity.

33

Shadows

Dottie and Roy Heller arrived the day before Thanksgiving and stayed until Sunday morning. Lightly dusted with snow, Fire Valley wore a picture-postcard face and made an unforgettable holiday for the newlywed couple and their hosts.

"I never spent a Thanksgiving or a Christmas away from southern California," Roy said when they arrived. "Now I see what everyone gets excited about."

By Saturday, after touring Fire Valley and meeting a few of the Lowells' friends, Dottie and Roy better understood the allure of the area. "If I had to lose you to a Denver or a Chicago," Dottie said to Janet as the Hellers were leaving, "I'd be pretty angry. But this I can't argue with!"

Before the Hellers had arrived, Janet had been worried her friends would pick up on her anxieties about Bonner, sparked by the violence of the autumn. Yet seeing the valley afresh through their eyes, she was able to put those fearful memories away.

The rampage of Jeff Rand fell more than a month into the past. Bonner was spared further disaster, and its rustic charm assumed a firmer hold on both her and Greg. Greg finished his work on Jeremy Hunter's newest, biggest *Gold Rush* novel, and was in the process of negotiating a new contract with Burton Faraday's agent. Janet, her skills growing, reveled in her unquestioned value to the medical center. She entered every formal 10K run in the region, and was even looking ahead to the half marathon Bonner was sponsoring in the spring.

And the quality of Greg and Janet's time together was better than they could ever recall. The darkness that had troubled them was pushed back in their minds. They became more in touch with the rural lifestyle after realizing how much they missed some of the daily chores. Among their plans was to purchase more milk cows, and maybe other animals.

Mark, also maturing, shed the surliness that had clouded him since his uncharacteristic eruption. Greg had spoken to him, as had Craig Morley. Although a hard loser, Mark understood what they had to say. He made peace with his friends and teammates. Returning to the mainstream, he showed interest in things other than football and began to date, which pleased Janet and Greg.

If it hadn't been for the dreams.

Greg would toss restlessly, then sit up and flail at some unseen intruder. Occasionally he stood in front of the bedroom window, staring into the night. . . .

Janet, held deeply by slumber, watched Jeff Rand swagger out of the barn, saw herself . . .

She was naked.

. . . following, her body streaked with his semen, begging for more.

It happens.

Catching up to him . . .

. . . *out there by the well.*

Not Rand now, but Otis Perry, the bloated walking corpse of Otis Perry without a face . . .

. . . *probably something in the water.*

Climbing into the well, beckoning Janet to follow, grabbing at her with a bony hand, causing a . . .

. . . *purplish bruise on her wrist.*

Janet plummeted into a darkness even blacker than her sleep.

By mid-December, thick snow covered the mountain summits, but the lower slopes and valleys had seen only occasional brief flurries. By Bonner's standards, the late fall had been mild. Barring a sudden front, it would stay the same through Christmas.

The Lowells would not have minded spending their first Christmas in Fire Valley. Even with the move, though, Janet had continued to save for the trip to Pennsylvania. She made plane reservations in October, and all of them were looking forward to it. Their flight, on December 22, was from Reno to Pittsburgh.

On a Monday afternoon, while driving to town, Greg

spotted a lone figure on the side of the road. It was not an unusual sight, and he assumed it was a hitchhiker or someone waiting for a bus. Yet there was something familiar about this slight shadowy figure. He slowed, then stopped and backed up to speak to the person.

No one was there.

"What the hell?" he muttered.

The road fronted a farmer's field, its boundaries marked by a low fence. The land was flat with no place to hide. No trees, no ditches. And there was a thin layer of snow on the ground from a recent light fall. Clean snow, no tracks.

He drove another mile and saw the figure again. He kept his gaze on it as he pulled off the highway. When he climbed out of the car, the person was still there. He approached slowly, not without some fear.

A veil was brushed back. It was the old woman he had seen—or thought he had seen—in town last summer. More bent and haggard, her face even more heavily lined with wrinkles. She wore black clothes and something like a wide skull-cap.

"Padgett," she uttered in a hoarse monotone, her eyes looking through him.

"My name is Lowell, Greg Lowell," he said.

"You chose not to heed, Padgett," she continued. "Now you see what your coming has done to the *sayka loluk.*"

"What are you talking about?"

"Your woman knows. You know also."

"You mean the things that happened? What did *I* have to do with them?"

"You are Padgett," she said simply.

"This is crazy!" he exclaimed. "And anyway, nothing's happened for a long time. It's over."

"What has already happened is nothing compared to what will come. It is only resting."

"*What* is?"

She shook her head. "You will learn that from another. My time is short, Padgett."

"Who are you?"

"You will know that too." She started to back away.

"Wait!"

"Yes?"

"Aren't you going to tell me to leave Fire Valley?"

"It does not matter anymore. It is too late."

"I don't understand."

"You cannot leave the *sayka loluk* again."

"I can't do *what*?"

"Not you, not your children. Not at the same time. It will not let you go again."

Greg scowled. "This is unreal. Okay, I'll play. What about Janet?"

"The woman does not matter; she is not a Padgett." The old woman turned. "I must go."

Greg watched her hobble away, then returned to his car. When he glanced back, she was gone. Bewildered, he drove off.

Two hours later, Greg returned home. He did not drive to the house, but stopped ten yards away from the old well. The parasol top and mortared stone lip were dusted with snow; the monument appeared more preposterous than ever. But through this facade Greg sensed the horror, felt the tendrils of evil that rose from the deep black vault, crawling like an enshrouding web over the land, polluting and enslaving the minds and souls of those within its forbidding sphere.

And he knew the old woman had been right.

Greg stared at the well. He stared until he could see nothing else, until all—before it, around it, beyond it—was hazy, indefinable shadows.

It was warm, stifling. There was no snow, but hard dry earth tormented by a throbbing sun in a clear sky. The distant mountains were brown, with green patchwork.

Greg saw three figures standing nearby. A boy and a girl, and a man in a wide-brimmed straw hat. The man was bending over; then he looked up. It was himself! No, not a mirror image, but a strong resemblance. Grim-faced, each of the three was purposeful in his actions. The girl stirred something in a pitcher on a small table; the boy set up chairs; the man fingered a rifle, then laid it down with other weapons. They were talking, but in a vacuum, for the sultry air was soundless.

Then the man pointed and waved. The boy and girl stopped what they were doing and waved too, yet the gravity of their expressions went unchanged.

Greg turned toward what had caught their attention but saw only a dim outline in a blinding white haze. Puzzled, he whirled to face the trio.

* * *

Allison was standing beside him.

Greg's coat was half off, but the 30-degree temperature changed his mind. He glanced behind him again, then faced his daughter.

"Hi, Dad," she said.

"Hi, honey."

"I was in the barn and heard you drive up. What are you doing?"

"Nothing. Is your brother home yet?"

"Uh-huh."

He started for the Camaro. "Get in the car."

"But, Dad, I wanted to finish—"

"Get in the car!"

They drove to the house. With the motor still running, Greg jumped out and hurried to the door. He called for Janet, who appeared from the kitchen.

"Hi, babe," she said cheerfully. "Wait'll you see—"

"Jan, where's Mark?" he interrupted.

"Upstairs, studying. Why?"

"Mark!" he shouted. "Mark!"

The boy's door opened. "Yeah, Dad?"

"Put a coat on and get down here. Jan, you get one too."

"Greg, what's going—"

"Just do it! I'll tell you later."

He led them outside and into the car. "Greg, where are you taking us?" Janet asked.

"I don't know. I mean, I can't tell you yet. Please, this is important."

He drove to the highway and turned north. One mile, two miles, his speed well above the limit. Without warning, the right front tire blew, and the Camaro swerved. Greg regained control and steered it off the road.

"Must've hit something," Janet said. "Your tires are practically new."

"Mark, come and help me," Greg said, opening his door.

They changed the mangled tire and drove off again. But this time, Janet would not remain silent.

"Greg, where the hell are we going?" she demanded.

"Jan, I told you—"

"I want to know, Greg, or you can let me out right now!"

"Come on, Dad," Allison said.

Hunched over the wheel, he said, "Just to the state line, okay?"

"Why?"

"There's something I want to see, something I have to know."

"But did you have to take us—"

"I wanted all of you with me!" he said sharply. Then, more calmly, he added, "Just bear with me. I promise I'll explain—"

"Dad, look out!"

Three men stood on the road, squat and black-haired, half-clothed and bleeding. Blood dripped to the road, forming glistening pools. Three men waving their arms, shaking their heads, warning. Warning.

Fighting the instinct to slam on the brakes, Greg drove through the grisly barrier. Janet, her head buried, screamed, and he slowed.

"Jan!" he cried, grabbing her arm. "Look back there!"

"No! Don't make me look. Don't!"

"Jan, turn around!"

She did, reluctantly. No blood, no bodies—nothing.

"Mom, Allison's getting sick!" Mark exclaimed.

Greg stopped the car. Janet opened the back door and helped her daughter out, then knelt by her while she vomited. When she finally stopped, Allison was pale.

"Greg, we've got to get her home," Janet said.

"Allison," Greg asked, "can you keep going?"

"Greg, for God's sake, leave her alone!"

"It's okay, Mom," she gasped. "If this is important to Dad, then I don't want to mess it up. I'm all right."

Janet surrendered with a shrug. "Mark, let's switch places, so I can keep an eye on Allison."

"Listen." Greg forced a half smile. "I promise we'll be home within an hour—one way or the other."

They set out again and were ten miles farther north when they heard sirens. Greg pulled over as a squad car and Rick Johnson's ambulance roared past.

"Wasn't that Winn?" Janet said.

"I think so. What happened?"

Two minutes later, they found out. An oncoming Aerostar van signaled them, and they stopped. The driver rolled down his window. "You folks don't wanna go that way."

"Why not?" Greg asked.

"A semi and pickup hit head-on, right smack on top of the Muddy Creek bridge."

"Lord, no!" Janet exclaimed.

Greg's hands tightened on the wheel. "How bad?" he asked.

"One dead that I know of. A kid. The pickup was totaled, and the rig's jackknifed on its side across the bridge. Fuel's spilling and everything. Cab's mangled, driver's trapped inside. Hey, gotta go. I'll never make Klamath Falls before dark."

More sirens—a CHP car and a fire truck. Other vehicles appeared, heading south. Greg did not follow but sat and stared. His hands, still clutching the wheel, began to shake, and the column rattled.

"It's true," he said. "Christ, *it's true!*"

Janet leaned forward from the back seat. "Greg, what are you talking about? What's wrong?"

Mark grabbed his father's wrists. "Dad, come on, lighten up."

The trembling stopped. Greg released the wheel and sank into the bucket seat. "We can go home now," he told his family.

On Friday, the last day of school before Christmas vacation, Allison stayed home with what appeared to be the flu. Larry saw her Saturday morning. By the end of the day, she had improved, but on Sunday she could hardly breathe. Her parents drove her to the medical center where she spent three days fighting pneumonia. She was at home even longer, recovering.

The trip to Pennsylvania was canceled.

34

The Old Year Passes

After the brief and ill-fated drive northward, Janet had no more doubts that something was wrong—something terrible. Greg said nothing at first; then, unable to keep it inside any longer, he told his incredulous wife everything. Despite her shock, she couldn't deny what he said. She'd been the first to hint at a connection between the string of disasters that had begun in September—and possibly before. But why *them*? she asked. Why the Lowells? What was doing this to them? How could they begin to fight it if they did not understand?

And what would happen next?

Early Christmas morning, Thad Wenges drove his pickup along a snowy highway to Len Grayner's farm. Thinking about the many presents stacked under the tree for his wife and son, he smiled. It had been a good year, and he'd allowed himself to spoil his family. But the best gift for six-year-old Timmy was not there yet. Len Grayner's German shepherd had had her litter over a month ago, and Marianne and Thad had been allowed the first pick, a frisky pup with oversized ears. That morning, appropriately, Timmy would meet his new friend.

Grayner had the dog ready. His wife had gift-wrapped a large box and secured a red bow to the top. Wenges, smiling, lifted the cover. The puppy wagged furiously when it saw him, then whined and yelped as the top came down.

"I can't wait to see Timmy's face," Wenges said excitedly. "Len, thanks for everything, and Merry Christmas."

"Merry Christmas to you. Hey, that's a great little pup there. Gimme a call later and tell me how it went."

Wenges carried the box to his truck and put it gently in back. "Hey, little fella, stop your crying," he said softly. "We'll be home real soon, and you'll see who's waiting for you."

With the box shimmying, he closed the tailgate and climbed behind the wheel. His tire chains carried him easily through the unshoveled snow of the farm road. Ten minutes later, he was back on the highway, which had been plowed. His own place was only three miles farther north; it would not take him long.

Halfway up the highway, the engine of the Ford pickup died. Wenges couldn't figure it out. He had plenty of gas, and the vehicle had been serviced a month ago. He poked around under the hood for a minute but found nothing wrong.

"Stupid darn machine," he mumbled, slamming the hood down.

When he'd gotten out, the puppy had been crying. Now the box stood motionless, and the only sound was a sporadic grunting.

"Not too happy about this either, are you, fella?" Wenges called. "Well, I'll try to move us out of here, the quicker the better. Darned if it isn't getting colder!"

He got back behind the wheel and turned the key. The truck roared to life. Still puzzled, he drove the rest of the way to his farm.

Timmy Wenges had been unable to wait until his father got home. A profusion of brightly colored wrapping paper and ribbon was scattered ankle-deep around the living room. The boy, his eyes dancing, could not decide whether to ride his new bicycle with the training wheels or complete the track layout for the racing set. But he abandoned both as his father walked in with the big box.

"Mommy, look!" he exclaimed, the paper crackling under his small feet as he scurried to intercept his father. "What is it?"

Smiling, Marianne Wenges rose from her chair. "Gee, I don't know, son. Thad, do you?"

"Nope," he said, winking. "Guess you'll have to open it, Tim."

He sat the box on the floor and knelt on one side of it, his wife on the other. Timmy, wide-eyed, put both hands on the lid and with help from his father, worked it loose. It was tossed away, and the family gazed into the box.

Their smiles faded.
"OH, MY GOD!" Marianne screamed.

The excitement of Christmas in the Grayner house began to abate by late afternoon. For the first time, Len Grayner wondered about the Wenges family and their new puppy. Timmy must have been thrilled, he figured. He knew that Thad would call sooner or later, but eager to know, he dialed their number. He got a busy signal.

One hour and four tries later, he was still unable to get through. It was strange, he thought. Neither Thad nor Marianne ever spent much time on the telephone. Even with this being Christmas . . .

Grayner dialed the operator, who tried the Wenges number. Again it was busy, but there was no one on the line, she told him. The phone was apparently off the hook.

Grayner was concerned. After telling his wife of his plans, he drove to the Wengeses'. The farm was still, disquietingly so, the only sound the occasional lowing of a cow in the barn. Grayner noticed that the fresh layer of snow that had fallen that morning and covered the yard between the house and barn had not been disturbed by any footprints.

He climbed the porch steps and rapped on the front door. "Thad! Hey, you in there?" he called. "Marianne, it's me, Len."

No one answered, and the front windows were fogged from the inside. He knocked one more time, then tried the door. Unlocked. But he could only open it a foot or so, for something blocked it on the inside. He called out once more, then squeezed his gaunt frame through the crack and entered the red screaming hell of the Wengeses' living room.

Timmy's small body lay sprawled next to his mother's. Both their throats had been ripped open; death had come so quickly, the blood had clotted over gaping holes. Thad had put up more of a struggle against whatever had done this. His corpse, which blocked the doorway, was crimson-soaked, mauled almost beyond recognition. His torn hand still reached for the phone that dangled from a table two feet away.

Grayner staggered deeper into the room, then heard a rustling sound. Something moved beneath the blood-spattered layer of gift wrap. He bent over, his trembling hand reaching for the largest piece. Casting it aside, he pulled back instinctively.

The puppy, sad-eyed and frightened, gazed up at him from a pool of its own urine and wagged its tail.

The sun was shining on December 30, but it was a brisk day. The midmorning temperature was only 35 degrees, with a wind chill factor of less than half that. The Juniper Mall parking lot was mostly filled, but to Karen Hennesey it seemed empty, for until the previous day, many of the stores had been innundated with the post-Christmas crush of returns and exchanges. Now the thoughts of most shoppers were on New Year's Eve. The Wine Shoppe and Stringer's were bearing the brunt.

Karen parked her Hyundai in one of the fringe spots utilized by mall employees and crossed the lot to Redby's Boutique, her high heels clicking loudly on the snow-free asphalt. Karen, twenty-two, tall, and reasonably attractive, had worked for Flora Redby, her aunt, for the past six months. "Decision time," she called it. Her boyfriend had proposed to her during their last year at Chico State and still waited for her decision in Sacramento. She loved him, and there was no one else; but she was devoted to her mother, who had been ill for a long time. Despite the woman's urgings, she could not yet give up her responsibilities.

Joe Franks, manager of the Stereo Shack next door, smiled a good-morning to Karen as she walked past his display window. Franks, married with two children, had tried to date Karen a few months ago, but she had refused. She was of a small minority who did not care for the handsome, curly-haired Franks, whose stylish clothes and reputed manhood tempted more than a few to risk the consequences.

Karen entered the boutique and unbuttoned her heavy coat as she walked to the back. Her aunt was behind the counter, putting change in the cash register.

"Good morning, Karen," the woman said cheerfully.

"Hi, Aunt Flora."

Karen removed her coat. She wore a long skirt and bulky wool sweater, but in spite of that, felt cold. "Aunt Flora, haven't you turned the heat up yet?"

Alone in his office at the back of the store, Joe Franks's flashy smile was gone. He had just gotten off the phone with a supplier who told him that his order of spare parts, due two days ago, would not be in till next week. His service department was already backlogged, and the long-denied customers were bitching loudly.

"Shit like this wouldn't happen if I was running a store in San Francisco," he grumbled. "I gotta get out of this horse's-ass town."

While pondering his future, Franks heard the door open. Thinking it was Dana, his new clerk, he said angrily, "I told you I didn't—!" He caught himself, and the overdone smile lit the room when he saw Karen Hennesey standing in the doorway.

"Hello, Joe," she said.

He stood. "Karen, baby! What can I do for you? Hey, come on in. Take your coat off."

She closed the door, and Franks saw her turn the lock. Her coat fell to the floor. She kicked it aside with the toe of one of her shoes—all that she was wearing. Bewildered, Franks tried to maintain his cool as she sauntered toward him, the nipples of her breasts firm with desire.

"Make love to me, Joe," she whispered, her tongue running across her lips.

"Hey, uh, Karen," he stammered, "I'm glad, you know? But couldn't we wait till lunchtime? We could drive down to—"

She pulled him to her, silencing him with her lips. Her tongue probed hungrily. One hand dropped to his zipper and released his manhood. Her reddish-brown hair, earlier tied in a ponytail, swept across her white shoulders and breasts as she writhed against him.

"Fuck me, Joe," she said insistently. *"Fuck me!"*

She leaned back across his desk, her feet off the carpet, long legs spread wide. Franks, after undoing his belt and lowering his pants, entered her eagerly, her tightly contracting vulva nearly causing him to explode prematurely. Over his initial surprise, he assumed his usual dominant role and began thrusting forcefully. Karen took all of it and moaned loudly for more as she straddled the brink of her own pending orgasm.

Alternating between either breast, Franks massaged them with his teeth while his tongue laved her nipples. Karen, who had been raking his back with her fingernails, knew that she was near and instinctively placed both hands behind her for leverage. Her knuckles brushed against a hard object on the desk. Despite her urgency, she raised the heavy thing to see what it was. Franks, gnawing harder, was oblivious to what she did.

It was an ornate sculpture, made from cast iron by a skilled artist. The metal twisted into thin Picassolike shapes, familiar and legendary: Don Quixote, holding a lance; the smaller Sancho Panza; two animal shapes, a horse and a jackass.

"Ooooh—God!" Karen cried as the white-hot magma poured from the crater of her passions. She made whimpering animal sounds as she twisted beneath Joe Franks, and in the midst of her climax, she drove Don Quixote's lance through the back of his neck and into his brain. His eyes bulged; his body went rigid. But she clung to him like a carnal parasite, and his death throes, his spewing gore, heightened her lusting frenzy. He was silent, but she screamed and screamed until it was over and, still holding the sculpture, she let him fall to the carpet.

Someone rattled the doorknob, cried out, then pounded on the door. Keys jingled, and the door was thrown open. Franks's clerk saw Karen, naked and covered with blood, then saw Franks. She screamed and ran from the office.

Karen caught the girl in the middle of the store and knocked her to the floor. Three horrified customers watched as she hit her again and again with the sculpture.

Again and again . . .

Three minutes later, when Winn Stanley and Les Curry arrived at the Stereo Shack, Karen was still battering the pulpy corpse, and she would have attacked them also had they not shot her down.

The old year passed unnoticed from Fire Valley.

THE
LEGEND

35

A Growing Awareness

Glenn Beechum's real-estate office experienced a boom during January as nine families, including some longtime residents of Bonner, packed up everything and left. Joe Franks's widow and children returned to her former home in Fresno. Len Grayner bought a farm in Tehama County. The Hennesey home also went on the market after Margaret Hennesey died on New Year's Day. Beechum sold most of the property at distressed prices, investing in some of it himself. All of the ownership remained within Bonner.

The slaughter of the Wenges family and the killings at the Stereo Shack horrified and anguished Janet and Greg. They hadn't known any of the people; they hadn't been near either place or on the run when the killings happened. No matter. As Janet had said, there was a link between all of the disasters that had befallen Fire Valley.

And somehow, they were involved.

Allison had recovered from her illness and was back in school. Returning one morning from driving his daughter and son there, Greg found Janet sitting on the couch, staring blankly at him. In the past couple of days, she had grown more withdrawn.

"You okay?" he asked.

"Yeah. How come you wanted to take the kids? They usually go with Billy."

"I wanted to make sure they got there okay," he said testily, then softened and sat down beside her. "On the way back, I drove slowly. I looked everywhere for that old woman, but I didn't see her anywhere."

"Greg, who is she? What's her part in this?"

"She said I would learn the answers from someone else."

"But *who*?"

"I don't know."

"So are we supposed to sit around and wait for someone to come to us?" Janet nearly shouted.

"I don't know that either."

"Why don't we try to get away from here again?"

"No!" he said frantically. "It won't work. We'll just be the cause of God knows what else."

Their joint fear and frustration simmered through the air. Too anxious to sit still, Janet leapt up off the couch. "Greg, why is this nightmare happening? We didn't come here for this! Good Lord, what is *happening*?"

"Jan, stop it!" Greg said sharply, standing and taking her hands. "Look, you're right. We can't wait to find out what this is all about. I'm going to get some answers."

She took a deep breath, calming herself. "Where will you start?"

"I'm not sure. I have this crazy idea. Let me try it before I say anything."

The next morning, while Janet was at work, Greg phoned Winn. It was an idle conversation, but by the time they were done, Greg had the name and phone number he wanted.

Janet was also busy. During her lunch hour, she drove to the Bonner Library where she spent the time going through back issues of the town's biweekly newspaper. She became so engrossed in the research, she was late getting back to the medical center.

After work, she returned to the library.

Professor Raymond Bradley, a gray and distinguished fifty-two-year-old man, had been dean at Modoc County College for eight years. He was a product of the region. Born and raised on a farm near Canby, he had spent most of his life in Modoc County, save for two years in the army, his junior and senior years at Stanford University, and his postgraduate work there. His grandmother had been a full-blooded Modoc, and his memories of her had long ago ignited his desire to learn of his heritage. Bradley's knowledge of Modoc history and culture was unmatched; his master's thesis had become one of the standard texts.

At ten minutes of two, Bradley returned to his office from a lecture. Julia Pratt, his secretary, smiled as he walked in.

"Hello, Julia," he said. "Anything doing?"

"Professor Stryker called to remind you of your racquetball game at three-thirty. Oh, and your two-o'clock appointment should be here any minute."

"Appointment?"

She looked at her calendar. "Mr. Greg Lowell."

"Oh, yes; he called. Just show him in."

Greg pulled into the Alturas campus at five minutes of two and followed the signs to the dean's office. "Mr. Lowell, the dean's expecting you," Julia Pratt said. "This way."

She led him to Bradley's door, knocked twice, and opened it. They found Bradley face down on his desk, his skin like chalk. There was no heartbeat. Greg began CPR, Julia Pratt called for help, but it was too late. Raymond Bradley had died of a massive coronary.

Modoc County mourned the loss of one of its most respected residents.

When Janet arrived home that evening, she found Greg sitting in front of the fire. She waved her folder of papers, then sat next to him.

"What's that?" he asked.

"The result of something you said once," she replied. "Look through it. Then I'll explain."

She had photostated copies of newspaper articles and marked those of interest in yellow highlighter pen. Each one of the dozen or so stories reported a grim event: brutal murders; accidents; an old workhorse trampling a farmer and his son to death; a woman, nude and laughing, driving a car through a crowd at a Fourth of July picnic, killing three, injuring ten. And, finally, the Harmony House fire, where Greg saw his father's name mentioned. Robert Lowell had helped save two people from the inferno before he was overcome by smoke.

"Did you notice the year?" Janet asked when Greg was through. "And all of it happened between March and September."

"While my parents were here," Greg said. "Oh, Christ!"

"You said the fire was probably a coincidence, but it wasn't. Not with all this before it. And another thing, the reason I thought of checking in the first place. You said that Bonner must've had its share of bad times, both before and after the fire. But, Greg, I had to go back two years—*two years*

—prior to this to find an incident of violence worse than a Friday-night barroom brawl. And after the fire? Typical small-town gossip and other news, but nothing else until eighteen months later when a farmer was killed in a tractor accident."

Greg shook his head. "It happened then, it's happening now, and I'm sure it happened when Wallace and Rebecca Padgett came here." He walked over to a window and stared past the barn. "That well," he muttered, pounding his fist on the sill. "It's the focal point of this whole goddamn thing. I don't think Wallace Padgett was ranting during those last couple of days. He knew what he was saying, and Martha interpreted it correctly in her letter. There was—*there is*—something in that well!"

"Greg, I called the water district today, as well as a company up in Klamath Falls that does soil testing and has business records back to the turn of the century. No one knows of any minerals in this region that might have affected the water—"

"I don't mean bad water!" he exclaimed. "I mean . . . Christ, I don't know *what* I mean. I know that it has something to do with the Modocs, but otherwise it makes no sense. Dammit!"

Greg's frustration exploded. He drove his foot into a magazine rack and nearly kicked it into the fireplace. In the crackling flames he thought he saw a faceless undulating shape. A low mocking laughter whispered in his ears.

"Leave us alone!" he shouted.

Janet managed to pull him down next to her and dispel some of his anger. "Babe, you said there was a connection between this and the Modocs. How do you know?"

Greg trembled, reluctant to explain what had happened. "I played a hunch, and I was right." He told Janet about his visit to the college that afternoon.

She buried her face in her hands. "No," she moaned softly.

"Bradley might have told me what I needed to know," Greg continued. "But what now? I don't dare try to ask anyone else, or the same thing will happen. I already feel like a . . . a murderer!"

It happens, Janet thought.

A bolt of lightning . . .

Baron killed James tonight.

Jeff Rand . . .

She was naked.
Walt Cunningham . . .
Perfectly sane loving husband and father goes berserk.
Merry Christmas and a Happy New Year . . .
Must be the water in the well.
Out there in the well . . .
Must be . . . *It happens.*
They heard Billy's truck pull up outside. When Allison and Mark entered the house, they found their parents in the kitchen.

"Dinner'll be hot in a few minutes," Janet told them. "Just some fried chicken and stuff that I brought home, okay?"

"Sounds good, Mom," Mark said, and he and his sister went upstairs.

Janet turned to Greg. "They'll have to know sooner or later."

"I know, but not now, not when *we* don't understand it. We'll try to maintain something like a normal life."

She nodded. "Normal."

Despite the cold, Greg went outside and stood on the front porch. He stared across the yard, and taunting laughter echoed in his head between whispered repetitions of his ancestor's surname.

After a minute, the cold seemed to touch his bones, and he went back inside.

36

Adrienne Gordon

On the second Friday in January, a storm out of the north exploded over the volcanic tableland. By the next morning, Fire Valley was buried under two feet of snow. With the wind chill factor, it was 25 degrees below zero. Strong winds blew deep drifts onto the roads. One motorist, missing for days, was found frozen to death in his car near Yreka. For once, Greg felt no guilt.

The wind and snow stopped late on Sunday afternoon. Fire Valley was reprieved for twenty hours. Then a second fury assaulted the region, and those who had been digging themselves out succumbed in frustration. Schools and businesses were closed. The Lowells were confined to their home for five days, five quiet days during which the evil lay dormant.

By Wednesday morning, the only snow that fell came in light infrequent dustings. Greg's new snowblower was put to the test by Mark, who was clearing the walk from the porch steps to the picket fence. Greg, having earlier wallowed through a four-foot drift to retrieve the blower from the barn, followed his prints back for the tractor. The road crew would be plowing up to his front gate, but he still had his share to do.

He was halfway there when he stopped in amazement. Dora Waverly stood at the well, knee-deep in snow. She had been there the week after her grandson's death and every week since. But *today*? On the other hand, Greg believed that had the morning produced a blizzard, the old woman would have been there.

Suddenly Greg realized that locked inside Dora Waverly's silent world—and likely to remain there—were the answers. More than Raymond Bradley, more perhaps than anyone else, this daughter of a Modoc squaw knew what was at the core of the horror that had stricken Fire Valley three times since its settlement. But her silence was probably her life, for how else could she survive standing so near it?

He had approached the woman once since Rand's death, to offer his condolences. But, perhaps blaming him for what had happened, she waved him away. He'd left her alone since then. The only reason he walked to the well now was his concern for her health. She had trudged through the heavy snow from the road, and her slight frame trembled despite the heavy clothes she wore. The least he could do, Greg thought, was to offer the woman a warm place to rest, some coffee if she wanted it.

Not wishing to scare her, he circled around. When she saw him out of the corner of her eye, he was fifteen yards away. Still her reaction was as if he'd come up from behind and grabbed her shoulder. She recoiled, her arms waving wildly as she backed away.

"Please, wait a minute!" Greg called. "I just wanted . . . Christ, who am I talking to?"

She continued to retreat, nearly stumbling, as he came toward her. Greg stopped. Looking at her face, he saw not anger, but fear, a terror more chilling than the northern wind sweeping around them.

He smiled, extending his arms and improvising a message to the woman. He gestured toward the house, then held his arms and rocked back and forth in mock shivering. He lifted an invisible cup from a saucer and tipped it to his mouth, but to no avail. She continued to wave him away, then turned and toiled back through the snow, glancing at him with fear one last time. Helpless, Greg stood still until she neared the front gate. Starting toward the barn again, he watched her disappear beyond a clump of snow-dusted trees that bordered the road.

Somebody had to bring her, he thought—a neighbor, a relative, someone. A minute later, when he heard an engine cough to life, he knew he was right. He stopped worrying about Dora Waverly but still wished he could probe the vault of her mind for the terrible knowledge she carried.

The sun was shining on Friday morning. Fire Valley, draped in a white cloak and ringed by snow-crested mountains, was breathtakingly beautiful. It was a scene Adrienne Gordon, despite her many paintings of the Padgett well, had not yet captured. She was determined to change that. Parking her customized Chevy van near the monument, she worked in stints of twenty to thirty minutes, transferring the image of the hoarfrosted well and the dripping icicles on its parasol to her canvas.

Neither Janet, who was at work, nor Greg knew Adrienne was going to be there. Greg had been busy with the galley proofs of Burton's novel since nine-thirty. By one, he was unable to look at another word. Stretching, he walked out of his office. He had to get some air.

It was 38 degrees outside. The air was crisp and smelled good. From the porch, Greg recognized the van parked by the well. Curious, he put on his coat and crossed the yard.

Adrienne was sitting in a director's chair, her canvas on a low easel. The van was positioned between her and the house, and Greg did not see her until he circled around it. Adrienne heard the crunch of his shoes in the snow and waved her brush at him.

"Hi, Greg."

"Boy, talk about dedication to one's art. You must be freezing."

"Actually, I'm enjoying it. I came prepared. How're Janet and the kids?"

"They're fine. Janet's working today. How about your men?"

"Eric's home with a cold. Joey's back in school, thank God. This is my first day out in over a week."

"You should've said you were coming."

Adrienne shook her head. "Just decided this morning. Besides, I only wanted to paint, not bug you guys."

"You know better than that," Greg told her. He looked at the half-finished painting. "Hey, that's coming along great."

She frowned. "It'll do, I guess. Well, the clock on the wall and the sight of my skin turning blue tells me it's time for a break. How about a cup of coffee? I've got a thermosful."

"Okay."

He followed her into the van, sliding the door closed behind him. The inside, warmed by a battery-operated heater, was plush, a shaggy brown rug covering the entire floor and climbing halfway up the walls. A small sink with a refrigerator underneath stood in one corner, and along the walls were two bench seats that could be converted into cots.

"Take your coat off," Adrienne said. "It's pretty warm in here."

"You really did come prepared."

Sitting on one of the benches, Greg couldn't look away from Adrienne as she poured two mugs of coffee. Wearing a bulky sweater, snug-fitting jeans, and brown leather high-heeled boots, she moved fluidly, gracefully. Against his will, he felt desire burgeon. It was the scene in the loft, but this time, Adrienne was one of the players. Turning slowly, she signaled her own wanting without words, and the coffee was forgotten as they came together hungrily. Clothes were peeled off, and he was inside her before they fell to the thick rug.

Their lovemaking seemed to go on forever. Greg's eruption was just as long, but nothing like Adrienne's loud, furious ecstasy. Afterward, gasping and beaded with perspiration, she pleaded for more.

They had fallen in at the same time, but when Greg emerged, he was alone. Horrified, he stared at the moaning, lust-crazed animal beside him. He tried to stand, but she held his leg insistently, her mouth seeking his now flaccid manhood.

"Adrienne, listen to me!" he said, pulling free. "I have to make you understand—"

The sound of the door handle clicking back was like a rifle shot. The door slid open; Eric stood in front of the snow's blinding whiteness. Greg leapt to his feet. Adrienne, still lying on her side, stretched like a cat and smiled dreamily.

"Son of a bitch!" Eric swore bitterly. "Greg, why you? I thought you were a better friend than that. And *you*!" He glared at Adrienne. "Never satisfied, huh?"

"Come in, dear," she said teasingly. "There's plenty for all."

He balled his fists. "Eric, *don't!*" Greg shouted. "You've got to hear me out! This isn't—"

"You shut your fucking mouth! Oh, don't worry. I'm not going to play the crazed jealous husband and blow your brains out. It's not worth it. I've been this route with her before, in Sacramento. She was fucking our attorney, her hairdresser, Christ knows who else. It was supposed to be different here. Bullshit! She's just a cunt. She always will be."

"Eric, listen," Greg pleaded.

"I'm going to take Joey back to Sacramento. I suppose

she'll follow. Ought to be a pisser of a custody suit. You can tell her that if she can ever take her finger out!"

He stormed away. Greg, freezing, pulled on his clothes. He'd just slipped his coat on when Adrienne's head snapped back. Moments later, she was groping for something to cover herself with. She was aware of everything that had happened, everything that had been said, and knew that the life she cherished was over.

"Eric!" she screamed, tears streaming from her eyes. *"Eric, please don't go!"*

She jumped from the van and ran barefoot through the snow until she stumbled. Eric's car threw spray as it wheeled out through the main gate. Greg helped Adrienne to her feet and back to the van.

"He's going to take Joey!" she cried. *"He's going to take my son!"*

"Adrienne," Greg said softly, "I—"

"Get away from me!" she cried. "Just get away! Oh, how did this happen?"

Greg climbed out of the van, and the door slid closed with an unnerving slam. Thirty seconds later, dressed again, Adrienne drove away from the place where, through the years, she had known peace, had felt inspired. Greg watched her go, then turned to look at the only thing she had left behind. The half-finished painting of the well.

37

Another Try

Greg told Janet everything. There was no reason not to. She tried calling the Gordons that night, but no one answered. She drove over on Saturday and found the house locked up. Glenn Beechum, like a hungry vulture, was already cruising the property, anxious to plant a sign in the front yard. Janet wondered how he knew. On the other hand, it was a small town. . . .

"Greg, we've got to get a hold of Eric," she said when she returned home. "He's got to know what happened. This is so damn wrong!"

Greg shook his head. "At least they're still alive. Besides, what would we tell him? 'The devil made us do it'? He won't believe it. I'm not sure *I* do yet. We've got to keep quiet about this, Jan. Maybe when it's over, we can try . . ."

On Sunday, Janet heard the news from Carol Staley. Eric had gone straight to Joey's school. After taking the boy out, he'd driven to Sacramento and left Joey with his brother and sister-in-law. Adrienne had followed. The inevitable confrontation occurred on Saturday in front of the brother's house. Angry words, some blows. But the greatest hurt, reflected in the eyes and heart of the child who stood at the window watching, was ignored. They would not listen to each other again, or to anyone else. The emotional gauntlet had been thrown down, and shattered. There would be no reconciliation.

No one had spoken to Eric since he'd left, and it seemed unlikely that Adrienne, in her brief conversation with Carol, would have discussed the cause of their breakup. Yet, Greg sensed something in Burton Faraday's abrupt greeting and dis-

missal when he stopped at the writer's house with the galleys.
And Janet felt it on Monday when Carol called to cancel the
weekly bridge game, and again on Wednesday from the Rubens when she returned to work at the medical center.

They wanted to tell them all what had happened, to
scream out the reason for this madness, but they couldn't.
Friends, acquaintances, strangers had been killed or emotion-
ally destroyed. They could not put more of this upon anyone,
especially those they cared for.

Thursday. Janet was at work for the second day in a row. In
the morning, Greg had picked up the galleys from Burton—
Donna had given them to him at the door—and taken them to
the post office. Later, he spent half an hour on the phone with
Valerie Kelton. He assumed he sounded the same to Valerie as
always, though she probably wondered about his mildly enthusiastic response to her news of Sabre Press's high sales
figures for the last quarter of the year. Like a true southern
Californian, she complained about the pollution, the freeways,
the recent flooding and mudslides that had plagued the area;
and Greg laughed, as one who was immune to it would.

And he knew that he would trade his soul to be part of it
again.

At two o'clock, with little desire to accomplish anything,
he walked around the ranch. It was unseasonably warm,
nearly 50 degrees, with no wind. The floor of the valley was
wet from melting snow; the high peaks and the lower pine
slopes were blinding as they shone back the sun's rays. It was
an incomparable scene, at once awesome and peaceful. Before,
it had thrilled Greg; now he felt nothing. Like a helpless moth,
he was drawn to the source of the evil, which was still, but—
he knew—waiting.

Waiting.

The sun burned brighter, and Fire Valley was green in spots
but mostly parched. People stood around the well, the same
man, boy, and girl as before, and others. Men, women, children. They talked, again soundlessly, first one at a time, then
several at once. Anger rose. Faces twisted with it, even the
children's. Men shook their fists, arms flailed, fingers pointed
at the well. Then a darkness, thin, ethereal, floated sinuously
through the hate-driven assemblage. Weapons were seized—
carbines, wood axes; hunting knives and pitchforks. Explo-

sions of crimson. Women murdering children. Men blowing men apart. The darkness throbbed, absorbing the blood. Blood! It soaked the cracked earth, ringed the rising mound of mutilated bodies. A severed head spun through the veil of death, plummeting into the waiting shaft.

And a boy, untouched by the carnage, crawled away, crawled toward the barn. Toward . . .

Greg.

"They killed each other!" he shouted.

Greg Lowell.

"God almighty, they killed each other!"

Gregory Lowell.

"The Modocs had nothing to do with it!"

(padgett)

"They were forced to do this by the thing in the well!"

(PADGETT)

"The goddamn fucking thing in—"

The phone rang. Greg heard it through the window he had left open. Turning away from the silent well, he ran across the yard. At the foot of the porch steps, he crumpled, his legs lead weights.

"No!" he cried. He touched them, but they were not there.

He pulled himself up the steps, the useless members hindering him. A sixth ring, a seventh. He stretched to reach the doorknob. A tenth ring, an eleventh, and the door flew open.

The ringing stopped.

A tortured cripple, he dragged himself halfway across the living room until the muscles in his arms screamed. He rested, and soon the phone rang again. He redoubled his efforts and at last reached the kitchen, pulling the receiver down with the cord.

"Greg, where were you?"

"Jan, I . . ."

"Greg, listen to me. I'm in Susanville, and I have Allison and Mark with me."

"Susanville?"

"I took a chance, Greg. I picked them up at school and drove out of Bonner. Nothing happened! They're free, Greg. Allison and Mark are free! It's just you now. Try to get out of there, babe, *try!"*

"Jan, my legs . . . I can't move them."

"Oh God, no!"

"Jan, you stay there. Don't leave! I'll get out of here if I have to drag myself . . ."

"Greg? *Greg!*"

A tingling fluttered through his legs, like a million pin-pricks. A liquid rushing of life, then pain. Red, excruciating pain—ligaments knotting, flesh and muscle tearing. Screaming pain, beyond any threshold.

"Greg, we're coming home! We have to come home!"

"*Jan . . . et . . . stay . . . there . . .*"

Blackness covered the red, and when it passed, Janet was running through the door. Allison and Mark were with her.

"Greg!"

"Dad, are you okay?"

He rose tentatively. His legs held him. He looked at his son and daughter, then at Janet. "Have you told them yet?"

She shook her head. "No."

He walked out into the living room. "Then it's time they knew what the hell is going on."

38

Dora Waverly

The Lowells, burdened by the dark knowledge they barely understood, were alone, isolated by necessity. Janet called the high school on Friday morning to say that Allison and Mark were ill and would be out for a while. She phoned the medical center and told Emmett Nicholson the same thing. Allison talked to Billy, canceling the movies for that night and a party on Saturday. Her excuses were flimsy, and in the face of his challenging tone, she hung up angrily, leaving their relationship strained. It was a hard thing for her to do; she was unapproachable for hours afterward.

They were alone, more alone than they believed possible. No one stopped by; no one phoned. They were frightened, yet determined to stand against this cryptic and destructive force that mocked them with its evil, this wanton horror that made them prisoners inside its own dark sphere. Prisoners, yes, but recalcitrant as they waited. . . .

Waited for what, they could not say. Still, they waited, and watched. There was nothing, and Friday passed.

Then, Saturday morning, the phone rang, shattering the void of silence. It was Winn—subdued, formal.

"Greg, I need you to come down to the station."

"Is something wrong?"

"No, it's not like that. I have something to give you."

"What?"

"A message."

"A message? From who?"

"Can't say. You'll have to come and pick it up."

"You can't say who left it, or you *won't* say?"

"Do you want it or not?" Winn asked, irritated.

"Okay. I'll be there soon."

"Just you."

"What?"

"Just you—by yourself!" He hung up.

Greg said to Janet, "This may be it."

"What is it?"

"I'm not sure, but I'm going to find out." His brows drew together in a frown of worry. "I don't like leaving you here."

"We'll be all right. Maybe even in less danger than you. Greg . . ."

His jacket was already on. He kissed her. "I'll see you later."

He drove to town in a light rain, without incident. Few cars were on the roads, and he reached the sheriff's office at a quarter after ten. Winn and Les Curry skipped the amenities.

"There's what you came after," Curry said, nodding at a folded piece of white legal paper on his desk. "A kid brought it by this morning, then ran out."

Greg picked it up, at first thinking it was a child's handwriting. The letters were large, slanted, lots of serifs. But the message was clear: *Sheriff Staley: Tell Mr. Lowell to come to office. Alone. Say nothing about this on phone. It is very important. Tell him come to 723 Crater. This no prank. Please. Send no one else.*

There was no signature.

Greg looked at the lawmen. "Do you know who lives at this address?"

Curry nodded. "It's Dora Waverly's house."

Dora Waverly! This had to be it! he thought.

"Greg, what's this about?" Winn asked.

"I don't know," he replied, shaking his head.

The two men looked at each other, and during the awkward silence, Les Curry disappeared into a back room. Finally Winn asked, "Greg, did you have an affair with Adrienne Gordon?"

"Winn, I . . ."

"Did you have an affair with Adrienne Gordon?"

It was his life! Greg told himself. He couldn't tell anyone! Couldn't try to explain. Not now! "Yes, I did," he said softly.

Winn clenched his fists and turned away. "Get the fuck out of here."

* * *

Crater Drive was a little over a mile from the sheriff's office, running west behind the Juniper Mall. From the 900 block down, it was the most shabby neighborhood Greg had seen in Bonner. An exception was number 723, a tidy brick house with flower boxes, neatly trimmed hedges, and an ancient towering juniper pine in the front yard. Black serpentine smoke curled upward from a stone chimney. The windows were covered with dark drapes, creating an ominous aura that seemed to envelop Greg as he stepped from his car.

How was she going to know he was there? he wondered, climbing the porch steps. He reached the porch, and the door opened. Peering inside, he saw only darkness, then the silhouette of a woman who beckoned to him insistently. He entered, and she shut the door behind him.

The small room was old. The furniture, pictures, frayed rug—all had been there since the house was built. A smell of age, sickly sweet and strong, swirled around him. He fought the instinct to gag, then drew breaths through his mouth until it bothered him less.

As his vision adjusted, he saw other things: amulets, fetishes, bits of tied fur, whole pelts of small animals, chunks of agate and jasper and obsidian hanging from strings and thin chains, most around the windows and front door. And on both sides of the fireplace, piles of stones, the one on the right three times the size of the other.

He turned to Dora Waverly. She was darkly dressed, as always. Her cream face was lined with the grief she had borne since the day her grandson was killed. But he saw something else—fear, a controlled terror verging on eruption. And more in her penetrating eyes. Bewilderment, curiosity as she studied her visitor intently.

Then she spoke, her voice unsure, rasping. "There . . . is much that . . . must be said . . . Padgett."

"You can talk!" he exclaimed.

"And hear also. No, Padgett, it was not deception. Since I was a young woman, I was without ears and tongue. Now, with little time left, they are mine again."

"I don't understand."

"You could not. But you know that something is wrong."

"Yes," he said grimly.

She nodded. "Then my task will be easier. Come, for we do not have long."

She sat cross-legged on the rug in front of the fireplace and motioned for him to do the same. "Listen now, Padgett," she said. "Listen and hear the seldom-spoken story of Montanni."

39

Montanni

Dora Waverly told her story in a swaying singsong, every syllable spoken clearly, in the same manner she might have heard it from her mother or grandmother. Her voice, growing stronger and more assured after decades of silence, rang with a lilt.

"Long past, before the *basdin* came with their sickness and their guns, the People roamed the land in peace, and lived in harmony with the beasts of the valley, the sky, the mountain, and the water. And *Subbas,* the sun, smiled on the land of *Wus,* the fox, and *Moi,* the squirrel, and *Kaiutois,* the wolf, and *Keis,* the rattlesnake, and even *Kuja,* the rat; and the sky of *Blaiwas,* the eagle, and *Ndukis,* the hawk; and the lakes and rivers of *Kewe,* the eel, and *Kulta,* the otter, and *Kowe,* the frog.

"Kumush, who is Our Father, looked over what he had made and was pleased. He walked with the People and the beasts and protected them, and he shared in their happiness until it was time for him to go to the Place-beyond-the-Lake, which was his home, to think of more miracles to make.

"It was when Kumush was away that a *monadalkni*—a demon—arose from his bottomless *ginrdgs.* He was Montanni, the One-from-Below, and when he appeared, it was in his terrible demon's guise, and he so frightened *Moi,* the squirrel, that *Moi* fell dead from its tree. Thus warned, Montanni changed his form until he was a handsome young man with a warming smile. And he caused the *ginrdgs* to be filled with earth and rocks, for he planned never to go back.

"Montanni walked the land but was unable to fool the beasts, who fled in terror before him and sometimes went mad and destroyed themselves and others. But the People could not see as the beasts saw. They greeted him and gave him food and shelter . . . and more. The young maidens, prisoners of his eyes, followed him, and they opened their loins willingly when he bade them, *'Kyew stem. Kyew stem.'* And he took them all, never satisfied, and when each one was done, he changed back to his demon form, slaying them in terrible ways, staining the land with their blood. But still they came, and Montanni grew more hungry, and he fed his bloating evil with them.

"After a long time, Kumush returned from the Place-beyond-the-Lake, and he heard the shamans summoning him to their temescals, their sweathouses. So he sat with them in the smoke, and they could barely see him. They told him what had happened since he left, and he was sad. He knew that it was Montanni. This was the first time the People had ever heard that name spoken, yet they knew that this was an enemy of Our Father from when Time was born. He vowed to help them but said that Montanni was a powerful enemy and asked them to put a new stone on the prayer pile each day until it was over.

"Kumush, in the form of a beautiful maiden, went out of the temescal to the *sayka loluk,* where he knew Montanni to be, and he made the ground tremble, and there was another *ginrdgs.* He covered the opening, making it invisible, and he waited until Montanni came. The demon came down a green hill, and he was handsome and smiling. He saw the young maiden, and his smile grew even more. Kumush saw the false-ness and felt the evil but did not waver and held his guise.

"Montanni came closer and held out his hand, saying in a quiet voice, *'Kyew stem. Kyew stem.'* And Kumush, knowing that Montanni was yet too far away from the *ginrdgs,* smiled a smile of captive innocence. Our Father lay on the ground and lifted the buckskin skirt, and Montanni was pleased with what he saw. He came on and on but stopped before the *ginrdgs,* and Kumush willed him to continue, but the *monadalkni* did not.

" 'Woman,' Montanni said in a petal-soft voice, 'I will come *oteg.* I will come deep into you and make love to you, and you will not resist, for you wish it too.' And Kumush sighed, 'I wish it too. *Oteg,* handsome one, come and take me.'

"Montanni walked nearer and was close to the *ginrdgs*

but suddenly leapt through the air at Kumush. Had Our Father not rolled away, he would have been set upon by his foe.

"Montanni laughed and said, 'Did you think to deceive me?' He waved his hand, and the *ginrdgs* was visible. 'Oh, my friend, Kumookumts,' he mocked, using Our Father's ancient name, 'look what you have done,' and he tried to close the *ginrdgs,* but Kumush would not let him. 'Well then,' the *monadalkni* said, his voice changing to a rumble, 'let us see who will be put to rest here.' And he changed to his true and terrible form.

"Kumush watched him come and changed himself to *Lok,* the bear, and they met. They clawed and wrestled for nine days. The face of *subbas,* the sun, turned black, and the earth and mountains trembled. Terrible storms rolled across the sky and beat upon the land. The beasts fled from the *sayka loluk,* and the People, though wanting to know the outcome, were scared and followed the beasts.

"On the ninth day, Kumush mastered his enemy and threw him into the *ginrdgs,* closing it over him. *Subbas* then appeared, and it was the sign that all had awaited. They returned to their land, and Kumush, in an insect's guise so that none would notice him pass, left the *sayka loluk.* He was pleased that his people were rid of the *monadalkni,* yet cautious, for it was not his first encounter with Montanni, and he feared that it would not be over until the death of Time."

Dora Waverly paused. Greg could not be sure she was finished. Then he noticed her face, which had grown pale, and saw her press a trembling hand against her side.

"What is it?" he asked, concerned.

She lifted her head and breathed deeply. "Nothing. I'm all right. But the time becomes shorter, and there is more that must be said."

"Then let *me* say something. Are you telling me that the cause of all that's happening is this Montanni? It's a pretty good fable, but—"

"It's no *fable,* Padgett," Dora Waverly said angrily, "and do not challenge it again. You did not come here to play the doubter."

"All right," he said, subdued. "But where do my family and I, and those before us, fit in?"

"I will tell you. There is more first. A season after the battle in the *sayka loluk,* Kumush returned to speak to the shamans. He told them that Montanni was not dead, but dormant. He told them to keep a vigil on the *sayka loluk,* to make certain that the Place-Where-It-Had-Been was never disturbed. And they obeyed.

"For years and years after, the People hunted and fished and roamed the *sayka loluk,* but only those who watched went near the Place-Where-It-Had-Been. Then the *basdin* came to take the land, but even they did not disturb the spot, not at first.

"The first Padgett, the woman . . ."

"Rebecca?"

"Yes. She was the instrument of Montanni's release. Something about her was different, and he was able to reach her mind."

Rebecca Padgett, Greg mused. Different. Grandpa Samuel had told stories about the early Padgetts. From New England. *Witch burnings. Different.*

"Knowing that the land was dry and the *basdin* thirsty, Montanni used her. He told her, 'Dig here, dig here—there is water.' And he told her again and again until he reached her. She showed the men where to dig the well, and they began. There were none watching, and when the People did return, it was too late, for they could not stop the *basdin.*"

"The three Modocs," Greg said.

Dora nodded. "You know about them?"

"Yes."

"And of their fate?"

"That too. I'm sorry."

"You know more than I had guessed."

"I've seen a lot, but until now, little of it made sense. It's clear that this . . . Montanni was responsible for the deaths of James Padgett and his mother, and subsequently all the settlers in the Fire Valley Massacre."

"Massacre!" She spat the word. "To have one's people blamed! But yes, it was Montanni's doing—and also his greatest error."

"What do you mean?"

She grabbed her side again as the pain struck her. Greg tried to help, but, grimacing, she waved him off.

"It had been a long time," she continued, "and Montanni was still weak. He destroyed two Padgetts before he realized that they were his strength, then nearly took the others in the mindless bloodletting that was the release of his long-sup-

pressed evil. Only at the last instant did he think to allow
Benjamin Padgett's survival. But it did not matter, for what
he'd done had drained Montanni, and he could not hold the
boy, who was taken away. And Montanni was again dormant,
for there were no other Padgetts, until . . ."

". . . my mother came," Greg finished. "Then it can
only manifest itself through Rebecca Padgett's descendants?"

Dora nodded. "When your parents came, it began again.
They were warned but chose to stay, and only became aware
of the evil when it was too late. Much happened then, though
not nearly as much as what has happened since you and your
family came to Fire Valley."

"Why is that?"

"Your mother, being with child, was not strong. As
Montanni drew from her, she grew weaker. You, as an infant,
were of no factor to him, save as a hope for the future. It was
the reason your parents were able to leave, for after the hotel
fire, Montanni was helpless and could not stop them."

"And what about us?" Greg asked, afraid of the answer.

Dora shook her head sadly. "You are strong, Padgett. So
are your children. And from his first two experiences,
Montanni has learned. He has strengthened himself slowly
and is now nearly as formidable as he was ages ago when he
walked the land of the People. You and your family cannot
leave, Padgett. I think you already know that. No matter what
evil Montanni causes, he will not weaken himself enough to be
unable to prevent it."

"Then how do we fight him?"

"That is for Kumush to say."

"Do you speak to Kumush?"

Dora nodded. "I was young when Kumush first spoke to
me. It was right after your mother and father came. He asked
me to be his eyes, to watch the Place-Where-It-Had-Been. I
did, and it was during that time, on a dark and bewildering
morning, when I imagined I saw Montanni emerging from the
ginrdgs. My ears and tongue were taken then and not returned
until today, so that I might tell you this."

"Will you speak to Kumush for me?"

"There's no need to. You've already spoken to him,
twice."

"You don't mean—the old woman!"

"Kumush's many forms include those of females. I already spoke of one, when he met the *monadalkni*. Kumush is a . . . I forget the big word for man-woman."

"Hermaphrodite?"

"Yes. He will find you again—and soon. But it must be away from your land."

"Why?"

More pain assaulted her—severe, wrenching. She fell prone, gasping. Then, fighting it, she took Greg's hand and pulled herself up.

"I have to get you to the medical center!" he said.

"No!" she said strongly. "My fate was decided when I asked you here. It's only a question of time."

"Isn't there family I could call?"

"My husband is long dead. My daughter and son-in-law were killed in an accident ten years ago. There was only Jeff. . . . Please, Padgett, go now. Kumush will find you. Maybe together you can do what must be done."

They walked to the door, the woman holding his arm. The daylight, although hazy, was a bright contrast to the dark interior as they walked out onto the porch. Clutching both her hands, Greg looked at Dora Waverly and said sadly, "Thank you for what you've done."

She nodded. "I will pile more stones and pray that you and your family be freed of this horror. May Kumush walk with you—*Greg Lowell.*"

He climbed into his car, and she waved as he drove off. But even when he was beyond her sight, she continued to stand in the damp chill, for the pain had come again and was worse.

(you told him you told him he didn't have to know it was better for him to be ignorant of the truth Modoc whore you told him)

Dora Waverly bared her teeth like a savage wolf. *"Montanni . . . may Kumush . . . tear out . . . your . . ."*

Winn had followed Greg from his office in an unmarked car, parking across the street from Dora Waverly's house. Having waited for a long time for anything to happen, he watched the scene on the porch curiously. There didn't seem to be anything wrong. Yet after Greg left, he saw the old woman double up in pain. He jumped from his car and hurried up the walk.

With a final shriek, Dora Waverly's frail body swelled and

burst. The front door with its fetishes, the porch, and Winn were spattered with blood and pelted with a rain of torn flesh.

Three minutes passed before the white-faced sheriff could stagger to his radio and call for help that he did not need.

40

Burton Faraday's Plan

Greg had heard Dora Waverly's story but still did not believe that the last hour had happened. Driving through town, then up the Bonner-Oregon Highway, he found his thoughts back in the small dark room on Crater Drive. Three times he nearly lost control of the Camaro, once stopping inches short of rear-ending a camper.

The enemy was revealed now, but did it matter? If Montanni, the One-from-Below, was real—and how could he deny it?—then could it be stopped? Destroyed, sent back, or whatever? Kumush, the old crone, the young seductress—the god. Kumush was the key.

Kumush. Our Father. The Creator. The Old Man. A god, the Modocs' god.

I talked to a god, he thought unbelievingly. *How ridiculous. People have been locked up for delusions like that. Who's going to believe such crap? Jesus Christ! Jesus Christ? Maybe I can talk to him too. Greg Lowell, this is Jesus. Jesus, Greg Lowell. Nice to meet you. Always glad for a chat.*

But all along the highway, he constantly watched, pleading silently to see the small figure. When he pulled into the ranch, barely glancing at the well, he still wondered how he was going to explain this to his family.

A Mercedes was parked in front of the house. Burton's car. What the hell was he doing there? Greg wondered, and hurried to the door.

Janet was waiting for him. She looked pale, older. Greg hadn't noticed it before. He supposed he looked the same. He felt it.

"Everything okay here?" he asked her.

"Yes. What about you? Did you find out—"

"Why is Burton here?" he interrupted.

The writer had been sitting on the couch but stood as Greg walked in. "I'll tell you why," he said. "I came because I started thinking about the way I'd been treating you, and I was . . . embarrassed. The grapevine had been buzzing about your affair with Adrienne—you're aware of that—and at first I bought it. But something didn't wash. I know you, Greg, even though it's only been—what, six months? I wanted to hear it from you. Now I don't have to. Janet told me everything."

Greg glared at his wife. "Why did you do it? Letting him in here was bad enough, but by telling him, you just about condemned—"

"Listen to me, Greg!" Burton interrupted as Janet, her eyes wet, turned away. "When I saw the way your family looked, I *had* to know. Janet kept putting me off, but I wouldn't let up. I should've guessed something was wrong after what happened to me at the well a few months ago."

"What was that?"

"I'll tell you later. In any case, you need a friend, Greg. Christ knows you need someone now."

Greg touched Janet's face; his eyes apologized. "You told him all of it?" he asked softly.

She nodded. "Yes."

"Burton, how much of it do you believe?"

"All . . . I guess." He shrugged. "I mean, it's not easy . . ."

"Then you'd better open your mind again, because I have more to add. Sit down, all of you."

For half an hour, Greg spoke without interruption. Janet and Burton listened, first in disbelief, then with a foreboding that gradually bloated into horror.

When he was finished, Janet gasped, "This can't be happening! This is the twentieth century! You're talking about . . . Oh Lord!"

"I have an idea," Burton said.

"No, don't stick your neck out any further!" Janet exclaimed. "Get out of here now!"

"Janet, my neck is already out as far as it'll go. Now listen. I want you to meet me at the airfield around four o'clock. My plane's in one of the hangars for an overhaul, but I'll drive there now and hustle things up. I'm going to fly you out of here."

"Burton, it'll be suicide!" Greg cried.

"No, it won't. If Montanni destroys you and the kids, then it condemns itself. It may stop us from leaving, but it won't do anything to you or your family. I think it's a chance worth taking."

"We'll never get to the field," Janet said. "It won't let us."

"You've got to try!" Burton insisted. "You can't sit around and wait for a hermaphrodite Indian god to save you! Christ knows what can happen before then! Look, I'm going. Four o'clock, all right? Maybe, by dark, this nightmare will be over."

Greg nodded. "Four o'clock, Burton. We'll try."

Burton walked to the door. Greg and Janet, drawn even closer by the terrifying truth of their legacy, rose and followed the writer outside.

The squad car tore up the Bonner-Oregon Highway. Winn was behind the wheel, Les Curry next to him. Aware of what his superior had been through earlier, Curry had offered to drive, but Winn refused. The deputy prayed they would reach their destination before he got them killed.

"Come on, Winn, slow down!" Curry urged as the sheriff swerved to avoid a truck that had been turning.

"You should've seen it, Les," Winn said, ignoring the warning. "God, you should've seen it!" And he described Dora's death in detail for the third time, to Curry's disgust.

"It's Greg Lowell," Winn continued, grinding his teeth. "That bastard knows! He had something to do with it. He's had something to do with a lot that's been going on here! We'll find out. We'll get some answers. I swear to God we'll get some answers!"

Tires squealed as he turned off the main road; they threw gravel as he raced to the main gate. Greg and the others, halfway to Burton's Mercedes, saw it coming.

The squad car screeched to a stop in front of the house. Winn, red-faced, stormed out. Les Curry scrambled around the front to catch up with him.

"Where the hell do you think you're going?" Winn challenged Greg.

"What?" Greg asked.

"You heard me, Lowell!"

"Winn, what's this about?" Burton asked.

"You shut your fucking mouth! We'll talk later about the company you keep. Now I asked—"

"Hey Winn, take it easy," Curry told him. "We can't talk to people like that."

"Oh no? How else do you talk to a murderer? Tell me!"

"Murderer?" Janet cried. "Winn—"

"Don't deny killing Dora Waverly! I saw you there! I saw you!"

"She's dead," Greg said blankly, a sense of defeat washing over him.

"Murderer!" Winn screamed. *"Fucking goddamn murderer! Just rape wasn't enough, huh?"*

Janet took a step closer to Greg. "Winn, stop this!"

"Shut your mouth, *whore!*" Winn growled. "Yeah, I know about you too. *Whore!* A murderer and a rapist with a whore wife! The whole fucking family is no good! They don't deserve to live!"

"Winn!"

Curry grabbed Winn's arm as he raised his .38 Special. The two bullets that he managed to squeeze off flew harmlessly over their heads, one shattering an upstairs window. Although stronger, Curry was sorely pressed to pull the weapon from the grip of the crazed sheriff. He finally did, but was set upon by a terrible and mindless beast. The thing that had been Winn Staley succumbed only after a gun butt had been driven twice against the side of his head.

"Winn, oh no, Winn!" Curry cried as Greg and the others, having fallen to the ground, pulled themselves up unsteadily. They watched as the deputy handcuffed the unconscious sheriff, then lifted him in his arms and placed him in the squad car.

"I've got to get him to town!" Curry said frantically. "I've got to get him *somewhere!*" And he drove off as Winn had driven in.

Burton stared in disbelief at Greg and Janet. "Montanni?"

Greg nodded. "It was just a warning. If not for Les Curry, you would have died, maybe one of us. That's all."

" 'That's all,' " he repeated blankly. "A couple more dead, Winn Staley's career—*his life*—ruined. That's all."

Janet and Greg turned and began walking back to the house. "I'll see you later," the writer called after them.

"I hope you do," Greg replied.

41

To the Airfield

Normally, the drive to the airfield took thirty-five to forty minutes. But it was raining harder now, and the temperature, which had been in the low forties all day, began to drop. For that reason, among others, Greg decided they would leave before three.

"Which car should we take?" Janet asked as the four of them sat with superficial calm in the dark kitchen.

"Both," Greg said. "It might give us more of a chance. You take Mark in the wagon; Allison will ride with me."

They left shortly after, bringing little with them. If the plan succeeded, the Faradays would close up the house. Janet pulled out first, then Greg. This time, when he passed the well, he stared at it with both dread and defiance. It remained silent.

Janet drove cautiously on the rain-slick highway. Greg dropped back a hundred yards, adjusting his speed to match hers. They caught up to no one and were passed by only three other vehicles during the first couple of miles.

Six miles from town, Janet braked to avoid hitting a herd of cows. They had broken through a low wire fence surrounding a pasture on the right, each one trampling the mesh farther into the ground. There were about two dozen, including some bulls. They engulfed the car rapidly, their lowing loud—and disturbing—even with the windows rolled up.

Janet leaned on the horn. "Come on, dammit, move!" The cows huddled closer.

"Stupid animals," Mark said.

"I don't believe this—Oh!"

A crashing sound, sharp, troubling. The station wagon

rocked from the impact of one animal's hooves against the side. A second lashed out, a third; then it was impossible to separate them, for they came often and from all directions. Janet screamed, Mark swore as they battered the vehicle. The bulls drove their horns against doors and windows; some of the red-eyed cows emulated them but succeeded only in splitting their heads open. One window was shattered, the rest stained with their blood.

"God, oh God, no!" Janet cried as a horn thrust within an inch of her face.

"Get away! Get the hell away!" Mark shouted, grabbing an ice scraper from the backseat and lashing out at the animal.

Seeing the station wagon surrounded by the maddened beasts, Greg shoved his accelerator to the floor. "Hold on, Allison!" he yelled, and raced toward the mindless blood-spattered creatures. He clipped two in a braking swerve, then circled around as half of them broke away to confront him. He drove a pair off the bumpers before they could close in front of him. This time, when he stopped, he could see Janet's terrified face through the hanging shards of her window.

"*Greg!*" she screamed.

"Move the car!" he told her. "Move it out of here, *now!*" And he accelerated as one of the bulls thrust at the right side of the Camaro.

Struggling to ignore the animals that still came at her, Janet urged the LTD forward. It slanted sharply as it rolled over the carcasses now littering the highway. Free of them, she sped away. She saw Greg emerge from the blacktopped slaughterhouse, his horn blaring, and she pulled off the road to wait for him.

Allison rolled down her window. Greg called, "Are you all right?"

Janet nodded. "Let's go."

They drove off. Within a minute, the rain assaulted the valley in dense sheets. Janet, barely able to see the road in front of her, was soaked through the windowless opening.

"Why the hell are we even bothering?" she said, slamming her palms on the steering wheel. "No plane could take off in *this*. We might as well turn back!"

But after twenty minutes in the relentless deluge, they were less than two miles from downtown Bonner. Janet again pulled off the road as the LTD, its radiator punctured during the attack, coughed and died. Greg stopped behind her.

"Oh, look at Mom!" Allison gasped as Mark helped a pale and staggering Janet to the Camaro.

Greg jumped out, and together he and Mark guided her to the front seat. Glassy-eyed, she shivered uncontrollably. Greg covered her with his jacket and ordered Allison and Mark in back. Without a glance at the LTD, he returned to the road.

The downpour eased, then stopped as they reached town. Janet was warmer and seemed more comfortable, though her face was still bloodless. The sky lightened in a few places, bringing a shred of hope.

Avoiding Juniper Boulevard, Greg followed side streets through Bonner. Even so, there were numerous vehicles to contend with, the end of the rain bringing them out. Tapping his finger nervously on the wheel, Greg wished this part of it was done.

They sat at a red light, waiting to cross Yellow Pine Road. A steady stream of cars passed in both directions. One was familiar to Allison: Billy Douglas's blue Datsun pickup. Billy was driving, laughing with his passenger, Cindy Barnes.

Cindy Barnes. Been laid more times than any girl in school. Carries more condoms in her purse than a pharmacy. She always wanted Billy; she wanted in his pants. But she won't have him. She won't!

Allison's gaze followed the pickup. Ten yards past the intersection, it suddenly veered across the median. Tires screamed, horns blared, glass exploded, and twisted metal gnashed together as car after car was demolished in the carnage. Blood stained windshields, vinyl seats, the street, as cries of agony rose.

Greg crossed Yellow Pine Road between the cars that had stopped and was alone on the street.

Airport Road was hardly a road but a dirt trail, barely drivable after the deluge. Three-quarters of a mile to the field. They were jarred repeatedly by concealed holes and twice got stuck in the mud. Ten minutes later, when they reached Bonner Airport, they knew they had surpassed the limits of their endurance. It had to end.

It had to.

Seven minutes to four. Greg had figured correctly. They pulled up in front of the main building, an old quonset hut with a small glass-encased control-tower structure on the roof.

The rest of the airfield was equally unimpressive: three hangars, a storage shed, piles of motors and other rusted parts, an asphalt runway stretching about twenty-five hundred feet toward a wooded area. Twenty or so planes stood unattended to the right of the runway, a commonplace aggregation of prop-driven Piper Cherokees, Beechcrafts, and Cessnas. A grease smell was prevalent, despite the recent rain.

Donna Faraday emerged from the office as the Lowells climbed out of the mud-caked Camaro. "Boy, am I glad to see all of you," she said.

"Did Burton tell you?" Janet asked.

Donna shook her head. "Only that you were in danger and needed help. That was enough. Jesus, what happened to Allison?"

The girl, being helped from the car by Mark, was paler than her mother had been earlier. Glassy-eyed, she stared through Donna and sobbed, "We have to get out of here! *We have to get out of here!*"

Janet put an arm around her daughter. "It'll be soon, hon. I think we're going to make it this time."

"Where's Burton?" Greg asked.

Donna indicated the hangar on the left. "In there still. He should be out any minute. I checked right before you came, and they were nearly done. He's had Charlie and Bill working with him all afternoon—"

Mark was thrown against the car, the others struck to the ground by the shock waves of the explosion. The roof of the hangar blew high into the air; the bared opening and the windows and doors belched red and yellow flames that sliced through dense layers of black smoke. Adjoining buildings were engulfed by the holocaust in seconds. The office was threatened by a rain of burning debris and shrapnel.

"Burton!" Donna screamed. *"Oh, no, Burton!"*

She tried to stagger toward the inferno, but Greg held her. She struggled, then fell unconscious. He carried her to the car.

"We have to get out of here!" he told his family.

"We killed Burton!" Janet cried. *" We killed him!* How many more, Greg? How many . . . ?"

"Jan, get up! Mark! Allison!"

They tried, slowly. Thirty seconds later, it did not matter. The sky darkened, and the rain fell again; hard, as it had on the highway. It drowned the flames, leaving the hangar smoking. The scattered remains of the three men, which would have been incinerated to ashes, sizzled into charred lumps of bone and flesh.

When it let up, they drove away, away from the final grim reminder that they could not—*must not*—try again to escape from Montanni.

42

Kumush

The longest day of their lives was not over yet. They drove Donna to the medical center, though it was difficult even to get near the building. The victims of the accident on Yellow Pine Road overfilled it. Two were dead, nine others critically injured, among them Billy Douglas, although his chances of pulling through were fair. Cindy Barnes had suffered massive head and internal injuries; she was not expected to live.

Everyone who worked at the medical center had been called in, as well as doctors and nurses from other towns. It still was not enough. Unattended gurneys and stretchers with bloodied but less severe casualties lined the halls. Seeing this, Janet told Greg, "I have to stay and help."

"Jan, you can't be serious! Have you seen yourself?"

"I have to do this. I *want* to. Maybe I can make up one damn bit for what's happened."

"But we can't separate now. We have to stay together!"

She put a hand on his arm. "It'll just be for a few hours. Besides, I'm the nonessential one in this. I'm not a Padgett, remember?"

"I know, and that's what scares the hell out of me. Since Montanni doesn't need you, why should he think twice about . . . destroying you?"

She shrugged. "I've lasted this long. Greg, I'm going to stay. Wait here for a minute."

She left, quickly reappearing in her scrubs. "I wish you didn't have to go back to the house," she said to Greg.

"There's no other choice," he replied grimly.

"I know."

"How will you get home?" he asked.

"I'll find a ride."

"No. I don't want anyone else out there. You call me, and we'll come for you. I mean it!"

She kissed him. "I love you. It'll be over soon." And she hurried off to help.

Five o'clock. The sky was still overcast, threatening, but at the moment no rain. They were far up the highway, past the derelict station wagon, past the dead animals, which had been dragged off. Mark sat next to Greg, quiet, sullen; Allison was stretched across the back seat, sleeping, or thinking.

"Dad, look!" Mark exclaimed suddenly.

The figure in the middle of the road was far ahead, so Greg was able to slow down without jolting Allison. The girl sat up as he pulled onto the shoulder.

"Allison, do you see that too?" he asked.

"Of course. Who is it?"

"Kumush," he replied with a mixture of fear and relief.

The crone hobbled off the blacktop as they got out of the car, stopping before them. "You know everything now, Padgett?" she asked in her raspy voice.

"Yes."

"Your attempt at escape was ill-omened, though I know you had to try. It would have simplified things greatly."

"Why did Dora Waverly have to die?" Greg demanded. "Why did Burton—"

"It is not necessary to call the roll," she interrupted. "The Modoc woman and your friend died for the same reason everyone else has died since you came to the *sayka loluk*. Montanni is unleashed, and death is his existence. I warned you—"

"Your warnings were vague! By the time we understood, it was too late. Why couldn't you stop any of it?"

"Montanni acted from his *ginrdgs* on your land and through you. I could not reach him."

"But you're supposed to be a *god!*" Mark exclaimed.

"Yes, young Padgett. But an old god—once strong, now tired, weak. I let the People down when the *basdin* first came, and in the lava beds. Then they were dispersed, their blood mixed and remixed until now I hardly know them, and they have forgotten me. Perhaps one day I may go to the Place-beyond-the-Lake until the death of Time. But not yet, not while Montanni stalks."

"Are you afraid to confront Montanni?" Greg asked. "Is that why you haven't appeared near the well?"

"Afraid, yes, but not in the way you think. Were I to return to the Place-Where-It-Had-Been at any time since the day I bested him, Montanni would rise. Then, again, it would be he and I. And were I to be beaten, then he would be free, unstoppable."

"It's not an easy choice you had, either way. But did you really think we could get away?"

"I had hoped so. I counted on your strength and persistence. It was not as difficult the last time, with the Padgett woman—your mother. Then, I trusted in her weakness, and although a price was paid, she did escape. I never thought another Padgett would return after that."

"What are we supposed to do now?" Greg asked.

The crone shook her head. "Your part is nearly done. Montanni has grown stronger and will soon rise from the *ginrdgs.* When he does, he will be as he once was and will need no one."

"You'll *have* to face him then."

"I should have faced him before. I should have taken the chance. But I was not ready."

"And now?"

"I am still not certain. But it hardly matters. It has to be done. Go home now, Padgett." She turned to walk away.

"When will you come?" Greg called after her.

"Tomorrow, or the next day. No later."

"Kumush!" he said sharply, and the crone, stopping, faced him. "Your failure could be devastating."

"More so than you can comprehend," she said darkly, then disappeared through some trees.

"Come on," Greg said to Allison and Mark, who stared after Kumush a few more seconds before climbing into the car.

They reached home. Ominous night had fallen. They stopped near the well, and now the hatred in their dark stares was not motivated unwittingly from outside but a real part of them. Their silent venom was noted, then mocked. Knowing they had lost even this confrontation, they drove wearily to the house.

Nine-fifteen; a few lights on, a fire burning. They had eaten, though not because they were hungry. Mark and Allison had fallen into a restless sleep, the boy sprawled in a chair near the fireplace, his sister on the couch. Greg was past sleep. He sat in a rocker before one of the windows and peered into the darkness. The phone rang.

"It's me, babe," Janet said. "Is everything all right?"

"Yes. How about there?"

"Things are finally letting up. I'll be done by the time you get here, and I'll tell you about it."

"Twenty-five minutes, Jan."

"Please be careful."

Greg woke Allison and Mark gently. They did not complain, knowing they had to stay together. Greg drove toward the front gate but stopped near the monument. This time, he got out, telling his son and daughter to stay put.

"Listen to me, you bastard," he muttered, walking toward the well. "You know where we're going and you know we'll be back, so just leave us alone. *Just leave us the hell alone!*" He thought he heard a faint hollow groan in reply, though it might have been a timber creaking in the shaft.

A calm, quiet night. No rain, no wind. Stars visible in an obsidian sky. They met no trouble on the drive to town where Janet waited for them on a corner near the medical center, alone. She looked tired, though perhaps less so than six hours before.

"Mom, how's . . . Billy?" Allison asked reluctantly as they drove off.

"He's stable. He'll be all right. I saw him an hour ago, and he asked for you."

"What about the others?" Greg asked.

"Cindy Barnes is dead. A couple are just hanging on. The rest will make it. Emmett Nicholson sent half of them over to the hospital in Alturas. We were pushed to the walls."

"And Donna?"

Janet shook her head. "Not good. Larry has her sedated."

"She's a strong woman. I think she'll make it." Greg slammed the wheel. "Dammit! *Dammit!* Why did Burton have to get himself involved?"

No one spoke. After a moment, Janet said, "I saw Les Curry. He has Winn locked up. Says he's like his old self now. Remembers everything he did but can't believe it. Les isn't sure yet what to do. He asked if we were going to press charges. I told him no, but he's still going to hold him at least another day."

Greg nodded. "How about you, Jan?"

"I'm okay. I was right. I needed to do this. But as bad as they still want me, I won't leave you again."

"You can't now, Mom," Mark said.

"What do you mean?"

Greg told her. Driving up the Bonner-Oregon Highway, he told her about the meeting with Kumush, pointing out the spot where they had met the crone. He was thorough, and Janet did not ask questions, for now it was clear.

"Then it really *is* almost over," she said softly as Greg turned off the main road.

43

Confrontation

Janet and Greg slept in the guest room upstairs to be closer to their children. But the Lowells knew little sleep that night. Restless turning and violent awakenings plagued them; an occasional piercing scream echoed through the purgatorial halls where they waited. Waited for the disturbance of their visions and for the horror of their real living nightmare to end.

Then, at dawn, the summoning.

A black and cryptic and ethereal summoning, yet existent, undeniable. They felt it, *all* of them. Janet too.

Down the stairs, slowly, blankly, still dressed in the clothes they had worn falling into bed. Janet and Allison barefoot, Mark in bulky athletic socks, Greg in loafers that had absently found his feet. Across the living room, past the final embers of a dying fire.

Out the door and into the frost-glazed chill of early morning. Across the silent yard, to the well. The Padgett well, the *ginrdgs,* the memorial to the Fire Valley Massacre (HISTORICAL SITE, COME ON IN), the Place-Where-It-Had-Been. Side by side at first, then apart.

Nearer to the well, Greg and Mark stopped first, ten yards away; Janet and Allison walked a few steps closer. Crushing silence, biting cold, surrounded them as they waited again. But this time, they knew, not for long.

The ground trembled beneath them. Softly, not enough to throw them off balance. A steady rumble, then another sound, the rush of escaping air. It rose from the well, blowing the wood cover and the upright beams and the parasol apart. The splinters, along with the commemorative plaque, scattered in a wide circle.

Over the lip of the mortared stones, a hand, or something like one. Gnarled, spastic. The wrong color, the right number of digits. Nails (claws?) too long, too sharp. A veinous bloated wrist and forearm.

The hand snaked across the lip in search of a hold. It grabbed finally, but it was too strong, crushing chunks of mortar and stone into powder. Then a firm grip, more rumbling, more rushing air, and a dark form sprang from the well and landed silently on two feet.

The *monadalkni.* The demon, Montanni, the One-from-Below.

A man. An inch less than six feet and slender, but imposing. Long dark hair, with no head ornamentation, and sallow-skinned. A bare smooth chest without markings; unshod feet, but the rest draped in tan buckskin leggings. Handsome, darkly seductive. Coal eyes, a sidelong half-smile that was just shy of a mocking sneer. Montanni, silent, curious, gliding in a broad arc around the transfixed Lowells, then returning to where he had begun, four steps from his place of exile.

His thin lips parted and he spoke in a soft voice, strangely warbling. "The Padgetts, my friends. Fitting that you be first to witness the rising."

Greg's body remained frozen, but not his tongue. "We'll see you back into the hole, too, you bastard!"

Montanni's singing laughter dripped ice shards into their veins. "The old fool Kumookumts was too late. He waited, and waited—until it was too late." His white smile grew as he eyed the four. "How does it feel, Padgetts? You're free now, as I am. Do you feel the lightness? You must!"

Greg ignored the taunting. "So now we're finished carrying you. Now we're expendable. What are you waiting for? Are you afraid of something? You mock Kumush, but maybe you're afraid of him. Is that it, Montanni?"

Laughter again, like wind chimes, but with a deep undertone. Montanni sat on the ground, his legs crossed. His quick, precise movements were those of a woodsprite. "Afraid of Kumookumts! As you are of the ant, Padgett, or the fawn." A sudden fire lit his eyes. "I revel in the thought of our meeting. It has strengthened my existence below during the forever-time that has passed. I *relish* it, Padgett!"

Greg was sweating in the cold. "Whatever the hell you are, you fucking—"

"Stop it, Greg!" Janet cried. "He'll kill you!"

"He'll kill us all anyway, so what does it matter? Isn't that right, Montanni? *Isn't it?*"

The challenge was ignored. The One-from-Below stood again and walked over to Janet. "You were of no use to me," he told her, "yet from the first day, I wanted you, so I let you live. I knew you through the Modoc called Rand, and"—he cast a smug glance at Greg—"through you, Padgett. But today I will need no one else, Jan-et." He luxuriated over her name, then whirled and pointed a finger at Allison. "And I will know *you* also."

"*Oh, no! Mom!*" the girl cried.

Rage matched Janet's fear, barely transcending it. "Don't touch her," she warned huskily. "Don't you *touch* my child!"

Montanni said nothing but turned and strolled away, a hand to his face as if in thought. Then he faced them once more. His smile dripped syrup, his eyes danced. He extended one hand with the palm up, reaching, wanting.

He spoke, his voice singing again, but insistent. "*Kyew stem. Kyew stem.*"

"Stop it!" Allison pleaded.

"No!" Janet whispered fiercely. "I won't let this happen!"

"*Kyew stem. Kyew stem.*"

The power of his sensuality overwhelmed Janet's will. "No-oo," she moaned. "No please, no please, no-oo. Yes. *Oh yes!*"

"Mom, don't listen to him!" Mark shouted.

"*Oteg,*" Allison sighed, unbuttoning her blouse.

"*Oteg,* Montanni," Janet echoed, and pulled off her heavy sweater.

"*Kyew stem. Kyew stem.*"

"Jan, *no!*" Greg yelled. "Allison! Don't let it happen! You can deny him! *You can!*"

A slight wavering; brief uncertainty. Janet and Allison struggled to glance at Greg. Still smiling, Montanni peeled off his buckskin garment, kicked it away. Instantly his manhood sprang erect—large, smooth, a glistening pinpoint on the dark head—a thing of urgency that would not be denied. The two stared at it, then at his eyes, and were his prisoners.

"*Kyew stem. Kyew stem.*"

Janet threw away her top, unhooked her bra. "*Oteg,* Montanni!"

"*Oteg!*" Allison twisted loose of her snug jeans.

"*Kyew stem. Kyew stem.*"

They were naked but didn't feel the cold. Wanting him as he came nearer, they shared what they found. Greg's and Mark's frantic pleas did not reach them. Montanni ordered them to the ground, saying again, *"Kyew stem. Kyew stem."*

Willingly, hungrily, they obeyed. They fell supine, thighs parting, probing fingers beginning what they could not wait for.

"Oteg!" Allison moaned.

"First me!" Janet demanded. "Oh, please! *Oteg,* Montanni!"

He straddled her, pointing at Allison. "The undipped pool will wait a while longer. I will come *oteg,* Jan-et."

Penetration, then a loud, furious, brief copulation. He turned to Allison. A girl at first, softly whimpering; then a woman—erotic, insistent in her wanting. Taking all. Demanding more. Writhing in a screaming red eruption while he satisfied another. And ready again.

"I trust you savored it, Montanni, for it stops now, and it may be hundreds of winters before you know it again."

The low harsh voice came from behind them, toward the barn. Greg and Mark twisted their necks to see, although they knew who it was. Montanni, his game interrupted, sprang to his feet and stared coldly at the pathetic bent figure standing there. Then, recognition, and a smile shattered his frozen mask.

"Old Kumookumts! It's been a long time. Is *that* how you would come to meet me? What a fitting guise!"

The crone's body heaved in something like a shrug. "It was convenient. Get away from them, Montanni."

The demon obeyed. Despite his leering bravado, he retreated to the rim of the well. Uncaring or unaware of Kumush's appearance, Janet and Allison crawled after him, still lusting, pleading for more from the thing that now ignored them. Then their bodies stiffened. They were free of the desire but not of the horror as they realized what they had done.

Adopting a swaggering stance, Montanni smiled his spurious smile again. He extended an arm, his coal eyes flecked with dancing fire.

"Ca, Kumookumts. Montanni *siwg!"*

"You would kill me?" Kumush laughed, an old woman's nervous grating laughter. Then it stopped, and the deep-set eyes in the jaundiced face met Montanni's. In a dark voice,

Kumush said, "No more words, *monadalkni*. No more words."

Kumush walked forward. No hobbling, no shuffling. A strong step that carried him toward the well. Past the Lowells, who watched and saw . . . something else.

Not a bent crone but a figure that was tall, broad, with a bullet head and rippling back. *Lok,* the bear, brown and shaggy. It penetrated the nebulous red haze that was to be its arena, an ursine titan gliding slowly toward something equally large and ominous. The *monadalkni,* Montanni in his demon form, a nightmare that appeared to be molded from insubstantial black clay. A manlike shape that altered with each undulating movement, except for the face. Two oval blood-red eyes over a coyote's snout and a mouth that was like a gaping wound, with things that should have been teeth but more closely resembled writhing human fingers.

Hideous gurgling sounds came from the demon. A counterclockwise swirling of blackness in the mist, then . . .

The giants met, like wrestlers in some ancient Olympiad. Yet in silence. A deathlike stillness fell over their arena, then reached out and clamped the *sayka loluk* in a vacuum.

And a cold, more biting than it had ever been. Gelid, penetrating slivers that cut them deeply, especially Janet and Allison, whose exposed flesh was discoloring.

Still they watched, sometimes seeing the flailing of a massive paw, or a dark dripping appendage like that which had arisen earlier from the well. They felt the unleashed power in the resumption of this age-old confrontation, and they waited for the outcome.

Waited.

And then, on the ground, something dark and viscous and noxious-smelling, trickled out from the edge of the hazy arena. A voice—from somewhere —like a deep rumbling. *"Padgett, help me!"*

Greg found his tongue again. "Kumush?"

"He's crushing me, Padgett. Help me!"

"I can't help you!"

"Padgett, you must!"

"But I can't move! I—!"

His left leg was free, then the right. His torpor lifted; blood flowed. He took a few staggering steps forward.

"Greg, no!" Janet screamed. "Don't go there!"

"Padgett, he's winning!"

Greg paused, uncertain. "What can I do? Kumush, *what can I do?*"

"*Try, Padgett! It will all be over if you do not!*"

A few feet closer. "I'll try. I have to!"

"*Greg, please!*"

"*Dad!*"

"HELP ME PADGETT, HELP ME! PAD-GETT!"

He couldn't turn back. At the edge, he looked back at the pained, pleading faces of his family. Then he rushed into the mist.

"*GREG!*"

He pushed toward the well, but the mist resisted him. At the edge of the well he saw Kumush—Our Father—and Montanni—the One-from-Below—fused in one shadow; then they separated. The ancient god struggled, thrashing futilely as the *monadalkni*, sputum dripping from its obscene mouth, lifted him high above the mortared stone rim of the hole that had been its prison.

Greg felt no more resistance. He ran, then leaped at them. Montanni dropped the bear, who scrabbled in the snow for a moment, then rose tall on its hind legs. The demon, enraged, ripped at Greg's body with its nails as Kumush, briefly looming larger, engulfed them. The three seemed to meld, then toppled together into the well. The red mist swirled in, the stones clattered down, and there was nothing.

"*GREG, NOOOOO!*"

The ground shook, but not gently this time. Nearby hills moved, and distant mountains moved. Fire Valley was jarred, the lava beds shifted, and the town of Bonner suffered considerable damage in the twenty seconds of the tremor and the aftershocks.

Then it was over. There were new fissures but no trace of the well, now sealed—perhaps—until the death of Time.

The dust settled on the *sayka loluk,* and it became still.

EPILOGUE:

Janet Lowell

Janet Lowell stood by a window on the tenth floor of the hospital and gazed across the San Fernando Valley. The usual smog lay over it, though it was not as bad as it had been all summer. But the heat! Only ten in the morning, and it was in the mid-nineties. She had nearly wilted running out to her car to get something.

Molly Albert, her charge nurse, waved to her as she walked down the hall. "Janet, there's someone looking for you. I told her you were on duty, but she was pretty insistent."

"Did she say who she was?" Janet asked.

"Donna . . . Faraday, I think."

"Donna!" Janet exclaimed. "Where is she?"

"Waiting room two."

"Molly, give me ten minutes, okay?"

"You got it."

Donna looked older, but better than the last time Janet had seen her. She was smiling, uncomfortably.

She nodded. "Janet."

"Donna, it's good to see you."

They gazed at each other awkwardly for a moment, then the barrier was lowered by their unique and terrible bond. They embraced and cried, and finally sat together on a couch.

"I wanted so bad to talk to you again," Janet said, "but I was afraid."

"So was I," Donna admitted. "I guess that was stupid."

Janet shook her head. "We both needed the time. But I'm glad you're here now. What brings you to L.A. ?"

"Just a stopover. Things to do, people to see. I'm flying to Phoenix tomorrow, to look at some houses. Been traveling around kind of aimlessly the last three or four months, and it's about time I settled somewhere."

"Your daughter will like that."

"As long as I stay out of their hair. I plan to."

Janet hesitated, then asked, "You haven't been back to Bonner in a while?"

"No, but I've been in touch with my sister. Talked to her last night, in fact. They're trying to sell the estate. Haven't had much luck. A lot of people left Fire Valley after the earthquake and all the other things, and not many have come back. But I understand it's been quiet up there since."

"What about the Rubens, and the Staleys?"

"Jill and Larry moved back to Portland. There's not enough to keep even one doctor busy. Carol and Winn are okay. Les stood up for Winn at the hearing, and he was reinstated."

"I'm glad for him."

"By the way, I was in Sacramento last week and saw Adrienne Gordon."

Janet looked at the floor. "How is she?"

"Better. I talked to Eric a couple of weeks after you left, when he came back to Bonner to take care of the house. He was really affected by what happened there, what happened . . . to us. They're still separated, but they've put off the divorce and are talking again. They agreed to joint custody of Joey for the time being."

Janet lifted her head. "I said I was afraid to talk to you, Donna. Well, I've been ten times as scared to talk to Adrienne. But I'm going to do it, soon."

Donna smiled. "It'll be what they need, Jan, what they *both* need. How are Allison and Mark?"

"Fine. They bounce back, you know? Mark's enrolled at a junior college here in the valley for the fall. And Allison's happy now that she can see Billy Douglas again."

"The Douglases moved down here?"

"Santa Barbara. Ellen has family there. But Billy will be starting Pepperdine next month, so I imagine we'll have a dinner guest a few times a week. I'm glad."

Again, an uncomfortable silence settled over them as Donna groped for her next words. "Jan, I think it's about time," she finally said.

"For what?"

"To tell me, to make me understand at least as much as

you do. I want to know why Burton and Greg died. *I want to know what happened in Fire Valley!*"

Janet walked over to a window and stared out absently. "Can you come to the house for dinner tonight?"

"Yes."

"Good. The kids will be happy to see you. I guess it's time I unlocked it." She nodded firmly. "I'll tell you everything."

Donna joined her. "Thanks, Jan. It'll be a long day, but then it's been a long year." She gazed out the window, frowning.

"What's the matter?" Janet asked.

Donna shook her head. "I know this is your town and all . . . but God, I don't know how you can live here! The color of the air, that traffic!"

Janet looked down at it, then at Donna, and smiled. "It's all right. It really is."

Bantam Spectra Horror
because every spectrum is shadowed by the colors of the night...

☐ **The Demon by Jeffrey Sackett**
(28596-3 * $4.50/$5.50 in Canada)
An ex-sideshow geek moves into a small New York town, and on his heels follows a string of hideous and inexplicable murders.

☐ **The Horror Club by Mark Morris**
(28933-0 * $4.95/$5.95 in Canada)
Three young horror fans learn the true meaning of fear when they invite a new boy into their club who unleashes upon their hometown a terrifying, consuming evil.

☐ **The Amulet by A.R. Morlan**
(28908-X * $4.95/$5.95 in Canada)
Set in a quiet Wisconsin town, this is the chilling story of a woman's desperate struggle against the terrible power of a talisman which controls and changes the people around her.

☐ **House Haunted by Al Sarrantonio**
(29148-7 * $4.50/$5.50 in Canada)
From the four corners of the earth, five people are seduced into a sinister web of madness, murder and supernatural confrontation by a powerful spirit who longs for a doorway into the physical world.

Look for these bloodcurdling new titles on sale now wherever Bantam Spectra Books are sold, or use this page for ordering:

The dark and stunning vision of
Alan Rodgers

Blood of the Children

For generations, every child in the small town of Green
Hill has belonged to an evil, magical, and entirely secret
cult until he or she reaches puberty, and then all evil,
and all memory of evil acts committed, disappears....
When Ben Tompkins and his son, Jimmy, move into
Green Hill to begin a new life, they know nothing about
the children. But Jimmy is about to discover their
terrifying secret...and pay the price for that knowledge.

Fire

"Splashy, flashy, wickedly funny, and breathlessly sus-
penseful. Rodgers' second novel is a winner." -- *Locus*

The end of the world has come. The legions of the dead
are rising. The Beast of Revelations walks the Earth.
And it's all been engineered by Mankind. With Arma-
geddon but days away, a small band of men and women
-- both dead and alive -- are being summoned to heart-
land America for the ultimate showdown between good
and evil....

On sale now wherever Bantam Books are sold.

AN204 -- 2/91

John Saul is "a writer with the touch for raising gooseflesh."
—*Detroit News*

John Saul has produced one bestseller after another: masterful tales of terror and psychological suspense. Each of his works is as shocking, as intense and as stunningly real as those that preceded it.